TITAN 10

TITAN 10

Peter Tonkin

Severn House Large Print
London & New York

This first large print edition published in Great Britain 2007 by
SEVERN HOUSE LARGE PRINT BOOKS LTD of
9-15 High Street, Sutton, Surrey, SM1 1DF.
First world regular print edition published 2004 by
Severn House Publishers, London and New York.
This first large print edition published in the USA 2007 by
SEVERN HOUSE PUBLISHERS INC., of
595 Madison Avenue, New York, NY 10022.

Copyright © 2004 by Peter Tonkin.

British Library Cataloguing in Publication Data

Tonkin, Peter, 1950-
   Titan 10. - (Mariners series) - Large Print ed.
   1. Mariner, Richard (Fictitious character) - Fiction
   2. Sea stories
   I.   Title
   823.9'14 [F]

ISBN-13: 978-0-7278-7639-3

Except where actual historical events and characters are being described
for the storyline of this novel, all situations in this publication are
fictitious and any resemblance to living persons is purely coincidental.

Printed and bound in Great Britain by
MPG Books Ltd, Bodmin, Cornwall.

For
Cham, Guy and Mark.
As always.

ACKNOWLEDGEMENTS

The background research to *Titan 10* began in March 1998 when the *Telegraph* delivered a magazine reporting the investment opportunities in Nizhny Novgorod and Bashkorostan. It was here that Bashnev Power and Computing was born; born but filed away for later use. It was (not for the first time) the *Today* programme on BBC Radio 4 that started the plot itself. A couple of years ago, the *Today* programme began to report that the Russian authorities proposed adapting their Typhoon series of submarines in the manner and for the purpose described in this book. I thought at once, now that's exactly the kind of thing Richard Mariner would get involved in! And the real research began. First of all, as usual I called Kelvin Hughes of 145 Minories, London, for the charts and Admiralty Pilots of the Barents and Kara Seas.

Then, as always, I turned to libraries and to my computer. Internet sites have given me the most intimate details of the composition, capacity, construction, crewing and current location of the Typhoon series. Of the organization of the Russian justice services –

7

knowledge extended by reports on Russian-based cases from all over the world, from the *L.A. Times* to *Pravda* itself – and to the BBC, of course. It gave me details of Murmansk, North Russia and the Kola Peninsula. Of the existence of a model of the Kara Sea designed to give the US Office of Naval Research and the Norwegian Ministry of Foreign Affairs warning of the environmental dangers it poses. Of Norilsk Nickel, the facilities they support, the work they do – and the agreement they have reached with the scientists in Moscow to create a hydrogen-based fuel. I also consulted on-line the work of Mats-Olev Olsson and Alexei V. Sekrev on the environmental damage to the Kola Peninsula and the seas that surround it. Also, of course, sites on cyanide poisoning, radiation dangers and dosages.

Research continued with *Modern Submarine Warfare* by David Miller & John Jordan (Salamander 1987) and extended further into Tom Clancy's classic adventure-thriller *The Hunt For Red October*, and John Mc-Tiernan's fine film. Important also were the two later Renko books by Martin Cruz Smith – *Polar Star* and *Red Square*. *Polar Star*, in any case, is a great favourite of mine, and I have read it many times.

The internal disposition of *Titan 10* herself owes a certain amount to Robert Moore's excellent, moving reconstruction of the *Kursk* disaster, *A Time To Die*. I also watched *K154*, and *K19 The Widowmaker* in much the same way as I consulted *Run Silent Run Deep* (Edward L. Beech's book and Robert Wise's film, both of which I love) together with almost every submarine film and TV programme you can think of. And most of the books about submarine warfare in theory and practice as well.

My books are always dedicated to my wife, Charmaine, and my sons, Guy and Mark – for without their understanding, help and forbearance I could not begin to get the work of writing done. This time, however, I must also thank Charmaine for her indefatigable editorial work. She went through the first drafts of *Titan 10* with a fine-tooth comb, working – as she so often does – not only on the secretarial level but upon the creative. When characters and prose have been given an extra polish, where relationships and plot twists are tighter, where the atmosphere as well as the action is effective and thrilling (especially that relentless tapping aboard the haunted submarine), you can see her hand at work alongside my own.

Peter Tonkin, Royal Tunbridge Wells

CHAPTER ONE

Ghost

Captain Morgan Hand reached for the emergency alarm at the very instant *Prometheus 4* rounded North Cape and as she did so, her navigating cadet whispered, 'There's the ghost again...' But only Richard Mariner heard.

Even as the helmsman bellowed the new heading over the battering bluster of the suddenly beam-on weather, the Captain's fingers moved for the red emergency button. Her hazel gaze flicked up to meet Richard Mariner's sea-blue eyes, reflected in the sloping clear view above the restless brightness of the main-bridge control panels, as he stood just behind her right shoulder, frowning for a reason she could not understand.

The supertanker's control section stretched through several workstations, including the helmsman's and the Navigating Officer's, right across the bridge beneath the sloping windows. With their clearview panels and heated, ice-clear sections these looked down the grass-green deck the size of a couple of football pitches – and marked like them with white lines designed to split them into various work areas. The line of the control panel – and some crucial pieces of equipment – extended out beyond the forward doors at port and starboard on to a pair of bridge wings that overhung the grey and restless sea.

Richard's reflection above the sparkling, space-age panel in the window was clear but disturbingly ghostly, thought Morgan Hand. It was as though his massive frame – bulked out by the cold-weather gear required for where they were and what they were about to do – were somehow part of the grey-white, ice-flecked wilderness of smoking ocean ahead. He nodded once.

The gesture was so intimate that they might almost have been alone on the supertanker's bridge, thought Morgan in the instant before she took action. The pair of them were certainly isolated in spite of the bustle all around them; isolated by their intimately overlapping responsibilities as Captain and Owner – here on the bridge, aboard the massive vessel itself, and away out in the icy, stormy, Russian waters of the northern Barents Sea. Though were she to be marooned alone with any man alive, Richard Mariner must stand up there at the top of the wish-list, second only to Pjotr Korsakov, she thought. No, *Peter* Korsakov, as he had insisted she call him at that romantic little luncheon at the spectacularly unromantic shipyard at Severodvinsk. He was the gorgeous captain of *Titan 10*, the submarine they had been refitting then, which they were coming out here to meet now.

'New heading one hundred and twenty-five degrees,' called the helmsman as the tanker's hull rolled a little under the beam seas. Then the Heritage Mariner Company's new flagship shuddered and settled as the North Cape current swept her relentlessly onwards – south-eastwards towards Russian waters. The change in disposition was as swift and unconsidered as the fleeting thoughts in the mind of her captain. Morgan answered, 'Very well!' And pressed the button.

The British owner and his slight American captain were by no means alone of course. Morgan had a crew of forty aboard *Prometheus 4* who looked to her for leadership. Richard had two guests berthed in the exclusive Company Suites on D Deck just beneath this one, whose combined fortunes could have bought and sold a good number of countries. And indeed, according to rumour at least, they had. But just at the moment, although they were berthed luxuriously below, both men stood on the bridge behind their massive host.

As the distinctive sound of the emergency alarm boomed up the wind and down – between the northern shores of Finland, as far east as Russian Lapland, and the southern fringes of the Polar pack-ice – Morgan and Richard each turned to their main responsi-

13

bilities. And how each one did this went some way to defining them.

Richard turned, with a reassuring smile creasing his craggy features. 'Nothing to worry about,' he rumbled. 'Routine drill. Let's get to our lifeboat stations and out from under the Captain's feet.' He opened his arms, bear-like, and swept the two slighter men before him. Even as he spoke, as though his whim could govern every routine aboard, the emergency siren stopped. The rest of the drill could proceed without it evidently. Cheerfully irresistible, he continued into the sudden quiet, 'I hope you appreciate this, Tucker. We've called drill early; thought you'd be more comfortable playing ducks and drakes in Finnish waters. We'll be in Russian seas by sunset. Though perhaps you'd have preferred that, Max.'

Tucker Roanoake IV and Max Asov each shrugged amenably. Both of them were twenty-first century entrepreneurs – though the American was Old Money and the Russian was New. The spare, angular, tanned Tucker was Texas Oil, whose massive fortune had been born with Rockefellers. The pallid, plump, ebullient Max was Bashnev Power, the ink on whose billions of roubles was still wet. Neither of them had any real worries about international borders on land or at sea; any more than the fit, fastidious, health-conscious Tucker feared a premature heart attack or the confident, self-indulgent bound-lessly energetic Max feared an apoplectic stroke. Their nightmares tended to be virtual ones; modern ones. Of financial dangers springing out of bursting dot-com bubbles and burgeoning computer viruses. Of corporate dangers from the Mafia, American and Russian, and the opportunistic mobsters that rode on their black coat-tails.

The rear exit of *Prometheus 4*'s bridge brought the three men into a lateral corridor closed against the elements at each end by a metal bulkhead door. Ahead of them stood a lift, its closed doors flanked by internal companionways leading downwards. 'The lift is closed for the drill,' warned Richard, guiding his guests into the right-hand stairwell. 'All the way down to A Deck, then out on to the weather deck, please. You remember which lifeboat you're in?' Their heavy wet-weather clothing made it clear that all of them had been given some warning – and some briefing – beforehand. So it was hardly surprising that both of the landlubbers as well as the sea-wise owner knew exactly what they were doing and where they were going.

Both men grunted in answer to their host's cheery question as they clattered on down together. As they did so, Richard heard Morgan's clear Southern tones ringing across the bridge, rapping out orders to First Lieutenant Skylerov as though she had gone back ten years in time and were completing her training by the book at the Marine and Petroleum Institute at Chauvin, Louisiana. 'Alexei, it's your watch, so you and your team stay here.

You keep the log of course. I'll radio details and timings up as usual. Alert the engine-room watch that this is just a drill. Routine. The Chief will have done it, I know. But I want the engines manned, remember. We will proceed to the stations on the weather decks but we will not launch. I don't want us slowing down. And I don't want anyone in these seas if I can help it...' These were the last words Richard heard as he ran down into the bustle of B Deck and, below it, A.

Richard was in the Captain's boat, as form and tradition dictated. Tucker was with the Chief Engineer – albeit in the Second Lieutenant's boat – and Max in First Lieutenant Alexei Skylerov's. Honours thus remained equal, a balance that matched the standing of the two guests. And they were safe in the knowledge that in the event of a real crisis, all that power and wealth would be spread out in the safest boats with the most experienced crew-members to guard and guide them.

The idea of safety became a relative thing as Richard swung open the bulkhead door at the starboard end of the lateral A-Deck corridor. A gust of wind come straight south off the Pole blasted sleet and spray into their faces. 'Jesus!' swore Tucker, used to Texan weather. Nevertheless, he did not hesitate, but stepped on to the wet green deck.

'Ha!' called Max cheerfully, stepping out over the raised sill at his side. 'As balmy as spring in Norilsk. I think I can smell the summer already!' Richard smiled, in spite of the

16

cold. A typical piece of Asov bravado. Particularly as what the Russian could actually smell was the stench of rotting fish.

'If summer in Norilsk smells like what I can smell,' countered Tucker dryly, 'then that explains why I've never heard of the place!'

Because this was a drill, Richard led the two men to their places himself, and made sure that each was standing beside a responsible officer before he returned to his own place beneath the pendant keel of the Captain's lifeboat. As he did so, he observed with wry amusement just how well served the two of them had been – their stations were on the lee side of the bridge house, out of the wind and weather. Under the shelter of their lifeboats it might indeed seem as balmy as spring in Norilsk. Round on the weather side, however, it was more like midwinter in Mys Zhelaniya – on the uttermost tip of Novaya Zemlya, one of the northernmost points in Russia and amongst the coldest he had ever heard of. Even now, in the middle of June, Mys Zhelaniya was likely to be fast frozen in the eternal ice on the northern edge of the terrible Kara Sea.

With these grim thoughts in his mind, Richard arrived at his emergency station at exactly the same time as Morgan herself arrived, sou'westered, lifebelted and narrow-eyed, clutching a stopwatch in one clearly freezing hand. 'All present?' she bellowed to the Second Engineer, her 2i/c aboard her lifeboat. He glanced across at Richard, pressed

17

the button on a stopwatch of his own, then nodded. She compared times, made a note, opened the channel to the bridge on a radio held in her other – gloved – hand, and bellowed something unintelligible. Then she was off, plunging back along the side of the bridge house, weaving a little in the intermittent blast of the Polar wind. Without further thought, having established himself as being 'all present and correct' and with nothing better to do, therefore, Richard followed her.

He caught her up at the second lifeboat and he stood upwind of her right shoulder as she compared times on the two stopwatches, made her second note, and shouted up her second report to the bridge. 'It's much quieter on the other side,' he bellowed cheerfully as they crossed on to the lee side. And at first it seemed that he was right. They got the time from Alexei Skylerov's boat – again from his 2i/c as he was on watch. Then they ran past Max and the rest of the personnel at that station going down to where the Second Lieutenant stood almost forlornly between the considerable powers of the Chief Engineer and Tucker Roanoake IV. No sooner had they completed their final routine there, however, than all hell broke loose.

It began with the emergency siren which blasted abruptly into the blustering air once more. It continued with the sound – and the sensation – of the motors being ordered into violent, emergency motion and of the helm

18

being thrown hard-over. An almost useless gesture in any supertanker – and a measure of the unknown danger. It intensified with Alexei's voice gabbling impenetrable garbage on Morgan's handset – and it ended with the Second Engineer tearing up to the Captain, his face white and his eyes wide. Or this section of it ended.

For, as soon as he spoke, things immediately went from bad to worse. 'Man overboard,' he reported, his eyes flickering wildly from the Captain to the Owner to the Chief. 'I've ordered the Captain's boat swung out so we can get after him at once. But we'll have to hurry. He fell off the bridge wing up above our heads and I don't know where he's gone! Man overboard.' He insisted, as the Chief at least stood frowning and hesitant in the face of the catastrophe. *'Man overboard!'*

CHAPTER TWO

Overboard

They held the uncovered lifeboat level with the deck-rail as the rescue team climbed swiftly aboard. Although it was Morgan's boat, logic and leadership dictated that her place was on the bridge. No such ties bound Richard, however, and he followed the

19

skeleton crew aboard without a second thought.

A lesser man might have been overeager; in the way. But Richard knew a well-trained team when he saw one and was content to keep clear of them and let them work. It was not too hard to keep clear for the boat was designed to seat a dozen – and was well prepared to take ten crew if *Prometheus 4* went down. There were only six aboard her now with Richard taking them past the half dozen. Alexei Skylerov was in command, with the Second Engineer to look after the powerful diesel motor and keep a firm hand on the tiller. The Ship's Doctor – a rare and dying breed – was aboard, as were two GP seamen, and the cadet.

Even as the lifeboat was still sliding swiftly down *Prometheus 4*'s vertiginous side, the practised crew were strapping in as though this were going to be a particularly hair-raising fairground ride. Richard, in the bow between Alexei and the cadet, was as swift with his straps as any of them.

The lifeboat slid gently on to the water, controlled by the winch-motors at her davits. These in turn were computer controlled like all the rest; governing speed and angle. At the first buoyant heave, however, men took over from machines – for the time being at least. Alexei hit a catch by Richard's shoulder and the falls sang free to whip away across the wind. The engineer gunned the motor and the lifeboat swung out from behind the breakwater of the great hull.

The lively bows exploded upwards through the crest of a white horse rearing in front of them and for a moment Richard could see the sea due north and dead ahead. The Arctic Ocean seemed to be marching down on them in relentless lines of grey. Richard was put vividly in mind of monochrome pictures from his schoolbooks showing the ranks of German infantry marching relentlessly across the Somme during the First World War. And there, on a distant, ragged advancing shoulder shone a bright badge, as vivid as a poppy. A life jacket. 'You see it?' roared Richard, without further thought. 'Five hundred metres. Dead ahead.'

'I see it,' said Alexei. Even as he spoke, he pulled out a hands-free headset and slipped the ear-piece home. 'Dead ahead, Murphy,' he ordered, and so Richard learned the name of the engineer in the stern. 'We have sight, *Prometheus*, five hundred metres dead ahead. Do you have GPS readout on his beacon yet?' The lifeboat swooped down the back of the wave and in that roller-coaster moment, everything ahead disappeared behind the onrushing face of the next tall sea.

The cadet slipped a second headset on, frowning with concentration. '*Prometheus 4*,' she said decisively. 'This is Nancy ... Ah ... Cadet Rider. Pass me the co-ordinates as soon as ship's GPS has them.' No sooner had she stopped speaking than she pulled a box from the bow-locker upon which they were seated, and slipped a little hand-held monitor out of it. 'Loading basic schematics now,' she said, and the grey screen lit up, webbed with lines – northings and eastings, degrees, minutes and seconds. She glanced up and saw him frowning down at her. 'Basic location grid, Captain Mariner,' she explained. 'When we acquire his beacon-signal I can narrow the field and go to headings and metres.'

The super-buoyant, super-strengthened bows of the lifeboat exploded through the second crest. Nancy leaned forward to protect her equipment from the water. Richard leaned forward to protect Nancy. His shoulder hit Alexei's and the two men exchanged a glance. But both were far too sea-wise to waste precious time on a wave-top looking at anything but the sea. And it was as well that Richard, at least, looked forward. For the outlook ahead had changed appreciably – and by no means for the better. The serried ranks that he had called so vividly to mind from his history textbooks were twisting, somehow, out of line, as though one of the watery regiments were marching to a different drum. The poppy-bright wound of the lifebelt was sliding oddly sideways in answer to this strangeness. As it did so, it turned slightly, revealing the whip antenna and the star-bright light of the automatic emergency beacon at the lifebelt's right shoulder. There was an emergency whistle there too, but the lost man was clearly in no condition to blow it. Richard had only an instant to register all this, for something strange and unexpected was rearing up behind.

'Did you see that, Lieutenant Skylerov? Alexei, did you see that?' Richard demanded as the lifeboat's head went down and the next wave reared skywards like an inverted guillotine. The Russian looked back at him, eyes blank. 'Nancy? Cadet Rider? Anything showing on that handset of yours?' But he could see that there wasn't. If he had had a headset he could have asked *Prometheus 4* but he didn't; and what he had seen was so strange and at the same time so vague it wasn't worth pulling rank over. Not yet, at least. He felt the lifeboat's hull bottom solidly on the trough of the wave and pitch upwards into her climb. He turned and focused all of his being forward, then, trusting his eyes and his experience far beyond the scope of the machines...

'*Alexei!*' Morgan's voice was so urgent that Richard could hear it from both of the nearby headsets, even over the rushing of their upward climb back into the blustering of the wind. '*There's something dead ahead of you...*'

'It is ice, Captain,' said Alexei grimly. 'But only enough to cool a little vodka.' He gave a dry laugh that reminded Richard of Max and the smell of summer in Norilsk. 'A growler blown south from the pack, I'd say. It's what Pugin was looking out for when he slipped off the bridge wing. Thank God he had on his jacket if not his safety harness. Has anything of either of them come up on the bridge systems yet?' There was a silence that even Richard could hear. 'We must be waiting for a satellite,' mumbled Alexei finally. 'Anything on your handset, Cadet Rider? Not even the emergency beacon? No, I thought not...'

Pugin ... Richard filed away the name of the man they were rescuing and focused on what was coming dead ahead. He saw the top of it over the creaming head of the wave. Square, solid-looking and dark. More like granite than growler. An odd ice floe for a strange sea on an extraordinary day. Black ice. He had heard of it; seen some once, far away and long ago. Black ice – but something very different to the winter driving conditions that made the phrase familiar. Real ice. Floating ice. Anything up to the size of *Prometheus 4* herself. And really black; all but invisible – as deadly to a modern vessel as its brighter cousin had been to *Titanic* herself. But this piece was here and now – and potentially dangerous. Almost impossible to see from any distance on a grey sea under a leaden overcast with only the northerly bluster keeping the fog at bay. It should have been dead long-since, for it was much shorter-lived than its bright cousins. Its dark sides soaked up sunlight where their white surfaces reflected it and black bergs went to spongy softness, all tunnels and caverns, and melted away in days or weeks instead of months or years. Or, they usually did. But there was no sunlight beneath this foggy, perpetual overcast; had been none for weeks – and seemingly no heat left north of Murmansk itself in spite of the fact that it was supposed to be summer here. So the black floe was still alive and still a threat in all kinds of ways.

These thoughts all flashed through Richard's mind in the time it took for the boat to crest the south-bound comber. For the shadowy floe to rear three metres, four, into the lower sky. For the blood-bright life jacket with its flashing beacon to bob against the outer edge of it, to hesitate where the waves were falling recklessly away – like battalions deserting wildly and *en masse*, covering their retreat in grubby white. For the sound of it to cut across the guttering bluster of the wind as they came into its wind-shadow. And for the stench of it to bring tears to Richard's eyes – and what Max had said about the smell of summer in Norilsk to his mind again. Time was disorientatingly slow in the intensity of the moment and the action.

'Who's running the stopwatch?' demanded Richard, and the Doctor held up his hand, focused on the timepiece too fiercely even to speak. Richard nodded once. Like everything else out here, time was dangerously un-reliable and it was crucial to know exactly how long Pugin had been in the water for when they began his treatment – or his autopsy. Ask any one of them to estimate the passage of minutes and seconds and you would likely get seven different answers. Eight, if Pugin himself could speak. Each

25

moment for him would seem an age as his vital functions closed down in an increasingly vain attempt to conserve the core temperature in breast and brain – where life and consciousness lay.

'We have a signal,' called Nancy Rider. 'I'll have a position in a moment ... Oh!'

'What?' demanded Alexei.

'There's the ghost again.'

Richard looked over her shoulder with a shiver that was not entirely due to the cold. And sure enough, on the little GPS handset, the bright signal that must represent the automatic beacon on Pugin's lifebelt was haunted by another one. It was far dimmer, apparently infinitely deeper, behind or below him. But it was strong enough to register. And must have registered on *Prometheus 4*'s equipment too, in the moment before the emergency drill.

Nancy shook herself. 'An echo coming off something in the ice, most likely,' she said bracingly, then she started calling off course and distance. But even as she did so the lifeboat crested a wave and her directions became of academic interest. For Pugin was there before them, sliding sideways down the flank of the strange black ice floe, three waves ahead. The grey mass rose high and hollow behind him. Ten or twelve sheer feet of it, and who knew how long or wide besides, seeming to soak life out of the dull afternoon and hold it, glittering dully, deep within itself. The north wind boomed and sobbed strangely in

26

whatever nooks and crannies scarred the thing. The stench of rotten fish intensified as the lifeboat pitched forward once again into an airless hollow between the waves.

The currents surrounding the strange floe took them then, as it had clearly taken Pugin, swinging the lifeboat's head over in spite of Murphy's steady hand upon the tiller. And it was just as well, thought Richard, thrown forward as their see-saw progress hesitated, and suddenly looking down through the strange clear water. For there, below and ahead on their old course, the sunken section of the ice reached out in a floating reef, wickedly sharp and seemingly solid enough to tear them open. The relentless power of the water swung them further over on Pugin's track, sweeping the buoyant vessel over a second sunken horn of ice and down towards a kind of backwater. The keel hit the ice hard several times as they slid into the strange bay, but the boat was tough and resilient – it bounced safely into the dead water.

And *dead water* was a terribly apposite phrase, thought Richard grimly as Murphy gunned the motor, bringing them swiftly down upon their objective. For collected within the wide, shallow throat of this strange, moving, transient bay, were the corpses of numberless fish. Heads, spines and tails floated in a slow, oily fluid, seemingly too thick and dark to be water. Thick enough to be holding Pugin and his rescuers unnaturally high, like the Dead Sea, where bathers

27

can sit and read newspapers, buoyed up by the salinity of the water. Almost jellified by the tight-packed bodies and the sub-zero temperature, the sea beneath the lifeboat heaved sullenly, threateningly, like some deadly swamp in fantasy fiction. 'What is this?' breathed Nancy, simply awed. 'What did this?'

'The question is not *what* but *who*,' grated Richard. 'These fish have been dredged up from the deep. Processed. Gutted. The fillets have gone from their sides. All that's left is head and bone – too little even for fish-oil or bonemeal. Some great trawler or factory ship has washed out her bilges and waste holds here. But more than that—'

'Here!' interrupted Alexei. 'I have him. Whatever this is or whoever did it, let's get poor Pugin out of it. Take him, the pair of you. Doctor...' Of course they had not been sitting idly as they talked. Even Richard's comments had been based on the fact that he had been stretching out beside Alexei, trying to reach Pugin's flaccid body – the one piece of brightness, warmth, entirety amongst this whole foetid floating graveyard.

'More than what?' asked Nancy as the pair of them heaved Pugin into the bilge. The Doctor was on him at once, calling instructions to his GP seamen helpers. 'What else is worrying you?' The life jacket was off in a twinkling, its useless beacon switched off as the three life-savers fell to work with practised urgency. 'I have a pulse!' he called.

Murphy was gunning the motor while Alexei reported in.

'No birds,' answered Richard. 'You'd have thought a feast like this would have had every gull in the Barents Sea feeding here. I haven't seen any seals either, or anything else that might be attracted to this much offal. But look,' he continued conversationally, 'this thing's still registering your mysterious ghost.' He held up Nancy's GPS handset.

'My God, so it is,' she said. 'Now how strange is that?' And as though in answer to her question, the engine died. The hefty little lifeboat slid backwards down the sluggish wave its own bows had created, and its stern slammed into the battered spike of half-submerged ice they had ridden over to get here. There was a *Crack!* worthy of a high-powered rifle, closely followed by a slow, rumbling sucking sound. The whole section behind and beneath them split away from the mother-floe. Released into the realm of its own physics, the submerged section began to surface, turning over as it did so.

The lifeboat slid away forward once again, surfing ahead across that strange dark bay, powered by the waves from the ice's massive movement as though the propeller was in motion once more. But almost immediately, she settled again and began to wallow, cheek-by-jowl with a new floe sitting a metre high for nearly nine square metres. And there, in the middle of the ice, spread-eagled face-down and half-buried in the strange black

substance, frozen immovably into place, was
a corpse.

Richard looked at the bright life jacket –
largely in tatters now and spreading across
the black ice like fresh blood – with its whip
antenna dangling forlornly from the shoulder, then he glanced down at Nancy and the
GPS handset in her convulsed and shaking
fist. 'And there's your ghost,' he said quietly.

CHAPTER THREE

Recovery

Richard's grim words echoed down the wind
towards the dark, distant bulk of *Prometheus
4*. The little lifeboat heaved up the back of the
next grey wave, rolling the comatose Pugin in
the bilge under the Doctor's busy hands.
Only the half-drowned, nearly-frozen seaman
was not looking at the body on the floe. Even
the Doctor's gaze was following Richard's to
the strange sight on the black ice.

The dead man lay spreadeagled, face down
as though frozen in the act of crawling across
the strange surface, thought Richard. No, not
crawling, *digging* – for the corpse was half-
buried. Face, chest, stomach, hips, thighs,

knees and feet were all held deep in the ice. And, noted those keen mariner's eyes, hands. At first glance it seemed the corpse had no hands at all – but no. The hands had dug themselves deep into the frozen stuff and lay there, almost invisible, buried to the wrist. In the waves' wash, the burst life jacket stirred and spread like endlessly oozing blood. At the left shoulder, an antenna wavered like the broken leg of a spider-crab. Was it only the shadowy light – or did the emergency beacon still glow, as ghostly as the signal still whispering from the last dregs of power in the battery?

Without looking away from the terrible sight, Richard said, 'We must get Pugin back aboard. Then we have to come back and recover this poor beggar, somehow.'

Twenty minutes later, Richard and Morgan were standing on the port bridge wing, looking down from the very point where Pugin had fallen overboard. Skylerov had the con, restless and impatient with the delay, but still, like Richard, in his bulky emergency gear, ready to go over the side again.

Even Morgan seemed to be tense, thought Richard, shrewdly suspecting that, had he not been here they might well have slid past the strange berg with its stranger burden. Their priorities, after all, were dictated by their tight sailing orders and tighter budget. And by the demands of the computer programs designed to guide and monitor – and cost and budget

31

– them every inch of the way to their rendez-vous. Were computers capable of showing frustration, he thought, the whole ship would be trembling with ill-contained fury now. And he bore some responsibility for that himself. If this voyage went right, there would be many thousands more – but fortunes would only be made if each subsequent voyage came in on budget, with profits secure. Richard knew to within a penny how much it cost per minute to make the trip. He knew he had already watched tens of thousands of pounds vanish. But he remained what he had always been – a man to whom certain principles stood so far above money that the accounts were never considered. Though, he suspected, he would have to talk his actions through with the two financiers currently so remarkable by their absence.

'How will we do it, then?' asked Morgan quietly.

'The floe is too small and restless for any-one to get securely on to it and chip him free,' answered Richard decisively. 'So we'll have to manoeuvre *Prometheus 4* alongside and lower a net. You con her and I'll go back down in the lifeboat. With Skylerov and the same crew as before – except for the Doctor, of course.'

'We'll have to reset all the computers...'

'We'll have to do that in any case. We're more than forty minutes out of whack. And yes. I know what that's doing to the budget. It won't be coming out of your pay cheque.'

'That's good,' she said acerbically, turning

away. 'We've pissed away next year's salary already – for me and the rest of the crew.'

Another crew's salary later, Richard was standing in the bow of the lifeboat, trying to balance himself. This was a difficult task, because the little boat was pitching and tossing increasingly wildly in waters worthy of the fiercest rapids. The stately southward progression of the waves was thundering against *Prometheus 4*'s side and returning in a vicious backwash. At the same time, the waves that were slipping off the side of the larger berg were cutting across these. And, this close, the wavelets generated by the floe itself were adding to the mess. All this was complicated by the fact that they were upwind of the tanker's hull and the gale came and went as confusedly as the waves.

But Richard was well-practised at handling the chop by now. He had already staggered across the floe, Nancy Rider wide-eyed and sure-footed at his side, looping lines and dropping nets, calling orders to both lifeboat and ship. He had already secured the voluminous skirts of Kevlar-strengthened webbing around and under the rapidly shrinking floe.

Now he hung on to the nearest of the great lines holding the net that connected it to the lading gantry high above. And as he did so, he secured the last of it, one-handed, round the crumbling ice. 'Heave away,' he ordered into his hands-free headset, and staggered back as the great winches above took the strain.

'That's it,' he continued to Skylerov. 'Back to the lifeboat falls and get us winched aboard. Captain Hand, you may turn back to your original heading as soon as we are all secure.'

'I don't think I can,' came the distant reply.

'Why not?' he bellowed, far more loudly than the sensitive equipment required.

'The computers won't let us take back the con. We have all our life support and comfort systems OK, but we seem to be shut out of propulsion and navigation...'

Twenty minutes later, Richard was back on the bridge with Morgan on one side and Alexei Skylerov beyond her, both broodingly angry. On his other hand was Max Asov, stoically cheerful, like a man enjoying the bracing winter breezes in Norilsk.

Richard had bought everything aboard except the computer system. In spite of all his years and experience with most modern vessels and command systems, he had felt himself nowhere near competent to deal with that most vital hardware. Particularly as whatever computers were purchased had to interface with the systems aboard the fleet of newly refitted, redesignated Titan submarines with which they were in constant communication. The system therefore had to be both state of the art and Russian. A system that Max had supplied – and Alexei had been trained to use. Lengthily and expensively trained. As Lading Officer he had to be the most computer-literate aboard.

To be fair, Richard had sailed in – owned – ships that used the most advanced technology. From his own Katapult series of computer-rigged trimarans upon which so much of his company's fortune was still founded. Through his even more modern Jetcat Ferries that plied their trade on routes between Dover and Calais across the English Channel, from Thunder Bay to Chicago, across the Great Lakes. To ships such as this, container ships and tankers, which carried the name of Heritage Mariner all across the world.

And, more advanced still, Richard had been famously aboard the great Russian cruise liner *Kalinin*, whose control systems had all closed down at the Millennium, so many years ago and exactly half a world south in the deepest of Antarctic waters. Then, more recently still, the super-freighter *New England*, aboard which he had gone with the British and American Special Forces to recapture her from terrorists intent on mayhem at New York's Hell Gate. *Kalinin* and *New England* had computer officers whose only task was to oversee and maintain the massively complex, intimately vital systems that controlled everything from engines to kitchens, from radar to radiators.

But on a working tanker such as *Prometheus 4*, communicating with vessels such as *Titan 10*, the task of understanding and using the computers simply had to be added to the other responsibilities of the Chief Lading Officer. The First Officer and Lading

Officer's vital, main, responsibility had to be to get thousands of gallons of crude oil safely into and out of the massive tanks both here and in the submarines. And do it in the middle of the stormy, unpredictable and dangerous Barents Sea.

Richard looked from Max to Alexei. 'What do you think?' he asked.

Silence.

'We have to be able to depart from the navigational protocols in case of emergency,' he persisted gently. 'That is absolutely vital, of course, especially in waters as dangerous and unpredictable as these. We agreed that this would be put into the programs, Max.'

'Indeed. And so I ordered. This is a simple glitch, I am certain. Nothing more.'

'Okay. So how do we fix it? Alexei? You need a spanner? A hammer, perhaps?'

'No, Richard,' soothed Max as Alexei frowned, wrestling with English humour. 'We need do nothing here. We simply contact our Novgorod headquarters via email and their computers will diagnose our computers over the Net, like the Doctor is doing with that unfortunate seaman in the Medical Room. Then they will fix them automatically. It is only a matter of programming, after all. It will take mere moments, I am sure, and then we will be free to proceed...'

CHAPTER FOUR

Underside

But half an hour later, *Prometheus 4* was still sitting solidly in the water downwind of the black iceberg when Richard and Cadet Rider stepped over the sill and out of the bulkhead door at the end of the A-Deck corridor on to the green of the weather deck outside. The overcast was thinning to allow watery sunlight through. Light, thought Richard, but precious little heat. It was still freezing out here, especially in the jaws of that vicious Polar northerly. Particularly after the subtropical fug down in the sickbay where he had been checking on Pugin immediately before being summoned aloft by Nancy – whom he had left in charge of the filthy floe with its mysterious passenger.

'The hose was an inspiration, Captain Mariner,' she said as they hurried down the narrow path beside the bridge house, under the projecting wing. 'I did have to watch the pressure, but the water is not only melting the ice but it's washing away the mess at the same time, which will please Captain Hand. And starting low then working higher seems to be just the ticket. The body will be free soon, and then...'

At this point they rounded the corner forward of the bridge house and the central section of the deck was revealed to them. Here two less-than-ecstatic General Purpose seamen were wielding the ship's main hose. The half-power setting Richard had suggested and Nancy had ordered was washing salt water over the last remnant of the floe, whose thick, dark, oily life blood was writhing sinuously across the green deck and straight away under the safety rail where, in a lesser vessel, the scuppers would lie.

Face-down and still frozen, the corpse lay on a piece of ice about the size and depth of a coffin. Around the body itself, the ice had fallen back into gutters and these were full of water, so that the drowned man seemed to be floating, no longer so fiercely gripped by the ice.

Deep in thought, Richard crouched beside the black ice box, his eyes seemingly consumed by the body on top of it. Nancy gestured to the seamen and the water stopped abruptly. The wind seemed to die and an actual sunbeam fell down upon the macabre little scene, like moonshine through primrose glass. 'Look,' he said so quietly that Nancy had to strain to hear. 'It isn't just the life jacket. Nearly all the clothing on the back is in rags. No boots of course – he'd have kicked them off before escaping – standard practice.

But see, here, where the ice held him, it is complete. Face-down he seems almost naked. If we laid him face-up he would appear to be fully dressed.'

'Is that important, Captain?' Nancy's gaze was riveted by the strange flesh of the corpse's back, as it had been since the hose first spat briny foam towards it in the instant that the netting lifted free. It was mottled ivory-white and bruise black. But as she looked, so a pattern seemed to emerge. The highest points – shoulders, buttocks – seemed darkest of all. It seemed so waterlogged, soft, flaccid. And yet the way the matted, glistening hairs were bound to it, the way the water ran sparkling off it, showed it was rock-hard; still frozen solid. Only the vivid threads of clothing seemed softer, somehow, moving in the water like hair blown by the wind...

'God knows what's important,' said Richard but his words were drowned by the tannoy as Nancy was summoned to the bridge.

When Nancy Rider returned, Richard was still crouching beside the oozing block of ice, but the GP seamen had vanished – putting away the hose no doubt. 'Welcome back,' he said. 'Can you scare up those GP seamen again if you'd be so kind. They'll just be finished stowing the hose, I expect. I need a clean tarpaulin to wrap Captain Birdseye here in and a stretcher to carry him below.'

'I don't think ... ah ... Captain Birdseye ... will actually go on any of the new body-moulded stretchers,' she mused. 'Not unless we wait for him to thaw. Or break his arms and legs to make them fit. I think we'd be better with something like a door.'

'Good thinking. Or a ladder. Might be easier to carry – they can hold rungs or up-rights like handles.'

'Yes, Captain.' Nancy turned once again.

'Oh, and Cadet Rider...'

'Yes, Captain Mariner?'

'If the Doctor could be spared from Pugin's bedside...'

Nancy sent the Doctor up first from beside Pugin's bed in the outer sickbay, then went in search of the seamen. When the three of them arrived back on the deck, armed with a sheet of clean, clear heavy-duty plastic sheeting and an ancient wooden ladder, property of the ship's carpenter, the two men were leaning over the body like vultures, their heads low and almost touching, their hands gently busy, side by side.

'Yes, Captain, I believe you may be correct,' the Doctor was saying as Nancy neared. 'One scarcely likes to consider such a terrible cir-cumstance, but what you have observed here certainly seems to point that way.'

'We'll be able to tell more when we get him down into the sickbay,' growled Richard. 'Even getting him over on his back will give us a whole new series of clues...'

The strange pair stopped speaking as Nancy brought her men up close, but that one word rang most disturbingly in her mind.

40

'Clues...' You only got clues in a crime. And a crime involving a dead sailor must mean murder. She frowned, rearranging all her assumptions. For up until that moment she had thought the dead man simply lost overboard – perhaps from the trawler that had left all the fish beside the strange black berg. A lost man accidentally dying in the icy embrace of the terrible Barents Sea. But no. Apparently this was murder.

The five of them eased the dead man out of the ice as gently as if he had been carved by Michelangelo. And he was indeed cold and stiff and heavy enough to have been made of marble. The front of his body, face and clothing remained caked with a thick black layer and Nancy found herself thinking, not of a marble statue, suddenly, but one of those terracotta soldiers Chinese emperors had buried with them to protect them in the afterlife.

The others wrapped the body in the plastic and laid it on the ladder – arms and legs still stubbornly akimbo. The Doctor went first, then the seamen, one on each end of the ladder, then Richard and Nancy beside him, with their filthy jars. 'Murder?' he answered her immediate, whispered question. 'No. There's no immediate evidence of that. Why do you ask?'

'Because you were talking to the Doctor about clues. I thought...'

'Ah. I see. No. Clues as to cause of death. Though when we know how and why he died we might well know whether it was murder or not. We might well know a lot of things, for that matter.'

'But it was something...'

'Something strange? Certainly. Something tragic? Probably. Something criminal? Maybe. Murder? Possibly. Just possibly.'

And that was all he said on the subject as they hurried down the companionways, having seen the other three – four – just crowd into the lift. But what struck Nancy was Richard's certainty. His authority.

When the pair of them arrived in the sick-bay, they found the body already lying on the stainless-steel operating table of the inner room, with Pugin craning to see round the inner door-jamb. Putting the corpse on the operating table was a practical move made unnecessary as yet, for the gutters and runnels remained empty. The corpse was still cold enough to be dry. But the heat of the little room was enough to make Richard, for one, certain that the outer layers at least would not remain so for long. And the heat was being intensified by the number of living bodies here – each one, he remembered inconsequentially, emitting as much heat as a two-bar electric fire. The seamen were waiting aimlessly, one of them clutching the plastic sheet and the other the carpenter's ladder. The Doctor was already bending over the body, sponging the crusted filth away, his eyes as wide as the marble-solid orbs in the gargoyle of the dead man's twisted face. And,

42

as she watched, Nancy was suddenly, sickeningly, struck with an unexpected truth. The horrific face was black. Shuddering, she too leant forward. The features were Western, not negroid. And yet the skin of his face was dead, dark, black. The lips were even darker, and strangely folded back from black-edged horse's teeth clenched in the rictus of death. The staring eyes were grey. From nostrils and mouth corners, black worms, slightly darker than the surrounding flesh, oozed. Or seemed to do so, frozen in the midst of their serpentine progress.

Richard's eyes swept up over the Doctor's and the corpse's face to the other faces here assembled. All, like he had been, seemed enraptured by the horror of what they were seeing. Max had come down from the bridge. Whatever his headquarters in Novgorod was doing to the ship's computers clearly did not require his presence any longer. Nor did it require the Captain's, for Morgan was here as well. And so was Tucker, his lean face twisted almost to gargoyle in distaste.

'He's black,' whispered Tucker, awed. 'I didn't think they had any blacks in the Soviet Union.'

'They do,' said Richard grimly. 'But this poor chap isn't one of them. It's oil. And whatever else that foul berg is polluted with. Look at the mess it's made of his clothing, the front of his life jacket, that emergency beacon. He might just as well have been tarred and feathered.'

There was a moment's silence as they all digested the grim truth of Richard's words.

'You were right, Captain Mariner.' Nancy Rider broke the silence. 'He does look fully clothed now he's lying on his back. Except for his boots. Or the lack of them.'

'And,' pursued the Doctor, smoothly reasserting his authority in his own domain, 'you were correct about some other things as well. Look at those emissions at nostril and lip-juncture. They are clear even against the stained skin. The lungs are certainly ruptured. When we get his mouth to open I'm sure it will be full of blood. But the damage does seem more catastrophic than even drowning might explain. And the finger-tips! Precisely what you said we'd find...'

'So, Richard,' purred Max. 'Your experience suddenly stretches out of money houses into morgues...'

'From *Prometheus 4* to post-mortems,' mused Tucker, equally suspicious.

'How do you know all this?' demanded Morgan Hand, typically forthright. Though it might have been her junior deck cadet speaking, so much agog was Nancy.

Richard paused, almost nonplussed. Should he tell them about his experience with the United Nations and the Special Forces? Of the years of training he had received as a First Officer and acting ship's medic? That this training had been extended latterly by First Aid training up to Accident and Emergency level – as demanded by his work with his own

44

company Crewfinders, which specialized in sending replacement crews to vessels stricken by any kind of catastrophe short of actual sinking? That this experience had been further extended by his most recent experiences in Thunder Bay? Here he had even worked closely with the Canadian Criminal Pathology Service as well as with the Mounties, marrying his expertise with theirs to uncover the identity of a serial killer aboard a death ship loose on the Great Lakes.

'I've been around,' he said, modestly, almost dismissively.

'Your assessment of the situation certainly seems sound,' said the Doctor, oblivious to the byplay. 'The lungs are ruptured. The finger-ends are traumatized – there are no nails left. To get more detail we must wait for a full post-mortem, but everything you have said to me seems accurate. And therefore...'

'And therefore what?' demanded Morgan. She challenged Richard but it was the Doctor who replied. 'Therefore this unfortunate fellow, whoever he was, came up from some considerable depth before he arrived at the underside of our iceberg. I have no doubt that, when a full post-mortem is possible, we shall find an excess of gaseous nitrogen in his blood.'

'What?' demanded Max. 'What is this you are saying? *Came up from a considerable depth?*'

'Yeah,' added Tucker. 'I mean, look at the guy. He probably fell overboard one night off a trawler. The trawler you say gutted all those

45

fish near where he was found. They get pretty tanked up on those Russian factory ships, so I've heard. Use vodka the way our guys use Perrier. So he got wasted. Fell over the side. Landed in the water. Set off his automatic alarms whether or not he was actually awake. Crawled on the ice when it hove into view and froze there. I'd guess he never really woke up – did it all on automatic pilot like any terminal drunk. If he was missed, someone radioed in to Norilsk or wherever, and he's already been signed off as lost overboard. Case closed.'

'Perhaps,' said Richard. Then he frowned, suddenly angry that Tucker could dismiss this man's death so casually. 'Except for one or two things.'

'Such as?' enquired Max.

'Such as the look on his face. He didn't die asleep on the ice, tanked up and oblivious. He died fighting.'

'Fighting?' demanded Tucker. 'How do you know that?'

'Because of his fingernails. And, now I look at them, his toes. He died clawing and kicking. You have to see that!'

Their silence assured him that they did.

'So what?' asked Morgan at last. 'He died in some kind of seizure. Maybe he fell overboard in the middle of an epileptic fit. What has that got to do with us?'

'Well,' answered Richard. 'Nothing. If it was as simple as that, it has nothing to do with us. But it *isn't* as simple as that. And, therefore, it

46

may well have something to do with us. The blood in his nose and mouth shows that he came up out of deep water. His clothing is standard overalls and modern life jacket but it's far too light for a walk on the deck of a factory ship, drunk or sober. Where's his sou'wester? His pullovers, the rest? Where are his boots? Max, how long would he last like that, taking a stroll in Norilsk?'

'Ten minutes,' admitted the Russian businessman. 'No more.'

'And why would a drunk put on a life jacket anyway?' continued Richard. There was a stir of answer. He held up a hand. 'Unless it was standard procedure. Yes, I grant that. But even so, if he did end up on the ice, why on earth try to dig down into it? Not even an Eskimo would try to get that kind of shelter with his hands and feet. And remember...' He paused, frowning. 'We only found him when the floe turned over. Until then he was on the underside. So, he didn't fall down – he came up. And when he arrived at the surface, his lungs bleeding with decompression, beginning to drown in blood as well as water, what did he find? Air?'

He looked around them but no eyes would meet his own. They were looking down at that desperately twisted face, to whose bulging eyes the warmth was bringing the first hint of a tear.

'No,' continued Richard, his voice as cold and grim as its terrible subject. 'He found ice. He found the underside of the black berg.

47

That was what he was trying to claw his way through when he died.'

'*Came up...*' persisted Max, his voice almost dreamy.

'Yes,' said Richard. 'And from some depth. He came out of a submarine, Max. You must see that.'

'But,' whispered Morgan. 'Men don't just go overboard from a submarine. Not alone...'

'Exactly,' concluded Richard. And he looked away through the walls of the sickbay as though his piercing gaze could still see the black berg upwind of them. 'The underside of that berg out there could be covered with drowned submariners...'

CHAPTER FIVE

Bob

They stood and stared at him, stricken by the horrific image his grim words had conjured up.

'The whole of the underside...' whispered Morgan with a shudder that set her brown curls shaking.

'Yes,' answered Richard. 'It's been known, after all. More than twenty major incidents involving Russian submarines in the twenty years before the Kursk went down. Average of more than one a year. It's certainly been known. Max. How many crew does a submarine carry?'

'Oh. Ah ... Depends on the submarine.'

'A Typhoon class, say – one of the subs the authorities have just refitted with our help and to our specifications and reclassified as Titans. They were the biggest, weren't they?'

It was Tucker who answered as Max frowned, clearly caught off guard by Richard's question. 'One-fifty. The old Typhoons had a complement of one hundred and fifty. Two full crews as standard. You know our Titans carry half of that because they're oil tankers, not attack vessels.'

'Right you are,' said Richard, still apparently looking through the walls away towards the black berg. 'There could be another one hundred and forty-nine of the poor souls out there.'

'Not likely,' said Max, more firmly than his earlier hesitation made Richard expect. 'There aren't any Typhoons left outside dry dock in Severodvinsk. We have them all now in Yard 402 except for *Titan 6* and *Titan 10,* which are out there somewhere, adapted, ready and waiting for us. All ten of the original Typhoons are already Titans – or are being refitted as Titans.'

'Mind, there's lots of other old Arctic Fleet subs out there still,' persisted Tucker thoughtfully. 'There was that November-class Kilo 159 sub that went down a few years ago while it was being towed across to Kola for break-up. And of course the *Kursk,* way back in summer 2000. Your people say they've de-commissioned what, nearly two hundred now, Max? But the old Northern Fleet's not quite history yet, is it? There's still Alpha-class subs out there, with their liquid-metal nuclear reactors and titanium hulls, sneaking about in the deep, dark trenches. Good old-fashioned fission-powered Charlies and Deltas – Delta 4s especially. Old diesel Kilos, nuclear Oscars, – *Kursk* was an Oscar 2, wasn't she? – Sierras and Victors, though they were superseded by the Akula class, weren't they? Still and all, there were one hell of a lot of Victors and Akulas. And, like you say, the old Typhoons they're refitting as Titans for us. Lotta hardware. Lotta men.'

'Just so,' said Richard. 'And as the Fates seem to have conspired with Pugin and our computer system to keep us here at the crucial moment, I suggest that we had better get under that berg and have a damn good look.'

'What?' spat Morgan. 'Waste more time?'

'When time really is money?' said Richard quietly but increasingly forcefully. 'Yes. We aren't going anywhere for the time being. And we have enough daylight left to set up the equipment. And, because of what we are and what we are about to do, we have the equipment we need. It can be done, so let it be done. We are able to do it and so we should do it. We must do it.'

Morgan's eyes narrowed and she looked at Max and Tucker, every inch the captain about to enforce her will.

'Look,' persisted Richard gently. 'Captain Hand. I know this is your command and therefore it is ultimately your decision...'

'For as long as you keep your command,' breathed Max mischievously.

'But let me make a suggestion. We set things up and get prepared. That'll take an hour and more. If *Prometheus 4* still can't proceed when everything's ready then we'll go over and take a look-see. But the instant the computers are fixed and we can make way then we will. I'll bring everything back aboard in short order and we'll be gone, whether I'm ready or not.'

'And,' whispered Max, still happily making mischief, 'I'll tell Peter Korsakov why you were late for your little date. Eh?'

Richard's eyebrows nearly joined his hairline: he had never seen a tanker captain blush before. Morgan looked around for Alexei to back her up as First Officer, but he had gone off somewhere.

The original design of *Prometheus 4*'s remote-controlled submersible was based on the US Navy's unmanned micro-DSRV series and had gloried in a long and eminently forgettable technical name until someone who had seen the film *Titanic* caught a glimpse of it in choppy water and had rechristened it. Now they all called it *Bob*; though whether the name was a description of its buoyancy or a tribute to Mr Ballard the underwater explorer, no one could tell. *Prometheus 4* needed *Bob*, or something like it, not as a rescue vehicle but as a remote-control docking facilitator. The tanker was designed to link up with Titan submarines that had filled with crude at deep well heads far beneath the stormy surface of the Kara Sea. Richard had seen from the outset that this would be no simple task that could be taken for granted – especially in the middle of the Barents, where contact was due to be made. Hence *Bob* had been brought aboard because it was designed to catch, hold, marry and tighten things everywhere from the surface to the floor of the East Barents, 350 metres down.

In almost every respect, *Bob* looked like one of the giant Kamchatka crabs – exponentially enlarged by nuclear pollution in the Kara Sea – that invaded Norwegian waters in the early summers of the new millennium, except that it had more claws and fewer legs. Still, it was well over a metre from claw-tip to claw-tip and if its eyes emitted steady beams of light as it bustled through the dark, grey waters, that was nothing more than some Norwegian fishermen claimed of the crabs in the bars from Hammerfest to Tromso.

To do its job, *Bob* was remote-controlled from a portable control panel that could work independently, given a reliable power-source, or could be married into *Prometheus 4*'s power and control systems. As the afternoon began to gather in, therefore, *Bob* was swung aloft on the already well-used gantry and lowered over the side. Richard and his little team ran up on to the bridge and snapped the relays home as though they were connecting a particularly bulky laptop to an even larger system. Abruptly, the panel's main screen lit up, as did the spare weather monitor on the left extremity of *Prometheus 4*'s main navigational display. Young Lieutenant Murphy, the Second Engineering Officer, eased himself into a chair and leaned forward to grasp the control sticks. Richard crouched behind him, and the watch officers, with nothing better to do themselves, looked on.

The monitor that was *Bob*'s eyes wavered and steadied. Water washed over it, and established itself as a choppy surface. A smaller monitor on the left gave a schematic of the little vessel's disposition while one on the right gave a clear picture of all its functions and actions.

Richard looked across at the only officer there not focused on *Bob*'s vision of the Barents Sea with the black berg looming in the background. 'Captain?' he asked, his voice only just loud enough to carry to her. She nodded once without turning her gaze from the darkening distance ahead. Richard's hand came down on the young engineer's shoulder and squeezed.

'Let's go then,' said Murphy. His hands moved. *Bob* angled down and began to move forward. On the left screen and the right, figures appeared: pitch, yaw, speed, rate of descent. The red lines of its schematic glowed as tiny propellers whirred and arrays of claws stirred, adjusting themselves apparently automatically against water pressure while preparing for action. But everyone except Murphy and Morgan Hand watched, entranced, as the central monitor showed the upper levels of the water, all agleam with star-bright specks catching the bright beams of *Bob*'s twin lights. How swiftly the darkness gathered ahead, as though the water became molasses in an instant. Molasses or crude oil, thick and black. Yet, above the intrepid little machine there remained just a hint of wan daylight. Just enough faint brightness to define the black loom of the berg as *Bob* was swept under it like a skiff under a storm front.

At once, Murphy angled *Bob* upwards so that the beams of its twin lights let the video-eye begin to scrutinize the underside of the iceberg. 'There you have it,' he whispered. 'The belly of the beast.'

'Let's hope it's an empty belly then,' said Richard bracingly.

After that one, brief conversation, silence fell at this side of the bridge as everyone concentrated on the central monitor and its slave, the second weather monitor. Outside, the Polar wind continued to gather with the darkness, throwing itself like a restless monster against the bridge. On the right side of the bridge, nearest the distant Russian coast, a quiet bustle persisted as Morgan and the recently returned Alexei Skylerov grimly continued to battle the computers. They were getting their orders directly by radio now, double-checking the work done by the computers at Novgorod, like a pair of pathologists checking where some fatal piece of brain surgery had failed.

But the gloom engendered by their ever-mounting frustration was matched on the port side. For *Bob*'s remote eye revealed a depressing desolation of lifelessness. There was nothing moving here except rags of some dead grey weed stirred by the current or by *Bob*'s intrepid bustling. But the ice itself was crusted, obscenely cankered. It had rotted into foul excrescences like huge heads of black brain coral. It sagged and swung in the current as though it were hung with hammocks containing corpses, or some huge foul submarine bats. Time and again someone would hiss with shock and Murphy would send *Bob* in for a closer look at some half-human formation. Time and again the seeming brain coral appeared to be a hanging head. More than once, a sheet of obsidian crystal tricked them into thinking that there were screaming faces frozen just behind it.

After half an hour, *Bob* appeared to have found nothing. Nothing, certainly, as absolutely human as Captain Birdseye slowly defrosting in the sickbay down below. Richard's hand tightened on Murphy's shoulder once again. He opened his mouth to say, 'That's it. Time to call it a day.'

But before Richard could get the words out, before he had even drawn breath enough to say them, Nancy Rider hissed, 'What's that?'

The instant Nancy spoke, before Richard could even see what she was talking about, Alexei Skylerov gave a hoot of joy. 'That's it,' he hallooed. 'We're back in! The computers are back on line, Captain.'

'Right!' snapped Morgan, her voice buoyant with relief and decreasing frustration, every inch Captain Hand, master of the vessel; as brisk as Captain Bligh. 'We're off. Murphy, bring *Bob* back aboard. The rest of you, get to your posts. I'll be calling for Full Ahead in five minutes.'

But even she was interrupted. 'Captain!' called the Radio Officer, popping his head out of the old-fashioned radio shack to Richard's left, right at the rear of the bridge. 'I have an urgent signal incoming!'

'Tell Novgorod we're up and running now. Tell them the boys at Bashnev Power have done the trick. Tell them thanks but we're fine now.'

'It isn't Novgorod. It's Murmansk. And it's not Bashnev Power, it's the Regional Prosecutor's Office in Murmansk.'

'What? Put it on the intercom.'

The Radio Officer complied at once. Richard's hand tightened on Murphy's shoulder and the engineer used the momentary confusion to send *Bob* towards what Nancy had seen.

'*Prometheus 4*,' came a voice in heavily

56

accented English. 'Please remain where you are. We will be with you within the next twenty minutes. If you have landing lights you must switch them on at once...'

'What is this?' called Morgan, her tone rising as this new frustration was added to all the others. 'Sparks, what's going on? This isn't Murmansk.'

But the oddly accented broadcast cut her off. '...say again, this is helicopter Kamov KA32 designation Tango Zulu Five Nine inbound to *Prometheus 4* from Murmansk. I have on board Special Investigator Rusanova of the Regional Prosecutor's Office. We will be landing in approximately eighteen minutes. If you have landing lights please switch them on at once...'

Morgan turned to Alexei, her face blank. 'Special Investigator...'

'*Police*,' he spat.

'Police? But what on earth...'

'Perhaps someone told them about Captain Birdseye,' drawled Tucker, and in the gloom his eyes gleamed, flickering across towards Max.

Richard missed most of this, for his considerable attention was focused on the central monitor, where *Bob*'s steady gaze was fixed on a piece of debris that seemed to be floating steadily into close-up. It had caught Nancy's eye for the simple reason that it was coloured. It was bright, emergency red, the same colour as Captain Birdseye's life jacket. And, as *Bob* got closer still, Richard could see that it was

57

obviously human in origin. But it was only when the intrepid little vessel extended a gentle claw and grasped the thing that Richard realized exactly what it was. It was another emergency beacon, like the one on the dead man's shoulder.

'Bring that bloody thing back aboard,' called the Captain impatiently, unaware of the latest development; and Murphy was at last pleased to obey. With its new discovery held safely in its claw, *Bob* turned for home.

Fifteen minutes later they were all on the brightly lit foredeck. Richard was down there with Murphy overseeing the recovery of *Bob* and her precious cargo. Morgan was forward of them, on the edge of the helicopter landing area, formally at attention, with her Captain's uniform coat-tails flapping in the wind. Nevertheless the dark-blue, tailored serge emphasized things she usually covered with a less formal workaday oilskin. Things, clearly, she wished to emphasize right from the start with Special Investigator Rusanova.

Richard was suddenly struck by how lonely her tall figure looked, outlined against the glare. In spite of all that had happened this afternoon, she was *his* captain after all, he thought. His captain as *Prometheus 4* was his ship. For an incredibly poignant moment he imagined his wife Robin – a ship's captain like Morgan – standing where Morgan was standing, subject to the same stresses, torn with the same frustrations, suffering the same

58

nameless fears, equally alone. Two seconds later, he was at her shoulder, pulling his hastily donned cold-weather gear into some sort of formal order; abruptly aware that clothing suitable for *Bob*'s recovery might not impress a Special Investigator in quite the way he hoped.

But it was too late to do anything about it now, he thought grimly as the relentless bellowing of the wind suddenly became the thudding of twin rotor blades and the strange, stubby body of the helicopter settled down into the light.

A door in the side of the thing just behind the articulated wheel assembly slid back. A set of steps fell out and crashed into position. A tall figure stepped purposefully down them, one hand keeping firm control of a flight bag and laptop case hanging from one shoulder, the other keeping the fleece-lined hood tight about the face.

Stooping under the complex battering of the two sets of rotors, Investigator Rusanova ran forward. At once, the steps slammed back up and the door slid shut. A white face glanced down from the cockpit, masked by a mouthpiece, and the Kamov KA32 lifted off.

Richard stepped forward until his shoulder almost touched Morgan's, then he froze, nonplussed.

Investigator Rusanova was straightening, eyes level with Morgan's and mouth moving in some formal words, impossible to hear above the noise. The hand came down from the hood and thrust forward in a Western handshake. The wind blew the hood back, revealing to Richard a tumble of jet-black hair and the face of the most beautiful woman he had ever seen in all his life.

CHAPTER SIX

Rusanova

If anyone had asked you to imagine what a Special Investigator of the Regional Prosecutor's Office in Murmansk looked like, thought Richard some moments later, the last person on earth who would have come to mind was Investigator Rusanova. She seemed in almost every regard the opposite of expectations. Indeed, had she not been so punctilious in producing her IDs, warrants and authorities, he might have supposed this was all some kind of a charade. But then, it was far too early in the adventure for him to suspect anything deeper or darker.

She was willow-slim, elegant, dressed in a beautifully tailored business suit that would hardly have been out of place in the boardrooms of Cardin, Versace or Ralph Lauren.

As the Investigator stripped off her heavy, hooded windcheater and folded it carefully over her flight-bag in the warmth of the bridge a few moments later, so the two women discussed the disposition of the ship and how Rusanova's investigation would fit into the voyage she was allowing to proceed. Or rather, thought Richard, observing silently and listening closely, how the voyage might be allowed to fit in with the investigation.

'No,' said the Investigator, courteously but immovably. 'I am afraid I am not at liberty to discuss either how this investigation began or where it is likely to proceed. But I see quite clearly your legitimate concerns, Captain. And I assure you it is not my purpose – nor the objective of the Regional Prosecutor – to inconvenience you further in any way. I am certain we can achieve a *modus vivendi* which will allow both of us to do our jobs.' Her gaze met Morgan's and Richard could have sworn he heard just the faintest ringing of steel, as though two swords had just been crossed at the beginning of a duel.

What Rusanova had in her capacious flight-bag to supplement clothing so unsuited to a cruise on a tanker, Richard could scarcely imagine. But he followed the courteously intractable Investigator and the thoughtful but relieved Captain back out of the bridge, as *Prometheus 4* got under way. He stood squarely between them while they sighed down in the lift and then remained between them as they proceeded to the last of the guest suites on C Deck, like a referee.

Precise, courteous, charming – disarming,

indeed – Rusanova spoke English with a Boston accent that made Richard think of Harvard Law School. And with this gentle but irresistible weapon she continued to lay down the law of her requirements, eventually falling back upon the laptop to bring up the documentation that underlay her authority here – once they were in her cabin and out of the public eye, where final details might be agreed. Decreed.

The ship might proceed to its rendezvous while she investigated the death of the seaman slowly thawing below, she repeated. But these were Russian waters and the contract negotiated by Richard and his partners with the authorities made it clear that the Regional Prosecutor's office had some jurisdiction here. For Russian personnel, passengers – and corpses plucked from the Barents Sea.

Morgan finally agreed with brisk formality, then hesitated, clearly on the horns of a dilemma. She was bursting to probe further the important facts of who had alerted the authorities to Captain Birdseye's existence – and why they had reacted so swiftly. But she was also bursting to get back on to the bridge and con her ship eastwards and southwards towards the rendezvous with *Titan 10.*

It fell to Richard, therefore, to lead their less-than-welcome guest down to the sickbay and to the primary object of her journey. In the lift once more, he probed with gentle, intractable, courtesy almost the equal of her own as to why the Regional Prosecutor's Office should have sent an investigator – and clearly their best investigator – on such an apparently trivial investigation.

Her only answer was a brief frown. 'Oil is never trivial, is it, Captain Mariner?' she observed. Then she met his gaze and gave a dazzling smile that kept him quiet as far as Captain Birdseye's bedside, until courtesy and practicality required that he introduce her to the Doctor.

It was not until Rusanova removed her pinstriped jacket, shrugged on a white lab coat and leaned down over the black-crusted corpse, that Richard managed to kick his mind out of its peculiarly English chauvinist blinkers and begin to see her for what she really was.

Over the ebony perfection of her hair she placed the band of a hands-free microphone. She attached its cable end to a CD recorder which reminded Richard of an old-fashioned make-up compact. She pressed 'Record' and slipped it into her pocket.

'You have gloves?' she asked.

The Doctor supplied white latex surgical gloves and Rusanova pulled them on without taking her eyes from the corpse. While this was happening she dictated the date and time, the circumstance and the names of those attending, starting with her own. Her first names, it seemed to a wryly smiling Richard, were 'Special Investigator'. But then he stopped smiling, for she knew his names and the Doctor's. Somewhere along the line she had done a lot of homework on *Prometheus 4* and her complement.

Still talking quietly, she went first to the feet and began to examine the ruin of the toes. 'He has clawed right through these socks,' she observed. 'And the socks are of oiled wool and heavy. The nails and toe-tips are gone. I can see the phalanges of bone. The same as with the fingers. Tell me exactly how this man was found...'

As Richard told the story, so she worked, probing, testing, washing, wiping; weaving her dulcet commentary into the rougher growl of his words. She checked the length of her silent subject. First the front and then, rolling him on to his side with the Doctor's help, the back. Then, having returned him to his more comfortable, face-up position, she began to ease back sections of the coveralls he wore. Her dictation on to the CD recorder never varied, but Richard, watching her, saw – or thought he saw – a deeper range of emotions go flickering across her perfect face. As she worked, and talked, it began to occur to him that the Investigator wasn't just looking at the corpse. He began to suspect with a gathering certainty that she was looking for something. Not just a clue as to who he was, where he had come from or how he had arrived beneath the black berg – or why. But something particular. Something specific. Something she was expecting to find – but hadn't. Yet.

64

Only when she got to the dead man's life jacket did her measured calm waver. Whatever the black stuff that covered him actually was, it had not reacted well with the plastic coverings and contents of his safety gear. As her search became brisker, so the very matter she was searching seemed to take a life of its own and began to fight back against her. White foam life-jacket lining panels gave off waves of disgusting odour as they became glutinous and sticky, like lately beaten whites of rotten eggs. What seemed solid plastic went semi-liquid under her touch.

Even the casing of the now-dead beacon stuck to her fingers like filthy red syrup, dripping in strings until, in exasperated disgust, she pulled off her first pair of gloves and demanded another. And that too was just as well, observed Richard, for within moments of being placed on the gutter beside the corpse's shoulder, the gloves too began to dissolve.

Half an hour later, Rusanova's first examination was complete, though clearly not to her satisfaction. A third pair of gloves joined the first two beside the dead man on the table. She scrubbed her hands in the stainless-steel sink beside the table, turning the big taps on and off with practised nudges of her elbows. Thoughtlessly, she crossed to her jacket, which was hanging on a coat stand by the door, and pulled out a cigarette pack. She flicked it open one handed while pulling off the headset with the other, then she lifted out a cigarette. Such a woman might have been expected to smoke Sobranie Black Russian or multicoloured Cocktail cigarettes. But these were thin, white and cheap. As functional as her attitudes and actions, Richard thought, with his first glimmer of real insight, and oddly at odds with her clothes and appearance. There were hidden depths here.

Neither man pointed to the 'No Smoking' sign as she lit up and exhaled a cloud of acrid fumes. Through the grey veil, she looked at them.

'What on earth are those?' asked Richard.

'Belomors,' she answered briefly, putting the pack on the stainless steel; leaving him mildly distracted, trying to read the Cyrillic letters, as she took up the main thread of Richard's testimony so far. 'You're right,' she said. 'He came up from some depth. The blood at nostril and lip-junctures shows that. Though you have noticed that his teeth are tightly clenched? He came up quite recently, of course, because his emergency beacon still had just one last vestige of power in it. This is not a particularly reliable guide because the batteries in these things are of enormously varying power. They can last from no time at all to a couple of weeks – under the right conditions. It is a pity that the oil and other matter in the ice has damaged the casing of the beacon itself. That might have given us something more with which to work. But on the other hand, he must have been in the water for a good while for the back of his clothing to have perished so. Perished or been nibbled away. What do you think?'

The abrupt question seemed to be addressed to the Doctor. So he answered. 'Eaten away, I would have thought. By something tiny, like shrimp, perhaps. We may find more evidence when he is sufficiently thawed for a full post-mortem. But if his clothing was eaten, why did whatever it was stop there?'

'Because by that time his flesh was frozen?' hazarded Richard.

'Possibly. And also, possibly, because the toxicity of the melting ice in which he was frozen killed them or drove them away. But either way, the destruction of the clothing could have happened quite quickly. But the body remained warm enough for long enough after death for the blood to drain into its lowest parts, making the shoulders and buttocks so dark. And then he froze. It's a difficult time-frame to calculate. I wonder how fast the body might be expected actually to freeze under those conditions. Talking of which, did anyone take a water temperature near where he was found?'

Richard shook his head, before he remembered the bright schematics on *Bob*'s screens. *Bob* would know exactly what the water temperature had been, he thought briefly. Or, rather, Murphy would. But he didn't mention it because it didn't seem all that important.

'You may have hit on something when you mention the toxicity...' said Richard instead of answering her question. Then he went on

67

to describe the striking absence of all animal and bird life anywhere near the berg – in spite of the apparently plentiful supply of food.

'Interesting,' allowed the Investigator. 'And it adds a new element, does it not? A factory ship close by...'

Then she shrugged, almost shivered, and flicked her cigarette end into a waste bin that was mercifully empty. 'Or it might be an irrelevance. A distraction.'

'Only time will tell,' said Richard.

'But we have little time to waste.'

'We have some, surely,' temporized Richard. 'We have to wait until Captain Birdseye thaws before we can get much more detail from him. That will take overnight at the very least. And of course, we have until *Prometheus 4* reaches the rendezvous point with *Titan 10*, and that will take another twenty hours or so, as long as the computers stay on line.'

Rusanova frowned at him, suddenly narrow-eyed. 'What makes you assume I will stay aboard until the rendezvous?' she asked.

'Nothing in particular,' he said, much struck by the realization that he had, in fact, made just that assumption quite automatically. 'I just supposed you would do the round trip back to where you came aboard.'

'Perhaps. Perhaps not. My helicopter has a long range. It can come and get me, no matter where I am. Besides...'

Rusanova's further thoughts – and Richard's simple wonder that an investigator for a Regional Prosecutor should have a helicopter at her beck and call – were cut short by a gentle tapping at the sickbay's outer door. Second Engineering Officer Murphy popped his head in. 'Ah, Captain Mariner. Can I have a word?' he said, his Irish eyes all wide and innocent. 'It's about that thing that *Bob* found...' Richard was nonplussed for a moment, for Murphy should have been on engine room watch as the Second Navigating Officer was on the bridge. But *Prometheus 4*'s great motors went on to 'Unmanned' at eighteen hundred hours – so the engineers were free in the evening.

Bob's treasure lay on the desk in Murphy's tiny cabin. With Richard and Nancy Rider both in there, the place seemed impossibly crowded. But there was room for the cadet to sit on a chair while the two men shared the bed. All three of them craned forward over the bright-red emergency equipment equally eagerly. 'From what I can see,' said Richard slowly, 'it appears to be perfectly standard. The kind of kit you might find anywhere. Except that it's the Russian version rather than the Western one.' He picked it up a little gingerly, remembering the way the corpse's had dissolved to sticky strings under Rusanova's gently inquisitive fingers. But it stayed solid, felt firm and icily cold; and surprisingly light.

'It's exactly what Captain Birdseye was wearing on the shoulder of his life jacket,' Richard continued. 'Except that it's in better condition. All except the battery, I assume, because it's dead as a dodo.' He turned it over, eyes busy. And froze.

There on the back of it, stencilled in black, were some letters. They were clearly some kind of an identification code, and the letters seemed familiar – except that Richard had had enough experience to know better. This writing, like that on Rusanova's cigarettes, was probably in Cyrillic. He recognized what it was – but not what it meant. Whatever, the actual ID number of the equipment – or of the vessel that had carried it – must await the arrival of someone who could read them. Perhaps, thought Richard suddenly, it had been these figures – or others like them – that Rusanova had expected to see on the dead man's clothing and equipment. But the corrosive properties of the oil had fooled her. His eyes flicked up to Nancy's breast. There on her work overall *'Prometheus 4'* was stencilled. And it was on all the equipment around and aboard. Yes. Yes indeed. They had better get someone who could translate these Cyrillic cyphers as quickly as possible! Or, he thought suddenly, grown a little paranoid perhaps and unwilling to share too much information with too many people as yet, perhaps not some*one*. Perhaps some*thing* would do. 'Has either of you got a Russian/English dictionary?' he asked.

But before either of them could answer, events once again overtook them. The ship's chimes sounded. It was time for drinks and dinner. 'Go and get ready,' he ordered Nancy Rider. 'Got pencil and paper?' he demanded of Murphy as soon as she left. It was the work of a moment to sketch the lettering on to the back of an envelope and shove it in his pocket. Then, 'Hide this,' he ordered, pointing to the bright beacon as he left.

CHAPTER SEVEN

Cyrillic

Richard had no time for the shower and shave he normally took at this hour. He satisfied himself with a quick wash and brush-down, and a secret glance at the Russian writing, before descending to the old-fashioned officers' ward room, where pre-prandial drinks were being served.

Max and Tucker were already there, drinks in hand, discussing the day's events with the junior officers over a range of beverages from Pepsi to Perrier; from Stolinskaya vodka to sour-mash bourbon. Richard accepted his single Tallisker and looked around. He felt isolated, suddenly, out of step and out of touch. Was this how spies felt? he wondered, never being quite what they seemed – always playing a part. Always in a position where the slightest slip would give away some terrible secret and put their lives – and more – at risk. He shivered and, affecting easy normality, he slipped his hand in his jacket pocket – only to find the envelope and it shocked him as though it had been electric.

Morgan arrived, with Alexei at her side, the Second Officer entering the second dog watch up on the bridge – unlike Engineering Officer Murphy, who was on his way. As the hum of conversation built, Richard inevitably fell in with Tucker and Max – who were the main reason he was here rather than sitting in the library looking up the letters. Instead he forced himself into normality, discussing matters that were obviously of immediate and considerable importance, such as what difference the day's delay might make to *Prometheus 4*'s carefully calculated schedule.

But Richard felt distant, preoccupied. As he made courteous small talk, he found the conundrum of the second emergency beacon's Cyrillic ID nagging at the back of his mind like an unsolved crossword clue. Especially as he noticed everywhere he looked the name of *Prometheus 4* stencilled, painted, engraved and embroidered on everything – and almost everyone – around him.

The only thing that distracted him for any length of time was Rusanova's entrance. It had not really occurred to him, preoccupied as he was, that the Investigator would join in with *Prometheus 4*'s social functions. But just

72

as things got heated with Max about whether *Titan 10* would be willing to wait for six hours beyond her schedule at the rendezvous, the ward room suddenly went silent.

Richard turned, to find Rusanova hesitating coolly at the door, if anything more *chic* than she had appeared so far. He crossed to her at once and swept her into the social circle of the ship. She accepted a Wolf Blass Black Label Shiraz that looked almost as thick as blood and sipped it as she mingled. At first Richard remained close by her side. But, although she was clearly an outsider here, Rusanova seemed able to hold her own on any subject and in any company. So Richard watched her increasingly distantly through the rest of the drinks session and then through the excellent dinner.

Prometheus 4, like all of the Prometheus series – like all of Richard's tankers, prided herself on the quality of her cuisine. The only variable from one of them to the next was the culinary taste of the Captain. It had been one of Morgan's first duties this morning – as it was every captain's every morning in the Heritage Mariner fleet – to approve the galley menus. Today, in deference to their entry into Russian waters, Morgan had chosen a feast with a Russian flavour. Blinis piled with sour cream and caviar were followed by Scha-velnik, a creamy vegetable soup delicately flavoured with sorrel. The thick, hot soup was followed by a cold pudding called Viets-Putra made with fresh white sea-fish and served with a range of salads and bowls of steaming potatoes. There were cherry dumplings for pudding and honey biscuits with coffee and tea.

Richard sat between Max and Tucker, feeling not a little trapped. The three of them were opposite Morgan, who had the Chief Engineer on one hand and Rusanova in Alexei's usual seat on the other. Alexei was in the Second Officer's place – and clearly none too happy with the demotion. Richard's eyes narrowed as he fleetingly wondered about Alexei's thoughts on Rusanova.

Richard himself continued his courteous exploration of her real reasons for being here, her orders and her plans; but she remained courteously evasive and soon Max and she were discussing the latest Moscow scandal – the detention of the third richest man in Russia for a range of nefarious activities from tax evasion to contracted murder. Such were the dangers, said Max airily, of getting and of keeping such fortunes even in the new Russia. Richard watched and listened, hoping Rusanova would let something slip – but she didn't. Over pudding, he finally dismissed her from his thoughts altogether as she had dismissed the factory ship – as an irrelevance. A distraction. As soon as dinner was over, he thought, he would find a way to take action on the much more pressing matter in his pocket. Unconsciously, his bright-blue gaze sought out Nancy and Murphy – and was disturbed to find how closely his fellow-conspirators were watching him.

Richard was a man used to handling events, controlling almost all the circumstances in which he found himself. But the one thing that a man like him in a place such as this found almost impossible to get was some privacy. Short of being brutally rude – an action that would be far out of character and suspiciously at odds with his cheerful emollience so far – he could get no time at all on his own. As the evening wore on seemingly endlessly after dinner, he talked American politics with Tucker. Then he switched the subject with Max to Norilsk Nickel's new project with the Moscow Academy of Science to try and power sources and fuel cells using hydrogen gas.

At ten he was scheduled to hold a nightly meeting with Morgan to check over the day's progress and the morrow's plans. Alexei sometimes joined them – but he often caught a couple of hours' sleep then before taking the midnight watch. Tonight, thought Richard, he would certainly be there, given today's adventures with Captain Birdseye and the black berg and tomorrow's crucial rendezvous with *Titan 10*.

Those aboard who knew Richard's routines, however, granted him one window of privacy without a second thought – at 9.45 local time. As his ancient, steel-cased Rolex Oyster Perpetual showed 9.44, he eased himself away from the still animated group and stepped out of the ward room, his mind racing. At this exact moment, all through the voyage so far, he had retired to his cabin, taken out his personal phone and dialled the international call code for Ashenden, his home on the cliffs of Sussex. Each night he was away from the place, he called, fondly imagining Robin, his wife, sitting curled upon the long sofa in the sitting room that over-looked the Channel, waiting for the contact he always made. It seemed something of a sacrilege to use the precious ritual of this moment as a cover, but he could see no other option.

As he hurried down the corridors away from the lift – in the opposite direction to his usual evening route – he pulled out his phone and started dialling. By the time he got a faint and intermittent ring-tone, he was at the door to the ship's little library. And the moment he heard Robin's distant, ghostly voice, he stepped into the darkness of the place.

For once in his life he did not hang upon Robin's every word and was so distracted by his search that he would never remember even what he said to her. Like Rusanova and the factory ship, the great love of his life became a distraction for the next few minutes as he closed the door behind him and felt for the light switch. As he crept across the room and searched the shelves. As he pulled out the biggest Russian/English dictionary there and began to search for the Cyrillic letters.

He started by opening the big tome at the index and then leafed through the introduction, looking for a page that would give him the Cyrillic letters and their Western equivalents. The task should not be too hard, he thought. He said again 'Yes, dear...' into the phone and pulled Murphy's envelope out of his pocket and the pencil with which he had written upon it.

Yes. The letters seemed quite clear:

$$T K - 20$$

they said, apparently in English – or any other language with Romance-based lettering.

'Really, darling?' he mumbled, as, eyes narrow, he started to check down the columns.

A really was *A*. Good start.

But then a kind of upside-down *Q* was *B*. That wasn't quite so good.

And *B* was in fact *V*...

Richard sat down and began to con centrate. He stopped talking to Robin. He even stopped listening to her as he pored over the dictionary, tracing the letters down.

He found *K* first. That was in fact *K*. Then he found *T* and, miracle of miracles, that really was *T*. The start of the designation on the beacon, therefore, was *TK*. That fact alone made his blood run cold, as he wrote the letters on the envelope beneath the Cyrillic originals.

TK-20

it said, in English now as well as in Cyrillic.

'My God,' he breathed as he sat back. 'That's very bad indeed.' Perhaps fortunately, his forgotten phone had broken contact several seconds ago. Automatically, still completely consumed by what he had been doing and what the designation on the envelope meant to him, he picked up the cellphone and put it to his ear. He was too preoccupied even to register the noise that it was making beyond that it was not Robin's voice. He switched it off.

'What in God's name does this mean, though?' he asked himself. He slipped the phone into his pocket and tensed himself to rise, still looking down at the envelope resting on the open book.

'Ah,' said a voice immediately behind him, so close that it made him jump. 'Captain Mariner. Captain Hand sent me to find you. It's after ten...'

Then Alexei Skylerov also stopped speaking and his shadow fell across the envelope on the little library table.

'*TK-20*,' he said. 'Now what in the world made you look that up, Captain Mariner? In Roman and Cyrillic. *TK-20*. You know what it means?'

'Yes,' said Richard. 'Yes, I do. It's the designation of a Typhoon-class nuclear submarine...'

He turned in his chair to face the frowning Russian. 'Indeed,' confirmed Skylerov, clearly supposing that Richard was just about to complete the sentence himself. 'It's what

78

Titan 10 was called before she was refitted and redesignated. It's what *Titan 10* was called before she became *Titan 10*.'

CHAPTER EIGHT

Conference

So it was that neither the day's adventures nor the morrow's rendezvous formed the first order of business at the late running ten o'clock meeting between the First Officer, the Captain and the Owner of *Prometheus 4*.

The three of them met in the old-fashioned chart room that sentiment had led Richard to demand right at the rear of the bridge. The little room felt scarcely bigger than Murphy's cabin, packed as it was with a chart table covered in clear Perspex beneath which lay Admiralty Chart 2962, across which their course was marked in blue chinagraph pencil.

There was just room to allow a narrow bunk designed exclusively for the Captain's use. It fitted like the filling of a sandwich beneath the shelves full of blue-bound, gold-lettered British Admiralty Pilots, and it lay above the great deep drawers full of charts to every water on the earth. The little bed was exactly like the room it occupied – cramped and uncomfortable, but private. Not even the helmsman seated at the supertanker's helm could hear them in here.

'No,' Richard was explaining. 'It wasn't on Captain Birdseye. All his kit was perished or destroyed as far as we could tell. Not even Rusanova could find any ID markings on it as far as I could see. And I was watching her pretty closely. This was floating a good way away from him under the main bulk of the berg. *Bob* brought it aboard just as Rusanova arrived.'

'That's perfect, as coincidences go,' laughed Alexei grimly.

'And you think it gives a clue as to where the body came from?' persisted Morgan, frowning her officer into silence.

'Yes and no. Because although *Titan 10* and *Typhoon TK-20* share the same hull and many of the same fittings, they are of course entirely different vessels. And in all sorts of ways. One is a commercial oil transport vessel and the other was a military nuclear attack submarine. And that's just the start of it. It's taken some time to refit *Titan 10* and recommission her. There's no way the corpse could have come off her when she was still *Typhoon TK-20*. I mean, his beacon was still giving out a signal and the batteries last for days, not years. But on the other hand, I've never been aboard *Titan 10*, so I don't know how much of the original kit is still aboard her, still marked with the old ID.'

'I'd say quite a bit,' said Alexei. 'You know how they are at Severodvinsk, Captain Mariner. Or maybe you don't. You do, Captain Hand. You can say if I'm right or not. It's "Waste not, want not" down there. And unless the people in charge of the refit had someone going in to dot every *i* and cross every *t*, no one would ever think of re-marking the survival equipment with the ship's new name.'

'But what on earth would *Titan 10* be doing out here? It's supposed to be in the Kara Sea filling up with oil and getting to the rendezvous.' Morgan demanded.

'Two thoughts,' said Richard. 'First, whatever happened to Captain Birdseye could have happened up to two weeks ago. Two weeks, if Inspector Rusanova can be believed. Because that's how long the batteries on his beacon could have lasted. Secondly, just because the berg was here today, there's no saying it was here that long ago. It could have moved a good distance in that time and old Birdseye at least would have come along with it – he was hanging on tightly enough, God knows.'

'There's a strong west-flowing surface current that comes off the top of Novaya Zemlya,' said Morgan, crossing to the chart and looking down. 'It comes just south of Franz Joseph Land, here, and then turns south straight into the Barents. That could have picked our berg up almost anywhere and brought it down here to us.'

'And there was that storm last week,' added Alexei. 'That came out of the Kara Sea and blew westward with hurricane force. We thought we were going to have to sit and wait it out. Remember?'

'So,' said Richard, thoughtfully, 'the black berg could have come one hell of a long way in a week, let alone two. The conditions sound right enough. But you've been in contact with *Titan 10*, haven't you? Surely they would have reported something like this.'

'Yes. I was speaking to Peter Korsakov exactly a week ago – though I haven't been on to him any more recently than that. Wouldn't have expected to if he's running submerged, of course. That's part of the point of letting the computers control everything down to the last inch and second, of course. He doesn't need to be shoving up radio buoys every hour of the day and night. He didn't say anything other than how glad he was that he'd be well away from the weather – on the bottom of the sea. There was nothing about anyone going missing. The most sinister thing he mentioned was a slight stomach infection...'

'That seems to be that, then,' said Richard. He looked around the other two faces, frowning. 'Now we need to move on to our next decision. And this one will be the first step down one road or another, so we need to think quite carefully and weigh the implications as best we can.

'Do we turn over all we've found here to Rusanova? Or do we not?'

'Are we the only ones who should be involved in that decision?' asked Alexei quietly. 'Should we warn Mr Asov or Mr Roanoake what is going on?'

'Good thought, Alexei,' said Morgan. But after a glance at her lieutenant, she turned to Richard. 'What do you think?'

'It spreads responsibility. Gets more of us into trouble if anything goes wrong,' he observed thoughtfully. 'And what would we gain? Two new heads – but not a lot more knowledge...'

'Mr Asov would have a well-founded view.'

'Well put, Alexei. You should be in the Diplomatic Corps. Perhaps we will refer it to his experience. Or perhaps we should also give it all to Special Investigator Rusanova. Time will tell. But I don't think we want to rush things. I think we need to sleep on it. I certainly do. So we'll leave it quiet for a while, I think.' Richard's bright gaze rested on the other two until they nodded agreement.

'Right,' he continued. 'Now, about tomorrow...'

The next day dawned brighter and clearer – bright and clear for the Barents Sea. There was no fog – but no real horizon either. The cloud was high and occasionally broken, allowing a dazzling sun to slope through and strike off the water and any other available surface with blinding intensity. The low overcast that came sweeping out of the east just before noon came as a relief to everyone – but it brought a biting wind to the air and an increasing chop to the sea.

Richard had slept unaccustomedly late and then called home instead of going down to breakfast. Unlike last night – for which he was trying to make amends – he did manage to communicate with an extremely sleepy Robin as she pottered around in the kitchen, fortifying herself with strong cups of English Breakfast Tea against the gathering prospect of feeding her teenage twins. And having cleared his conscience thus far, he felt ready to have the shower and shave he missed the evening before. Once in the shower stall, he felt moved to sing selections from Gilbert and Sullivan. All in all, it was a calm and peaceful time.

It was nearly ten, when Richard came on to the bridge. Because this was the hour that rendezvous with *Titan 10* had been planned originally, everyone who would have been involved in that extremely experimental manoeuvre had somehow made their way here, as though drawn by the unfulfilled prospect. Max and Tucker were there; Alexei of course, though it was the Third Officer who held the 'forenoon watch. There was a helmsman, alternating his steady gaze between the course-finder equipment in front of him and the dazzling and ill-defined horizon just above it. And there was Cadet Nancy Rider in her usual station where she could see both the collision alarm monitor and the weather monitor.

'How are we doing?' Richard asked Morgan.

'We made good time through the night. Rendezvous in four hours,' she said, squinting at the brightness of the low sun on the steady grey water. 'Come into the chart room and I'll show you the precise bearings and timings.'

'That's good,' he said loudly, following her into last night's privacy. Then, lowering his voice he asked, 'Anything else I should know about?'

She nodded. 'The Doctor says the corpse is almost defrosted. Rusanova will be taking another look at it soon, if she hasn't already started.'

'No surprises there. She handles herself with some authority around dead people. But I don't suppose for a moment she'll be doing a post-mortem herself.'

'She might ask the Doc, I suppose.'

'Unlikely. He's a GP with some extra training, not a pathologist. If she's going to do things properly, she'll need to fly one out or take Captain Birdseye back with her.'

'Logic would suggest that she'll make that decision when she sees what her second examination with the defrosted corpse brings to light. And whether she ever discovers about *Bob*'s treasure trove.'

'Yes. That's something that occupied me through the long night watches. If I tell her, is

85

she likely to get the rest of the Regional Prosecutor's Office out here mob-handed?'

'Or is she likely to take her bag and her facts and her body and chopper them all off my ship and out of my hair?'

'That seems the least likely of the alternatives. But it's certainly what Alexei or Max could advise us on. Or Tucker, come to that. He certainly seems to know one hell of a lot about the Russian Northern Fleet.'

'Well, they're all out there on the bridge.'

'Let's not rush, Morgan,' he growled.

'That's wise, Richard,' she said, and turned on her heel.

'Two o'clock. Fourteen hundred hours on the dot,' he said more loudly as he followed her out. 'That's very good news indeed. And have we heard from *Titan 10*?'

'Nothing yet,' she said, also more loudly.

'Max?' Richard's bright gaze took them all in now – Max beside the radio shack, Tucker beside Alexei near the helmsman – but where he could see the weather monitor over Nancy Rider's shoulder and the navigational aids as well as the computer-controlled course finder, whose green schematics were the helmsman's guide. Though, thought Richard, to be fair and as yesterday had shown, the computers both here aboard and ashore in Novgorod that guided the course finder were more in control of the ship than the helmsman or the helm. Push come to shove, they could probably get *Prometheus 4* to her destination with no further human help at all.

'Anything in yet, Max?'

'No,' said Max, picking up on the conversation with lightning speed. 'Nothing from Novgorod.'

'But he won't be broadcasting until he surfaces in any case, will he?' said Tucker. And although the words were a question, his tone of voice was not.

'But then, sir,' said Alexei, 'he should be surfacing right about now. It is we who are late, not Captain Korsakov.'

'We'll know when *Titan 10* surfaces in any case, whether Korsakov feels talkative or not,' said Max in answer, his voice ringing with justifiable pride. 'The satellites that track all our vessels will know. Just as they know we are running late and make adjustment through the computers at Novgorod.'

'Good,' said Richard, looking round them all again then out at the dazzling day. 'When the news comes in, please tell me. I'll be down in the sickbay with the Doctor and our two most recent guests.'

CHAPTER NINE

Naked Truth

Special Investigator Rusanova had not quite begun her second examination, but the disposition of her subject on the operating table – and the peculiarly piercing smell within the sickbay – attested to the fact that Captain Birdseye was ready and ripe. His arms and legs no longer lay frozen akimbo, but had been arranged more decorously. The legs lay with their ankles touching in the sopping ruin of their toeless socks. His arms lay precisely at his sides, held in the running gutters on either side of the table. The Doctor – Richard assumed it was the Doctor, for it seemed unlikely that Rusanova would have bothered – had closed his eyes. But water continued to run from under the bulging lids as it continued to run from everywhere on the stinking, saturated corpse.

At first glance it seemed to Richard that the Investigator was going to perform the autopsy herself after all, for she had tied a heavy green plastic apron over her white lab coat and was pulling on thick rubber gloves as he came in through the door. The outer room was empty now: Pugin had obviously returned to his duties. Given the stench, it was hardly surprising.

'Ah. Captain Mariner,' Rusanova said, tightening the second glove with a snap. 'I have been expecting you.' She fixed him with a piercing stare. 'It seemed so unlikely that someone who had taken such a proprietorial interest in our late friend last night would desert him this morning. And leave him to my tender mercies unsupported.'

'You make me sound like the best man at a stag party.'

'Best man at a wedding, perhaps. Though we deal here with the third great ceremony of life after birth and marriage. Death. Consider, however. Who was it that brought our friend aboard? Who caused him to be carried down here? Who examined him first? Who *christened* him?'

'Now, I had supposed, Ms Rusanova, that you were here to investigate our dead friend. And now I find you have been exercising your talents on me.' He made it sound amused. He did not feel threatened to be the subject of her scrutiny and did not wish her to suppose that he did.

'An investigator investigates, Captain Mariner,' she answered easily. 'That's what investigators do. There are no limits and no boundaries. An investigator investigates what needs to be investigated.'

Richard waited a beat. Just one beat. 'Then

89

you must have a very busy life indeed,' he said.

She smiled. Not the shallow, dazzling smile in the lift, but something deeper, that started in her eyes and brought out the most delicious lines at her temples and the corners of her mouth. 'You would hardly believe,' she said, 'how busy my life can get.'

'And so you have never married?' He approached the table on the opposite side from her, until only the corpse was keeping them apart. 'You wear no wedding rings,' he explained in the face of her quizzically raised eyebrows.

'You will need a lab coat, apron and gloves if you propose to come any nearer. Simply removing his clothing will be messy work. And, I would suggest, one of these.' She pulled out a face mask and slipped it over her nose and mouth, taking care that it fitted under the tiny point of her hands-free microphone.

Then, as Richard took off his jacket and followed her suggestions with the silent Doctor's help, she continued their conversation with unexpected candour. 'You miscalculate a little, however. Wedding rings are something of a luxury in Murmansk. Were I happily married I would not necessarily possess one. In any case I never wear jewellery when I am at work, so once again, there is no clue in my naked fingers. But as it happens, yes. You are correct. I am unmarried.'

'Ah.' Richard tried to make the mono-syllable neutral and noncommittal – but just enquiring enough to elicit more information.

Her eyes, darker than the plainest chocolate but given extra life and sparkle in contrast to the mask and full of unexpected passion, glanced up at him even as her fingers briskly began to test the corpse's joints for movement. 'Ah,' she echoed. 'You pity me. Typical male chauvinist. You feel that I am unfulfilled, just because I do not have a man to come home drunk to me and beat me with a big stick and rape me in the night. Because I do not have a brood of whining children to fasten themselves upon my back like vampires and drag me down, to turn me from success to slave. From financially independent worker to helpless pauper. From Businesswoman to Babushka. No. My work is my marriage and my boss carries a big enough stick for me.'

'I see.' Richard too picked up a hand and began to test how freely the fingers bent, struck again by just how much damage had been done to their tips where they had scrabbled helplessly at the ice.

'I doubt that you do. Nevertheless it is all that you are likely to see of my private life, so let us leave it there and concentrate on more immediate matters. His hands and arms are free-moving?'

'They seem to be so, yes.'

'Then let us look to his feet and legs. They are more massive and may take longer to become free. Ah. No. I see not. Very well. If we can sit him up with equal ease then we may proceed. Doctor, your assistance here, if you please.'

'Proceed with what?' asked Richard, suddenly a little unnerved by the speed with which things seemed to be moving. He half expected her to answer *To proceed with a full autopsy, of course. I will need you to hold the instruments, grasp the bone-spreaders, grip the walls of the thoracic cavity after I have made the first great incision...*

'To undress him. What else did you expect?' She glanced up at him again, her eyes dancing with mirth. 'We are hardly qualified to do even that. To go further without a pathologist would be unthinkable.'

'Your boss would get out his big stick?' The words were out before he saw the unfortunate double meaning.

Which she mercifully chose to ignore. 'Precisely. And Regional Prosecutor Lavrenty Michaelovitch Yagula is not a man you wish to upset.'

The three of them together heaved the dead body into a sitting position and he moved easily enough, his head falling back on a flaccid neck like a ball on a chain, then flopping forward with an unnerving looseness. Rusanova nodded and they laid him back down again. She pointed with what little of her chin was visible beneath her mask and the Doctor brought a big black plastic bag. Rusanova turned to the feet and began to ease the toeless sock off his nearly toeless left foot. Richard followed suit, easing off the right sock with all the care of a novice under the eyes of a famous master.

'Prosecutor Yagula is like the man the American President Roosevelt described,' continued Rusanova almost dreamily – and Richard began to wonder whether she had switched her recorder on yet. 'You remember the words? He walks very, very quietly and he carries a very, very big stick.'

'Oh,' said Richard, lightly. 'I thought perhaps you meant that he couldn't stand the heat in kitchens.'

She laughed. A single bark of dark, wry humour. She took the sock he offered with the words and began to fold the pair of them with all the fastidious neatness he was coming to expect. 'It was President Truman who said this, I think. However, I have never seen Prosecutor Yagula in a kitchen,' she said. 'I cannot even imagine him in a kitchen.'

'Perhaps he has hidden depths,' suggested Richard. 'Perhaps he cooks.' The pair of them stood face to face across the mess on the corpse's chest.

'We'll need another bag for this, please, Doctor,' said Rusanova.

'And we'd better make it a good, thick cloth one,' suggested Richard. 'Plastic won't last by the look of things. We'll be lucky if these gloves will.'

But as it turned out, the black chemical had done its worst. The life jacket, its back eaten away, lifted off in a section like a breastplate, and they were able to slip it, emergency beacon and all, into the doubled pillowcase the Doctor held for them. Richard nearly let it slip, however, as he looked eagerly beneath it to see if the telltale 'TK-20' sign was marked on the overall breast. But no. Although bits and pieces of the material remained largely undamaged, the central section solid enough to be buttoned, the two sections over the corpse's chest, the breast pockets and whatever they had contained, had perished after all and lifted away with the jacket revealing nothing more incriminating than a grey vest.

If Rusanova noticed his sudden clumsiness – or understood anything of the reason for it – she said nothing. Instead she seemed content to continue their discussion. 'Prosecutor Yagula does not cook,' she said with utter certainty. Then she glanced up with a tiny frown, as though she might have let slip something more intimate than she meant to. 'I have seen what he eats,' she explained.

'Ah,' said Richard again. 'And has Prosecutor Yagula no babushka of his own at home to cook for him then?'

'No,' she said, more guardedly, glancing up from where her fingers were loosening the last button on Birdseye's overalls above the belt.

'No doubt he is also married to his work,' he suggested lightly, reaching for the metal buckle of the corpse's belt.

Her answer was a little sigh. A sound almost of disappointment. As though Richard had missed something unexpected. As though he had shown ignorance of a basic rule in their strange little contest. As though he had spoilt the game, somehow.

'But I am very ignorant of the system that employs you both,' he admitted, hoping that apparent candour would serve to mend fences. 'And, indeed, of the society you live in. All we hear in the West is talk of endemic corruption, the work of Mafia and terrorists. That Russia is world capital of murder and drug dealing; that there are five times more murders per head of population than in Washington or New York and that the teenage and pre-teen drug of first choice tends to be heroin. That there is a black market for everything and ordinary citizens must queue for hours to get the most basic household items and groceries. But then, on the other hand, it is a vast engine for unimaginable wealth – especially in the fields of oil and gas, minerals and metals, gold and diamonds – and a corporate paradise for careful investors.'

'Such as yourself,' she observed quietly.

'And Mr Roanoake. But only through Mr Asov and his contacts and the good offices of your government, both central and regional. To be fair, though, it is Messrs Roanoake and Asov who are investing in Russia itself. It is they who have co-financed the Titan project with your government. It is they who have put the computers in the Titans, in my tankers and in the control centres in Novgorod and Murmansk. My investment is primarily in the Prometheus series of tankers.'

'So,' she accused, quietly. 'If it all goes wrong and they all go down like the *Titanic*, at least you can sail safely away on your *moveable assets* like this one.'

'That's the theory,' he admitted, very uneasily indeed.

'Let us hope it doesn't get put to any kind of a test,' she whispered, and pulled Birdseye's overalls wide, revealing a woollen vest and long-john combination that had clearly once been white.

They removed this with extreme care, and in a silence the Doctor was happy to share. But when he and Richard sat the corpse up again, preparing to remove the underwear, he observed quietly, 'You know, there's something odd about his face.'

Rusanova looked up from where she was neatly folding the overall into the bag with the socks. 'What do you mean?' she asked, but there was something in her tone that made Richard suspect that she, too, had noticed something. Something he himself seemed to have missed.

'Take off the top now you have him sitting up,' she ordered. 'We'll take a closer look when he's lying down again.'

The top was easy to slide forward over his shoulders and slip down his arms. Then a gentle downward tug from Rusanova was enough to remove the last garment completely – largely backless as it was – while Richard and the Doctor laid the flaccid torso back down on the table and arranged its flopping arms more decorously again. She then joined them at the head. 'Yes,' she said. 'You're right, Doctor. Most unusual.'

The dark eyes flashed up towards Richard and there was no longer even the faintest twinkle in them. 'You see?' she asked. 'The mouth and jaw?'

'The mouth is closed,' said Richard.

'Precisely. Would you care to open it?'

Richard reached forward hesitantly. As though dealing with a recalcitrant son refusing to take his medicine, he grasped the dead man's battered nose and took hold of his square chin. And pulled the two apart. Or rather, he tried to do so – unsuccessfully, for the jaw remained immovably fixed. Still with a father's gentle hands, he took the lower jaw and the forehead, seeking for some lateral movement. But there was none. 'It's stuck shut,' he said. 'Frozen.'

'Not frozen,' said Rusanova. 'The body is quite thawed, as we have seen with the ease of undressing him.'

'Rigor mortis?'

'In the jaw alone? The rest of the body is well past rigor now.'

'Well, whatever it is, you're stuck with it. You'd have to break the jaw to get that mouth open.'

'Ah,' said Rusanova. And there was a world of speculation in that one quiet syllable.

97

Just the sound of it set Richard's mind to racing. He stepped back and looked at the naked corpse, suddenly struck by the series of coincidences that now seemed to be falling into place. 'I don't suppose the Regional Prosecutor's Office goes in for DNA sampling,' he said at last.

'No. Nor do many of the Central Agencies, much. Not even the FBS.'

'Then you're scuppered, aren't you?'

'I beg your pardon? Scuppered?'

'Lost. Adrift. Helpless.'

'How quaint. Scuppered. I must remember it. Helpless to do what?'

'Identify him. There was nothing on him, was there? Nothing in his pockets, no watches, crucifixes, St Christophers or dog-tags. Not even a laundry mark on any of his clothes. I've not seen any scars, tattoos or obvious features. Not even his own mother would recognize his face in that state. And if you had any retinal scans – about as popular as DNA sampling, I'd guess – his eyes won't be in a fit state to use them after they finish thawing out. So if you have to break his jaw you'll ruin any dental records he might have had. And finally, of course, he hasn't any toe-prints or finger-prints left, has he? Not with all his digits clawed down to the phalange bones. So where does that leave you, Investigator Rusanova?'

'Precisely where you said, Captain Mariner. Scuppered. Scuppered, but with one more question left.'

98

'Did all this happen by chance?' growled Richard, asking the vital question for her. 'Or did someone arrange it on purpose?'

'Precisely,' she said.

And the ship's tannoy boomed: 'CAPTAIN MARINER, REPORT TO THE BRIDGE AT ONCE, PLEASE. CAPTAIN MARINER TO THE BRIDGE AT ONCE...'

CHAPTER TEN

Rendezvous

Richard was still buttoning up his jacket and shrugging it into place across his shoulders as he stepped out of the lift and strode across the lateral corridor that ran behind the bridge.

He was used to being summoned by the tannoy and was not concerned to have been called that way again. But he never forgot that this was exactly the way the next major crisis was likely to start and so he got a move on, too streetwise to think of slowing down until he knew precisely what was going on.

The bridge was unexpectedly gloomy. He had left it in migraine-making glare and now he returned to find that *Prometheus 4* was sailing into a lowering overcast. His wise seaman's eyes scanned the early afternoon as it appeared immediately outside his ship. The horizon seemed close ahead and murky. The sea looked like a huge rough metal file with triangular waves all black-faced; most of them white-capped. The only good thing to be said about the dullness was that it made the schematics on the control displays twinkle clearly, all of them easy to read. Which is what he did next, as he strode to Morgan's shoulder. 'You called?' he growled.

By way of answer she gestured to the helmsman. Richard was surprised to note that it was Pugin, but beyond that he could see nothing remarkable at all. But then he noticed the bright schematic in front of the man. When he had left the bridge for the sickbay it had been green. Now it was red. The last time he had looked at it, the computer-generated – computer-controlled – picture on the video screen had shown a bright diagram compounded of sea-bed topography overlain with sea and sky conditions explored in more detail by the specialized screens nearby. It was marked in red only for any items displayed also on the collision alarm radar, which existed both on a vertical screen and in a more traditional horizontal bowl nearby.

And through the whole of the Christmas-tree display had sped the straight green line of *Prometheus 4*'s course, unwinding inevitably towards the schematic line of the horizons the ship's sensors could see – horizons far beyond the reach of the watch keepers' merely human eyes.

But it was different now. For the line – no longer green but purple – did not end at the distant and retreating horizon. It ended at a bright-red point. And that point was on the upper end of something that looked for all the world like a large letter *L*. This too was red. And it was made all the more bright by the fact that it contained large square letters that filled the *L* from top to bottom: *TN10*. The letters and figures studied with so much effort the previous night rose before his eyes. So similar – but crucially different. '*TN10*,' he said. 'That's her ID. That's her. That's *Titan 10*!'

'Dead ahead. Maybe an hour away,' Morgan said, her voice shaking a little. 'Registering on our sonar right down to her ID beacon.'

'And running still submerged,' added Max exultantly. 'Still submerged, or our course would end at the angle of the *L* instead of at the top!'

'Most impressive,' said Tucker. And his voice rang with sincerity.

'You ain't seen nothing yet,' enthused the Russian. 'You know what we could do? We could all leave the bridge unmanned. We could all go down to lunch and leave no one up here at all. Now they have acquired each other the computers would bring us in as safe and sweet as you like. All on automatic pilot, you know? We'd sail down to that rendezvous point there and ease back automatically to a dead stop. And *Titan 10* would pop right up alongside us. And all her watch officers could be out to lunch as well. The computers will do it all, and better than humans. I kid you not one and all. Better than humans.'

'Of course, I'm tempted, Mr Asov,' said Morgan, no hint of irony audible in her voice. 'And please, the rest of you, feel free to go down to lunch. But my watch officers and I will be having a cold meal at our posts. Perhaps when I know your computers better I will come to trust them more. But this is our first time together, sir. And my mother told me always to take extra care on a first date.'

'Which may be why you're still a single girl,' said Asov, and the sneer in his voice was audible. 'Come on down you-all. It's lunchtime like the Captain says and the food'll be getting cold.'

He and Tucker went, side by side. 'Richard?' said Morgan. 'You want to go and smooth his ruffled feathers?'

'Later, maybe. After I've seen if his equipment stands up to his boast.'

'Alexei?' said Morgan at once. 'Captain Mariner is well able to relieve you if you want to go below. There's nothing to do on this watch but watch.'

'Thank you, Captain. Captain Mariner. Yes, I'll go down if I may. Things'll get pretty active in an hour, I should guess. And they'll probably stay that way for a good long while. Might as well stock up now. Can I take any of the juniors down with me?'

102

'Everyone except the helmsman and the Radio Officer. You and your lading team will be busy from the moment we make close contact. And, as you say, you'll be busy until we've transshipped the full load and broken away again. Warn the Engineering Officers as well. And Murphy particularly, in case we need *Bob*.'

'Aye aye, Captain,' said Alexei formally and he was off, with the others in tow.

'He seems a good officer,' observed Richard conversationally.

'Excellent,' said Morgan. Her eyes met Richard's reflected in the mirror of the dark, cloud-backed clearview windows and she glanced down towards Pugin at the helm.

'Indeed. Look, Captain Hand, that schematic thing is all very well, but I can't really seem to get my head round it. Can you show me the rendezvous point on the good old-fashioned chart, please?'

'Of course, Captain Mariner. It's just through here in the chart room.'

'You have worries about First Officer Skylerov?' demanded Richard in the privacy of the chart room, his voice as low as it had been last night when discussing the ID on the emergency beacon.

'Not really. It's just that he's always looking for an angle. It's nothing I can put my finger on. It's just that I wouldn't trust him a hundred per cent. If you hadn't brought him with you last night I wouldn't have invited him along.'

'Nor me, I must admit. But it was he who found me. He who saw what I was doing. And he understood the significance of the ID *TK-20* at once, too. After that there wasn't much choice.'

'Well, there's nothing we can do about it now. What did Rusanova's second investigation show up this morning?'

'More paranoia. Mind you, when you think about it, it is a bit of a coincidence...'

Richard was still explaining what had happened in the sickbay when the Chief Steward arrived with the watch keepers' meal. This was traditionally a mixture of hot soup in thick mugs and cold cuts with what salad was still available and lots of bread and butter so that anyone who felt so inclined could make themselves sandwiches. There were also flasks of coffee, tea, hot water and hot milk. And fruit. In the old days, the salad and fruit had been great luxuries; but they were less so now, of course.

As Morgan watched the Steward deftly setting up the meal on a little table beside the distant collision alarm radar, she said darkly, 'You know that really does make your information even more vital to the Investigator, doesn't it? That beacon is the only hint anyone has of where the poor man came from. Even if they never find out who he was or why he came up out of the sub, that at least would be something.'

And Richard, thinking of Rusanova's boss, Regional Prosecutor Yagula, with his strange ways and his big stick, felt that he was really betraying her. And yet, he hesitated – for there was something in the situation he still hadn't fathomed.

Richard and Morgan broke up their secret session and went out to make sure the helmsman and Radio Officer got their share. Then, as they were out again, they stayed out, chatting about less contentious things as they sipped their mugs of soup and ate their sandwiches and actually kept their watch. As they did so, the afternoon closed in around them, the clouds squeezing down as though they were sailing into a coal mine. But still that purple thread kept uncoiling ahead of them where the machines saw through the murk. The bright letter *L* with its Cyrillic *TN10* came relentlessly closer and closer, but the purple line remained attached to the top of the upright. Therefore *Titan 10* ran on straight towards them safely underwater, away from the steep-sided chop, the thickening murk and the gathering bluster of the wind. And the collision alarm radar stayed quiet. And the Radio Officer sat undisturbed, completing an old *Times* crossword.

At 1.25 local time the first wall of rain came lashing up the length of the main deck and Morgan reached forward to switch on the clearview wipers. As though this had been some kind of signal, the others began to come back then. Nancy Rider returned silently to her weather screen, and made a note of the worsening conditions for the log. Alexei brought the others up with him a minute or two later. The cheerful sound they made as they erupted from the lift jarred with the gloomy atmosphere on the bridge, but did nothing to lighten it when they came on through. Then Tucker arrived and for a moment Richard thought Max was going to stay below and sulk through the rendezvous itself. But no. Max appeared just as 13.45 came up on the local-time clock above the helm.

And the instant it did so, the steady grumble of the engines died.

Five seconds later the bridge phone rang. Richard was close enough to hear both sides of the conversation when Morgan picked it up at once. He glanced around as it proceeded and was quite relieved to see that he was the only person that close.

'Captain. Did you do that?'

'No, Chief. We're at the rendezvous. Fifteen minutes out. I assume the computers did it if you didn't.'

'We'll lose steerage way almost at once. We've been slowing and slowing through this last hour and more.'

'Well, there's nothing on the collision alarm radar, so we won't need to make any sudden moves. We'll have to come to a complete stop in any case. There's a buoy at the exact point. We'll go into full reverse just as we get there and come to a dead stop. We'll tie up to that and wait for *Titan 10*. You know the procedure.'

'I do. I'd just be happier if it was us that was in charge of it instead of those bloody machines.'

'You may say that, Chief. I'm afraid I couldn't possibly comment.'

Morgan hung up the phone. 'Engine room ready,' she said. 'Alexei, tell the Third Officer he can take his team down to the forecastle head now and secure us to the buoy he'll find convenient to our starboard quarter.'

'There's the light,' said Max.

'Two red lights over two white,' confirmed Richard.

'Radio beacon acquired,' called the Radio Operator.

'Computers have had it all along,' observed Max dismissively.

'The buoy is the size of a room, eight metres by eight metres,' said Morgan to Richard and Tucker. 'It sits high above the water and has a sufficiently high safety rail that part of it is roofed. The lights are on a mast above the roof.

'The thing is designed to facilitate oil exchange. We can tie up to it and secure our lading pipes to it if we want. Or we can tie up to it and connect directly to *Titan 10* when she arrives.'

'She's there already,' claimed Max.

'I don't see her,' answered Richard.

Abruptly, and with a roar that surprised them all the motors cut in again, just as Morgan had said they would.

Immediately the bridge phone rang again.

'Full reverse?' said Morgan as she put it to her ear.

'Full reverse,' confirmed the Chief, again only to Richard's ears.

'We're coming in perfectly,' Morgan soothed him. 'It's textbook.'

'Oh, that makes me feel better. That really puts my mind at rest.'

'Yes, Chief. I think it's very impressive too. You'll want to ready the pumps for oil transfer.'

'Now you mention it, I thought those bloody computers would have—'

'That's fine. Thank you, Chief.'

Suddenly four BMX bicycles appeared under the clearview, powering down towards the forecastle head, bearing four bodies wrapped in bright-yellow oilskins. The Third Officer and his crew on their way to secure *Prometheus 4* to Max Asov's buoy. They were enough of a distraction to lighten the atmosphere – sufficiently incongruous to raise a laugh. As they vanished beyond the grey curtains of rain, so the engines cut out again. This time the bridge phone did not ring, though Morgan's hand hovered near it on a reflex, like a gunfighter's above a Colt .45.

There was a *clang!* and a shudder that went through the whole of the ship. 'I believe we have acquired the buoy,' observed Richard.

'But still no sign of the submarine,' said Tucker, his voice almost as strident as Max's with the strain. 'Max, where in hell's name is it...?'

'Captain!' Pugin's voice cut across the bridge quite unexpectedly. His hand had left the wheel, so that one finger rested on the bright red *L* on the screen in front of him. The purple line that had guided them here was now a bright dash against the red *L*'s side. As they all watched, entranced, so the schematic under the helmsman's finger moved. The purple dash began to slide down the upright as the *L* rose inexorably up the screen.

'She's coming up,' called Morgan. 'Sparks, I want contact the instant her radio mast breaks water.'

'Of course, Captain.'

'They must be up at periscope depth now! Anything coming through?'

'Nothing, Captain.'

'Thar she blows,' said Richard. And the whole of the clearview filled with the sight of *Titan 10* coming up, as though on his order.

She came up level, with no pitch on her. She came up almost sedately, under perfect – almost too perfect – control. Her periscope and radio masts slid up through the surface like long, long daggers, then gave on to the sail of her conning tower, which slid up seemingly endlessly to reveal the whale's hump on which it stood. As if any whale that had ever lived could have supported a hump that huge. Then the massive bulk of her simply shouldered the sea aside.

It wasn't just her length; it was her width.

She was the largest submarine ever built, extra tanks in series widening her massively when she was already longer and deeper than most. Tanks designed to hold air and water ballast – strengthened now to hold oil. As were her nuclear missile sections. Her nuclear torpedo sections. Her attack and defence sections. As had been every spare cubic millimetre of space aboard her.

Up she came, and sat, as solidly as *Prometheus 4*, as though she had always been there, waiting.

'Sparks. I'd like to speak to Captain Korsakov.'

'Yes, Captain Hand. I'm doing my best. But there's no response.'

'What do you mean?'

'I mean what I say, Captain. She's there but she's not talking to us. She's not talking to anybody. She's dead, Captain. She's absolutely dead.'

CHAPTER ELEVEN

Surface

Everybody on the bridge looked at Max. He had been so proprietorial, self-assured and downright cocky when things had been going right all morning that he was clearly first in line to explain why they seemed to be going wrong now. But Max just stood there, pale and shaken, clearly as taken aback as the rest of them.

So it was Richard who took command of the situation. 'Right,' he said. 'Sparks, you'd better keep trying to raise some kind of contact. The rest of us can either wait and see what happens or we can send a party across to knock on their door and ask what's up.'

No sooner did he stop speaking than a little hand-held VHF two-way radio sitting on the shelf beside the bridge phone and the main address-system microphone began to buzz.

'In fact,' Richard continued smoothly. 'I believe we have a useful little recon party down at the forecastle head as we speak. Mr Skylerov, if you could ask the Third Lieutenant to give us an assessment of *Titan 10*'s current disposition as soon as he's finished securing us to the buoy...'

Alexei gave a half-amused grunt as he picked up the little radio. 'He'll take ten minutes tying up before he can do anything further, Captain Mariner. But there's a couple of BMXs left if you want a closer look yourself.'

The First Officer might not have been entirely serious, but Richard took him at his word. 'Good thinking! Max – you want a closer look?'

There was just room in the lift for the pair of them to shrug their wet-weather gear over their City suits. By the time the lift stopped at A Deck, they were both ready to go outside. The only thing Richard really regretted was the damage he did to the handiwork of Mr Lobb, who'd made his shoes. Although the yellow oilskins didn't make much of a job of protecting his turn-ups, he tucked these into his socks to keep them out of the chain. So it was really only his shoes that got soaked and scuffed as he crouched unhandily astride the adult-sized BMX bike and raced Max down the length of the deck. He won, but only because he had done this before and was able to lead the way across the footing of the bridge house, aft of the great housing where the central sheaf of pipes rose from the main tank system before falling to bisect the length of the deck. And he was confident enough to skirt the hazards – flights of steps, tank – tops, winches, lateral pipe-work and Sampson posts – as he sped along the equivalent of two full football pitches. It was only on the last straight run to the broad, flat blade of the forecastle head itself that Max – younger, fitter and better suited to the size of his bike – really began to catch up. And so they skidded, almost neck and neck, to a stop beside the Third Officer's team. Out of breath and filled with childish hilarity.

The Third Officer's name was Kem and he was another Murmansk man. Square, taciturn and seemingly humourless, he fitted well with everything in the current situation except his ultimate employers' childish laughter. 'I have put out fenders,' he reported. 'And I have dropped our main starboard line to the seaman on the buoy. On his signal I will winch it tight. You may go and see.'

Richard crossed to the safety rail and strained to see past the huge buoy to the even huger submarine beyond it. But the buoy's walls and roofed section – with the dazzling series of lights above – had contrived to stand between him and the conning tower. All he could see through the curtains of misty rain was the high tail fin and the granite slope of the afterdeck, mounting towards the huge whale hump that vanished behind the buoy. And what emerged on the other side was the broad, flat expanse of the foredeck, reaching massively down to the rounded, almost hemispherical bow.

Richard's thoughtful observation was interrupted by the winches grumbling into action, and the odd stirring of the whole of the forecastle head as *Prometheus 4* and the buoy were dragged together. No sooner had this process started than a bright figure surrounded by a halo of spray that looked like a yellow rainbow, came clambering up over the side. And Richard realized that Kem had hung a ladder down to the buoy's deck. Of course he had! How else would the seamen get down to attach the line?

With these thoughts tumbling through his mind, Richard was in action at once. He arrived at the top of the ladder swiftly enough to help the seaman up on to the deck and then he swung round to replace him on the rungs. The tanker's side was firmly against the buoy now and they were held tightly together, the ship's fenders squashed almost flat. *Prometheus 4* was steady in the water, far too large to be pitched or tossed by anything except the biggest of seas; and the line held the smaller, more lively buoy still as well. It was easy for Richard to shin down the ladder and step over on to the rock-steady railing round the buoy's side, therefore. And the railing was furnished with rungs allowing an equally swift and secure descent to its metal surface.

It was years since Richard had been on an oil rig, but the iron decking with its slip-proof pattern on to which he finally stepped brought that last visit vividly to mind. His footfalls echoed under the constant rumble and gurgle of the waters that surrounded the buoy. One of a series of bright metal capstans nearby groaned under the tension of the great hawser attached to it. Like the decking and the railing all around it, the metal capstan was bright, silvery and new. The housing that stood like half a hangar, door-less, wall-less on this side, was new too. At first glance it seemed quite flimsy, but as Richard hurried towards it he saw that this was an illusion. The whole thing was made of solidly secured metal. It looked like stainless steel, though sections of it were covered with thick all-weather paint. And it was all held in place by bolts and rivets almost as huge as those designed to keep his supertankers holding together.

The hangar was designed to give some protection to the pumping equipment that stood in the centre of the buoy, with a range of power connections and generators convenient to hand. Were this contact proceeding to plan, Alexei Skylerov and his team would be heading down here on Lieutenant Kem's heels, to get *Prometheus 4*'s great hoses connected so that the central sheaf of pipes could suck *Titan 10*'s holds dry. Two Titans would fill one new Prometheus when the system was up and running properly. And the Titans, sucked dry, would flood their tanks with water until the weight of the oil was compensated, then off they would go back to the submarine well heads deep beneath the Kara Sea where the water would once again be exchanged for oil.

115

But Richard was here alone and Alexei was still up on the bridge because things were not going according to plan. Richard grimly began to make his way past the massive pumps to the southward side of the buoy. Here he pressed against the safety rail, his eyes narrow, and looked up at the colossus sitting silently there. He knew her dimensions well enough, height above the water, draught beneath it – laden and unladen – her length and her breadth. It was her breadth that preoccupied him now. She was all but eighty feet wide. Forty feet to the centre of the sail from where he stood – allowing extra for the distance she kept between her sides and the buoy's. The sail – or conning tower as Richard persisted in calling it, mentally at least – was less than ten feet wide. Five from the centre, therefore. And the whale hump another seven and more. Then there was a square section more than seven again. Of the forty feet between Richard and the central hatch in the sail there were twenty maybe thirty square and level. Level if increasingly vertiginous – for the top of the sail stood nearly forty feet above his head. And everything else was slippery and sloping. And yet, he thought. And yet...

'Any sign of life?' demanded Max at Richard's shoulder, arriving so suddenly and silently that the words made the Englishman jump. 'There's still no signals. Skylerov told Kem and he told me. What do you think?'

'I think we should do what I suggested,'

answered Richard.

'Knock on the door and see who's home? How in hell's name?'

'Not like this,' said Richard, turning decisively. 'And not from here. The buoy is far too big. We need to think small.'

'This small enough for you?' asked Max a little less than half an hour later.

'It's certainly crowded enough,' countered Richard, grimly cheerful.

They were in Alexei's lifeboat. Alexei was in nominal command, as senior serving deck officer, with Murphy upholding the engineering section seated at the rear. But both Richard and Max had plans, if not actual standing in the command structure aboard. Their position, moreover, was by no means at the top of the pecking order, for Investigator Rusanova was aboard too, in Nancy Rider's place. And the only person there who had actually been on one of these submarines at sea – whether as Typhoon or Titan – was Seaman Pugin. So they were all likely to have to defer to him in any case, if push came to shove.

At Richard's suggestion, Murphy was taking them into the calm water between the steady buoy and the submarine itself. All of their passage so far had been in the wind-shadow of the supertanker and the water between the two great hulls was like a mill pond. The engine went from low revs to idle as the bulk of the sub gathered like a wall beside them. Murphy guided them in as though they were beaching on a tropic shore. The lifeboat slid through crystal water over the rounded grey reef of *Titan 10*'s submerged side until Alexei leaned forward and fended the slate-panelled steel with his hand. The lifeboat's bulbous, buoyant head bounced gently along *Titan 10*'s flank until it came to the exact point Richard had seen from the buoy above.

They were precisely level with the front of the square section forward of the whale hump and the sail itself. And here, reaching over the slope of the side – and then continuing up the front of the hump and the side of the sail – there were footholds. Set into the side of the sub, rounded and aquadynamic, they were fashioned like little caverns, each with a strong rung corrugated suitably for hands as well as feet. To the first of these, nearest the waterline, Alexei secured the lifeboat's line. Then he looked across at his passengers. 'Who's up first?' he asked.

He needn't have bothered. Richard was half out of his seat already and even Rusanova was willing to let him lead the charge. And Richard, for one, could see her point. The huge submarine gave off an atmosphere every bit as chilly, grey and forbidding as her own huge hull. The instant he took firm hold of the first rung, an icy numbness seemed to strike down his arms – and up through Mr Lobb's handiwork an instant later. He hung on and stayed still for an instant, looking back. 'Pugin next,' he ordered. 'He'll know what to do if anything unexpected turns up.'

And so they proceeded: Richard first, then Pugin. Max came next, shouldering dangerously in front of Rusanova. Alexei followed the Investigator, regretting, perhaps, the oilskins – which hid an otherwise interesting view of her rear. Then came Murphy, in case any engineering work was needed.

Richard clambered up on to the flat section that was as much decking as *Titan 10* seemed to possess and walked back down her length briefly until the footholds started again, like steps up the front of the whaleback. Eight steps took him to the narrowest of walkways around the port side of the sail. A dozen more led to the vertical ladder section that reached straight up the last twenty or so feet and over the top to the command bridge and the main access hatch in its floor.

Richard paused at the foot of this and glanced back at Pugin as the seaman rounded the front of the sail and started down the side towards him. The man's broad face was folded into such a frown that he resembled a battered old prize-fighter trying to work out the Theory of Relativity. 'Alright, Pugin?' asked Richard automatically.

The deep-set eyes looked at him as though he were a Martian. 'I swore,' said Pugin quietly. 'I swore I'd never come back aboard one of these monsters. Never again as long as I lived.'

Richard felt a sudden flood of sympathy.

But this was neither the time nor the place to indulge it. 'Well,' he said brusquely, 'the sooner we're in, the sooner we'll be out again.'

If we can actually get in, of course, he thought to himself as he hauled himself up the ladder towards the sail's narrow, rounded top.

The summit of the ladder proved a bit of a scramble, but Richard found a secure handhold and pulled himself over the housing as though it were a style in a fence between a couple of cow pastures. Then he stepped down into the port side of the bridge, crossing immediately to the starboard side to give Pugin room. Here he found himself beside a thin radio mast that reached a dozen or more feet into the air. He touched it automatically, wondering at its continued silence. Then he looked around himself.

The sides of the cramped little compartment came up to his armpits. Level with the welts of his shoe soles were runnels to let the water flow away. The decking seemed scarcely ten feet wide or six deep. In its centre lay the access hatch, shut fast and flush. He glanced down at it, then turned to look back along the sail, at the series of wells behind him to the periscope and three lesser masts in series behind it. Whatever they were designed to do, they seemed to be doing nothing at the moment, he thought.

Pugin scrambled over the rail and the little command bridge started to get more crowded. 'The hatch is closed,' Richard told him, feeling slightly foolish. 'I'd thought there'd be a mechanism. A wheel...'

'It's here,' said Pugin, reaching towards a sloping, covered section at the front of the bridge. He pushed back a panel and revealed a switch. 'If we have power, we may proceed,' he said, and pushed it.

The square section of decking at their feet swung upwards with a hiss, releasing a cloud of stale-smelling vapour.

'Power but no light, by the looks of things,' said Richard, looking down the black shaft at his feet.

Max arrived then and hesitated, at the top of the ladder, like a farmer waiting astride his style. 'We're in?' he asked.

'We're in,' said Richard.

CHAPTER TWELVE

Mary Celeste

As Richard talked to Max, Pugin swung on to the ladder and started down. Richard followed immediately, glancing up as his head went down into the dark shaft to see Rusanova arrive, pushing Max towards the access hatch in his turn. But when Richard looked up again it was her slim ankles and not Max's sensible hiking boots that were immediately above him. Her body blocked out the dull daylight and Richard abruptly found himself moving in almost Stygian darkness. He slowed automatically, putting his fingers at risk of Rusanova's impatience, but no sooner had he done so than he himself stepped on Pugin's hand.

'*Shtoi!*'

Richard stopped, and felt the Russian fumbling around beneath him. Luckily Pugin's order had got up as far as Rusanova, who stopped in her turn and called up to the others above her, 'Stop! Wait!'

Richard next heard a grating scream, and as it echoed up the shaft, a dull, tarnished yellow brightness struck up from beneath. The light came and went monstrously and he worked out that Pugin had opened some kind of inner hatch leading to a deeper but dully lit area, and gone on down. Then he followed, through a narrow opening, and almost at once he sensed the throat of the shaft easing away from his legs. Moments later he was standing face to face with Pugin, who was gesturing at a dimly glowing panel. 'We have power. We have light. Emergency light at least,' said the Russian tersely.

'But there's nobody here?'

'Nobody on the bridge or in the immediate command area,' he confirmed. Then he did the most unexpected thing – though the most logical perhaps. '*Hey!*' he bellowed at the top of his lungs. 'Is there anybody aboard?'

The pair of them stood and listened to the

echoes as they faded away into the corridors and cabins further and further away.

'*Strastvitye!*' he tried again. And in English, '*Hello!*'

Nothing. Not the slightest stir.

He turned and shrugged fatalistically. Richard shook his head with simple disbelief. But he couldn't stand around here just speculating. 'Will there be light in all areas?' he asked.

'Ask the electricians at Severodvinsk,' Pugin answered. 'When I sailed in these things, main priority was given to the command area. The two lower pressure hulls had to take their chances. Lightbulbs are rare and expensive.'

As Pugin explained this, Richard stood back to allow Rusanova room. Then she stepped back in her turn as Max arrived. Richard turned away from the gathering crowd, his eyes busy. Pugin was clearly the man to give them a guided tour if they had the time or the inclination to look through the whole of the massive hull.

But in the meantime, there was a good deal that an observant man could learn, even if he had never been aboard one of these things before. Starting with the most obvious, most shocking thing of all.

'There's no one here,' whispered Rusanova.

Richard turned to find her immediately behind him, so close that he could smell her perfume – a welcome sensation over the rank, dead odour of the place. 'No,' he said. 'No one close by at any rate, by the look of things.'

'It is like the *Mary Celeste*,' she whispered, a thrill in her voice, awed – for the moment at least – out of her hard-edged modern cynicism.

'Yes it is,' he agreed, surprised to find himself sharing a little shiver as he came close to quoting a line from the story as he told it to his children. 'A submarine *Mary Celeste* with never a soul left alive on board.'

'Then how on earth did the submarine get here and surface?' Rusanova was recovering quickly. 'And with never a soul left alive on board?'

'Best ask Mr Asov,' said Richard, brusquely. 'His computers could have got *Prometheus 4* here without our help. So he said. Perhaps they really did do the same for *Titan 10*.'

He turned again and started a wider sweep round the contained command area. As he moved, he wondered whether he really believed what he had said to Rusanova. He hadn't really believed Max's computers could have controlled *Prometheus 4* that perfectly. He had, indeed, remained on the bridge because he had not believed the Russian's boast. Now here he was, in effect, glibly saying to the Investigator, 'Oh, don't give it a second thought. It was all done with computers.' On the other hand, it was better than believing they had another *Mary Celeste* to deal with.

But even if it had been done with computers, then how had it been done? And why?

And where in God's name were Captain Korsakov and his crew?

It was at that point that an alarm bell started ringing. All of them jumped, and Richard, jerked back out of his reverie, swung round. The only one there who did not seem particularly worried was Pugin. 'Is radio signal alarm,' he explained tersely. 'We have incoming message.'

Waste of time shouting then, thought Richard. Anyone aboard would have heard that sound every time *Prometheus 4* had tried to make contact during the last half-hour at least. It was enough to wake the dead.

'Where's the radio?' demanded Alexei. Pugin led him off to show him.

Rusanova joined Richard again, and Max appeared just behind her. 'You know the layout of these things, Max?' asked Richard.

'Yeah,' said Max, with a little less confidence than usual. 'I was on and off them all the time when they were being refitted at Severodvinsk.'

'Is there another command centre?'

Max looked around the area they occupied. And so did Richard, his eyes wise enough to discern the most obvious pieces of equipment. It was a big open bridge and command area with the periscope housing in the centre of it and the access ladder over to one side. Forward there were the main navigational controls – obviously augmented by those required to make the vessel go up and down as well as forward and astern, left, right; fast, slow.

There was a large chart area with a collision alarm radar display extended to warn about bottom conditions and underwater hazards rather than floating ones. And there was another bank of instruments that seemed pretty familiar to him. Where the defence and offence armaments centres had stood no doubt, there were the lading and cargo-control systems, ill-fitting; smaller than the originals they replaced, and much newer looking than almost everything else.

'This is about it,' said Max. 'The main control area. The command area. The bridge. I mean there's a hell of a lot more of the boat, but this is it for command.'

Richard nodded, looking around. Abruptly, he became aware of a weird sensation. Two sensations, in fact, that were mutually exclusive yet both there at one and the same time. One was the vivid sensation of a huge construction of passageways and storerooms, power plants and oil tanks, stretching out all around the main command area, ready to react to any signal demanding power, motion, speed, heading, buoyancy, light, heat, air...

But at the same time he seemed to feel a great emptiness. For where the bridge was so obviously deserted, so surely must all those other areas. But that only brought him back to the central conundrum: Who had controlled the bridge during *Titan 10*'s voyage here?

Suddenly he wasn't so sure they were alone

aboard after all. And he felt the small hairs all along the back of his neck stand up. Oddly, Rusanova seemed to sense his disquiet, almost in the way his wife Robin would have done. 'You are concerned,' she whispered. 'What is it?'

'I can't believe this tub is deserted. It just doesn't seem to add up.'

'Then let us seek out whoever is hiding aboard.'

'We can make a start, I suppose, but we'd need Pugin or someone else that has sailed in these to help us get very deep. There must be enough little hidey-holes here to hide an army.'

'Pugin's off with Officer Skylerov, but you've got me,' said Max. 'I know my way around most of this ship. Around the main areas at least.'

'And I can probably feel my way around the engineering areas,' added Murphy. 'Though I know water-cooled nuclear reactors are a bit different to my Rolls-Royces on *Prometheus 4*.'

'But where to go?' wondered Richard.

'To their private areas,' said Rusanova. 'If you want to know who was here – maybe who is still here – and maybe where they went you must look at their personal effects. In the *Mary Celeste* was it not the half-eaten food that showed so much? And the personal effects left behind? Are not these the things that haunt us when we look into such mysteries?'

127

'That sounds good enough for me,' said Richard. 'Take us to the Captain's quarters. They'll be the closest at hand, I should imagine.'

'Immediately below,' said Max. 'The main bridge area and senior officer ward room and accommodation all in this central sealed pressure capsule immediately below the sail. Then there are two more independent sealed pressure areas running the length of the hull, side by side further down still. There's some accommodation there, but in the Typhoons those were the weapons areas, so they're mostly down to oil tanks now. Together with the ballast areas and so forth that were needed for military performance. We don't need that standard of course – and we do need cargo space.'

That little speech – rehearsed, thought Richard grimly, on many an eager sponsor visiting Shipyard number 402 at Severodvinsk – took them to a near-vertical companionway that led down into the dimness of the first lower deck – where emergency lights were fewer and farther between. Max led them down, sliding down the slick metal banisters like a submariner of the old school, still acting a part for those long-departed backers. 'The Captain's quarters are the closest, as you might imagine. The system was designed for efficiency in combat, of course, but we saw no reason to question its commercial efficiency either.'

Max gestured to a closed door. 'Captain's

quarters,' he announced. And for some reason they all hesitated.

Until Richard, with a hiss of impatience, reached across and grabbed the door handle, pulling it with a good deal more force than was actually necessary. The door slid open, screaming quietly on ill-oiled runners, revealing absolute, unfathomable darkness.

Rusanova pushed forward towards the threshold.

But right at the very instant she did so, Alexei called from the top of the companion-way immediately above them, 'There you are! What are you doing down there? I thought you'd all disappeared as well. That was Captain Hand on the radio. She wants us all off here and back aboard *Prometheus 4*. At once. You too, Special Investigator Rusanova. You've been outranked by the sound of things. Regional Prosecutor Yagula is apparently on the way.'

CHAPTER THIRTEEN

Motives

Max and Murphy turned at once, obedient to
Alexei's call, and began to climb the steep
companionway. But Richard did not move.
Instead, he waited tensely, his eyes on Rusan-
ova. She spat something in Russian that
Richard later loosely translated as, 'Sod
Yagula!' And she went into Captain Korsa-
kov's quarters. Richard followed her at once.

The light was dim but, once they were both
inside and the doorway clear, there was
brightness enough for their night-adjusted
eyes. For there was nothing at all to see.
Nothing to tell of any occupant whatsoever. It
was the absence of anything that was so
striking. There was a bunk, neatly made, with
no clothing on it, no footwear beneath it.
There was a tiny bedside table with a cupboard beneath, both as clean and polished
and as empty as a display in a furniture store.
There was a basic washstand with neither
toothbrush nor shaving kit upon it. There was
a modest cupboard with a shelf, a lateral pole
and some hangers. But it was empty. No case.

No clothes. No shoes. In its bottom section was a little chest of drawers. Again, all empty – no shirts, no socks, no underwear.

'Investigator!' came Alexei's voice, impatient and clearly unhappy at having his orders disregarded so flagrantly.

'The Investigator is investigating,' called Richard. 'Give her a moment.'

'I need to see another cabin. This is most perplexing.'

'Next one down is likely to be the Chief's or the First Officer's.'

'Let us look.'

'We'll have to be quick. Alexei's not happy and he's quite capable of taking the lifeboat back without us. Do you want Regional Prosecutor Yagula to arrive and find you here?'

'Would you not protect me, sir?'

'Of course. As far as I could.'

'Very gallant. And, if I may say so, very, very foolish. Here we are.'

This tiny room, whoever's it was, proved to be in some respects the opposite of the Captain's. The bunk was rumpled and unmade. Nameless personal effects were scattered across the little bedside table; a book in increasingly familiar Cyrillic script, a bunch of keys, a photo in a frame showing a strikingly beautiful girl wearing a bikini.

'Do not touch!' Rusanova hissed. 'We will be back with Lavrenty Michaelovitch and his men, I have no doubt. Just look.'

But there was surprisingly little else to see – clothing, footwear, even cases were striking

131

by their absence. Richard, however, was distracted by something completely irrelevant. Regional Prosecutor Yagula now had first names – but Special Investigator Rusanova still did not. It seemed strange to him that he should know one but not the other. But then, it spoke volumes of the manner in which he had thought about – and treated – the woman who suddenly seemed to be the lesser of two evils.

'What is your name, Investigator Rusanova?'

She looked up. In the near-dark, her eyes were black and dizzyingly huge. And yet they seemed to contain just the faintest hint of sparkle, like a light on a far horizon, warning of danger in the night. 'I beg your pardon?'

'Your name, Investigator. You know that mine is Richard. May I ask what your name is?'

She hesitated, but only for an instant. 'My name is Maria Ivanova.'

'Then we had better get a move on, Maria Ivanova, because things are very quiet upstairs. Alexei and the others have all gone.'

Things were not quite as bad as Richard had feared. Pugin was waiting for them at the bottom of the access ladder and he followed them upwards, closing the hatches behind him as he came. The afternoon outside was even duller than the security-lit cabins, and the atmosphere of gloom that hung about the strange submarine seemed to have settled over the whole of the Barents Sea. The crew and passengers in the little lifeboat were silent during the short voyage back, but their silence could not last. Even though the arrival of Regional Prosecutor Yagula and his team from the Murmansk Office was still a distant threat, those who had been aboard *Titan 10* all had a number of people eager to hear of their experiences.

Morgan Hand was first among these. In the shifting power structures aboard *Prometheus 4* – power structures likely to undergo another revolution when Yagula arrived – she was currently in undisputed command. There was something so strange about *Titan 10* and what was happening to her that *Prometheus 4* herself might well be at risk. And it was Morgan's duty above everything to assess and overcome that risk. And the duty of everyone else aboard – no matter what other preoccupations they might have – to help as best they could.

Alexei, Richard and Maria Ivanova, therefore reported directly to the bridge where they found the Captain, the Chief, most of the senior officers – navigating and engineering – and Tucker.

The First Officer's more technical report as to position and disposition of the submarine was extended by their versions of what they had found – above decks and below. Max, Murphy and Pugin followed hard on their heels and it was to Max that the Captain turned next, the pale breadth of her forehead folded in a frown between the level brown

133

brows and the curly tumble of her hair.

'Let's leave aside the possibility that there was one – or more – crewman or officer hiding aboard. Let us at least get all the alternatives to that one circumstance clear. Starting with the most obvious. Mr Asov, we all heard what you said about *Prometheus 4* being controlled by your computers. We all felt it. What happened was striking and effective. Now, tell me as accurately as you can, please. Could your computers exercise perfect control of *Titan 10*?'

'I believe so, yes.'

'Simply working pre-programmed? With no human interference?'

'That is their design. But to help, not to supersede...'

'Nevertheless. You are telling me that it is feasible that your submarine could be conned by her onboard computers alone. That those computers could be programmed to make her sail from one point to another point, submerged, and then to surface. On her own. Without human interference.'

'Yes,' said Max simply.

'With no one on board at all. And with no one outside having any access such as your computer engineers in Novgorod had to *Prometheus 4* and her computers when they fixed our own system over the Internet?'

'Yes. I have said ... Why do you persist with this point?' He turned to the others. 'Why does she persist with this?'

'Because,' answered Richard, 'it is crucial.

Think about it Max, it should be obvious to you. Once *Titan 10* is submerged, then random inward radio access is impossible. Any inward access – high frequency or low, radio, TV, mobile phone. Nothing. For no radio waves except very special frequencies can pass through water – and those frequencies cannot begin to carry the kinds of communication that we all take for granted. The submarine can put up radio buoys or she can surface and make contact with the outside world that way. But once she is submerged, then no radio waves can penetrate to her. She is beyond the reach of even satellite communication. Out of reach even of the Internet and your computers at Novgorod. She is utterly on her own.

'And if that is true, then only the on-board computers could have controlled her – with no interference or adjustment along the way, no allowance for changing circumstances or unexpected events.

'But if there was anyone who could have exercised any control, then they would have had to be aboard her. Would *still* have to be aboard her.'

'But there was no one there,' persisted Max. 'You saw that.'

'If there is anyone, then Yagula will find them,' warned Maria Ivanova.

Max shrugged.

'Well,' said Morgan. 'We seem to have covered that as far as we can. Was there anything else that anyone noticed?'

135

'Nothing,' said Richard. The others shook their heads.

'One thing,' Maria Ivanova corrected them at once. 'The one thing that none of you seems to have asked. The first question that came into my head: *Why?* Why would any of this happen? What would be the point? Where is the motive? *Why?*'

Morgan's light-brown eyes rested on the frowning Investigator. She frowned in her turn, but not because she was considering the question. She knew the answer, thought Richard, glancing round them all, shocked to discover how much they had taken for granted – how many suppositions and assumptions they had shared with each other. But not with the Special Investigator. Morgan, Alexei, Max and probably Murphy all knew the answer – knew it as well as he did himself. And Morgan's next words demonstrated that, though they seemed at first irrelevant.

'Alexei? I know my radio message distracted you, but did you get a chance to find or check the lading?'

'No, Captain,' he answered. 'Sorry.'

'Lading?' asked Maria Ivanova. 'What is it? Is this lading important?'

'I should say it is,' answered Richard dryly. 'We know the crew seems no longer to be aboard. The lading will tell us whether there's any *cargo* still left aboard. There were seventy-five of *them*. There were ten thousand tons of it. All top-grade Kara Sea crude oil. That's worth, what, $40 a barrel?'

'That would be a motive, you see,' said Morgan Hand. 'Even at a knockdown price on the black market, that would be several million dollars' worth of motive.'

And even as Morgan finished her explanation, the Radio Officer stuck his head out of the shack. 'Incoming message, Captain,' he said. 'Kamov KA32 helicopter inbound. It will be here in five minutes. Can we light the landing area?'

'That will be Lavrenty Michaelovitch,' said Maria Ivanova quietly to Richard, suddenly sounding rather nervous.

'He's got a good sense of timing,' Richard answered, amused alike by the unexpected drama and by her sudden look of almost schoolgirl concern. 'He's got a fine sense of the theatrical.'

She looked up at him, her face still, pale, almost alabaster. 'That's the least of what he's got,' she said.

And it occurred to Richard most forcefully then that, just as he and the others had taken so much for granted, never thinking to explain to her – no matter what the danger – so there was bound to be a very great deal between the Special Investigator and the Regional Prosecutor that she could not explain to him. No matter what the danger.

CHAPTER FOURTEEN

Yagula

The Kamov came clattering out of the overcast and on to the supertanker's foredeck precisely five minutes later. *Prometheus 4*'s Captain was there to greet the Regional Prosecutor, as formality decreed. So was the ship's Owner, prepared to discuss the Prosecutor's requirements as to accommodation and support. And, of course, the Special Investigator was there to greet her boss and brief him at his convenience about their seemingly burgeoning investigation. The three of them stood waiting as the chopper settled and squatted on its suspension. And waited while the blades slowed under their own momentum. Slowed and slowly came to a stop. Only then, only when the double set of rotors had achieved an absolute stasis, did the side door slide open and the hinged steps slam down towards the deck. Only then did Yagula descend.

The Regional Prosecutor, in his turn, had brought a pathologist, a two-man forensics team and couple of assistants who looked to

Richard more like Spetsnaz – Special Forces – officers than Militia, beat officers or CID. They climbed down to stand solidly at their boss's shoulders. These were military men, watchful, neat and smart. And very big indeed.

But Yagula dwarfed them. He was bigger even than Richard – fully six feet seven inches tall. And he was built like a bear, broad – square-seeming in spite of his great height. He gave off an enormous sense of power – and danger. If Pugin's face was that of a battered prize-fighter, Yagula's was that of the man that had battered it. His black bearskin hat sat absolutely on top of square, lowering brows that cut across his face immediately above the sunken bridge of his flattened nose. The eyes in the dark corners there glittered with surprising, unexpected intelligence – something disorientatingly beyond the low cunning one might have expected in such a face. The mouth was as straight as the brows and as lipless as a razor slash, pulled in a tight line between the off-centre nose tip and the great square, forward-thrusting shovel of his chin. Only when he spoke did you get a glimpse of great old-ivory tombstone teeth.

His hands were enormous, huge, scarred, ham-like things, hairy, misshapen and raw, and when Richard returned his handshake, they sought to crush his knuckles with automatic, unthinking, arrogant power. It was only when Richard held his own and answered the pressure ounce for ounce that the eyes really focused on him at all. 'A pleasure to meet you, Regional Prosecutor,' he said.

'Likewise, Captain Mariner,' said Yagula, his voice a rumbling *basso profundo*. Their handshake held, tightened. Lingered. Ounces of pressure became pounds.

Then Yagula, equalled if not bested, tired of the game. His gaze reached over Richard's shoulder and he smiled. 'Maria Ivanova,' he purred, slipping past Richard like a shadow to tower before her.

'Regional Prosecutor,' she answered in chilly counterpoint to his informality, standing rigidly at attention. 'My report is ready.'

'In good time, Maria Ivanova. In good time.' He turned, even as he spoke, his great right fist sweeping over the little group that had exited the helicopter on his heels. 'Captain Hand. Captain Mariner. I will not introduce you to my colleagues. Sufficient to say they are a pathologist and a CID forensics team associated with my office in Murmansk. Their English is unfortunately limited. My two foot soldiers here speak no English at all. Should you wish to communicate with them, you may do so through me.'

'Or through Investigator Rusanova,' suggested Richard.

Once again, those deep-set eyes measured him, as they had done during the handshake. 'Or through the Special Investigator. Indeed. But let us move. The pilot is not allowed to start his rotors until I am well clear. It is the tallest tree in the forest that always gets cut

140

down first, is it not? And I have no wish to be felled by a chopper blade.'

Or by anything else, thought Richard, watching the way the two Spetsnaz men, his 'foot soldiers', guarded his back, leaving the other, lesser, members of the team to carry all the luggage as well as their own bulky kit.

Of course there was not room for all of them in the lift. Unexpectedly, Yagula ushered the women and the load-bearers in and strode off down the corridor before turning nimbly up the companionways with Richard at his side and the bodyguards watchfully behind.

But then, perhaps more foreseeably, the simple act of climbing the stairs became a competition, with Yagula tearing ahead and Richard fighting to keep pace; both of them striving to talk without puffing breathlessly as they leaped upwards like mountain goats.

'I foresee that this investigation will last more than twenty-four hours And it will have to be centred here for the time being at least. So myself and all my team will need to rely upon your hospitality, Captain. I will require a private cabin for myself. I will require facilities to interview people in private should the need arise. I will require provision to dine in my cabin – alone or with company as circumstances and my further personal requirements dictate. The cabin will also need to function as an office. Does this ship support direct Internet access for laptops? Of course it does. Maria Ivanova has been on-line regularly. This should present no problems therefore. I shall also need an adjacent suite for my two closest associates. Adjoining if possible. The pathologist might well bunk in with or near your Ship's Doctor. Your sickbay might prove acceptable if it is otherwise unoccupied. Except for the corpse. Your Doctor has impressed Maria Ivanova, by the way; almost as much as you have yourself, Captain. And the forensics team will go where they are told. They too might share the sickbay if accommodation is tight. The atmosphere will not disturb them. Nor will the smell, which I understand is quite strong. Smell should not present a problem to them at all. I have visited their homes in Murmansk, you see. I know whereof I speak.'

'I may have to move Investigator Rusanova.'

'She will not mind. You have a female cadet aboard, do you not? Perhaps they could share.'

'That would not be suitable. I will contrive something for Investigator Rusanova.'

'You are courteous. She will be very grateful, I am sure.'

On this cheerily barbed note, Yagula bounded out of the companionway and on to the bridge deck. Three great strides took him across the corridor and into the bridge itself, where the others were hesitating, each set of them a little nonplussed, waiting.

'The quickest thing will be for Regional Prosecutor Yagula to take my cabin,' decided Richard forcefully. 'If he and his team can

142

wait in there I will organize everything else – or rather, delegate the organization. Cadet Rider, if you could show these gentlemen – and Investigator Rusanova – to the Owner's quarters, we can proceed. Captain, if I could have the microphone for a moment...'

The ship's chimes sounded – Heritage Mariner's equivalent of *'Now hear this'*. Richard's voice boomed through all the cabins, corridors and companionways, 'Would the Chief Steward please report to the bridge. Chief Steward to the bridge, please...'

It was pitch dark by the time Yagula was settled, and the weather was worsening rapidly. Nevertheless, when Richard knocked at the door to the Owner's suite just before Pour Out, he was greeted by the sight of the Regional Prosecutor testing the seams of the ship's largest set of wet-weather gear. But it was the Regional Prosecutor's head that gave Richard pause. The massive bullet skull was naked. Not bald, but shaved. The grey expanses of vigorous stubble showed like a four o'clock shadow; reaching from a widow's peak just above the point where his eyebrows joined, right back over the square cranium to vanish down his collar. There were even one or two razor nicks, to emphasize Yagula's shaving routine.

'Ah,' said Yagula. 'You are the one I want. Maria Ivanova and I will return to *Titan 10* now. We will require your services as guide. And those of Lieutenant Skylerov. Perhaps

143

also of Engineering Officer Murphy. My forensics team can search the boat with the guidance of ex-Submariner Pugin and the help of my two foot soldiers – and, by all accounts, some powerful flashlights, yes? But it is you and Lieutenant Skylerov, Maria Ivanova tells me, who can check something called the lading and tell me all about what is there and what is not.'

'So, this has all gone far beyond Captain Birdseye, then,' bellowed Richard into Yagula's ear as the lifeboat plunged through the blustery darkness. Even in the protected water between the ships, the turmoil of the increasingly stormy sea was making itself felt.

'Ah yes. Your joke name for the frozen man. You have named him for the American soldier who invented the first frozen food, yes? Birdseye Peas? Most amusing. Maria Ivanova warned me of such humour. It is very different to our Russian humour of course. Like naming your supertankers *Prometheus* after the Greek Titan who brought dangerous fire to mankind. But yes. Things perhaps have gone beyond Birdseye. My pathologist may tell us more. If he cannot, he had better look out for his job. Perhaps we will even be able to work out who he was and where he came from in the end. But he is one man. One man lost overboard and frozen in the Barents Sea. Not much in the scale of things – unless he is a small key to a much bigger lock. The lock to open wide a much larger puzzle. Eh? You see what I mean?'

When Richard remained resolutely silent, he continued.

'One dead stranger.' He shrugged. 'We find dozens such every morning in the lakes of our parks in Moscow and Murmansk. Men and women who drink too much vodka and fancy a swim in the night, or fall in – or merely fall asleep. An hour or two will do it in the winter. An hour outside on almost any night in Murmansk, in fact.'

'Colder than Norilsk? Or Mys Zhelaniya?'

Richard meant nothing in particular by his remark. It had been a running joke with the others, after all. And if he was testing anything in the Regional Prosecutor, it was his sense of humour.

But Yagula swung round as though slapped in the face. His bulk and his movement made the lifeboat rock dangerously. The movement made the foot soldiers reach for their guns. 'What do you know of such places?' he snarled, clearly not amused in the least.

'Nothing much. I know of Mys Zhelaniya because I am a sailor and it is a port – of sorts. It's written up in my British Admiralty Pilot for these waters. And I know about Norilsk because Max Asov has been there. That's all.'

'I see. Well. In answer to your no doubt joking question, no. Murmansk is the northernmost city in all the world – the only one north of the Arctic Circle. But both of the places you mention are colder. Much colder...'

It was hard to imagine anything much colder than this, thought Richard. It seemed that only salinity and restlessness were keeping the waves from freezing. The rain had turned to sleet. And this was the summer, for crying out loud!

By the time he had clambered up out of the boat and on to the submarine he could see all too clearly how Captain Birdseye might have frozen so solid under the ice. Even through his well-lined, heavy waterproof gloves, his hands were seemingly turning to ice. And as for his feet ... Only a man as driven, intrepid – powerful and intractable – as Yagula would have got them here in this weather, he thought. And even then, the expedition was only feasible because *Prometheus 4*'s huge lights at least made every tile step and hand-hold on the submarine stand out as though they were on some huge sound stage, making a James Bond film.

Pugin was leading, slowly and carefully. Alexei was next, then Richard followed by Maria Ivanova. Yagula was close behind her and the foot soldiers close behind him. The forensics men came most slowly and carefully of all, laden with their equipment. And Murphy brought up the rear, in case their work or their discoveries needed some engineering input.

The outer bridge cockpit was freezing and slippery. Richard nearly came a cropper climbing in over the stile and it was only the speed of his reactions that saved Maria

Ivanova as she tumbled head-over-heels – fortuitously into his arms. The sensation was deeply unsettling. She seemed to linger there on purpose, crushed against the steady safety of his breast. He put her down with some alacrity as Yagula heaved himself into view. With alacrity but with characteristic gentleness. Then he turned and followed Alexei down the access ladder to the first hatch in the top of the upper sealed pressure compartment. Then on down into the command area once again.

This time they knew what to expect – and had come in some measure prepared. So the dim emptiness of the huge vessel was less disorientating. After the weather outside, it was also comfortingly warm and dry, though it was never going to be cosy. As soon as he stepped down on to the bridge deck, Richard pulled out the big torch his waterproof pocket had been keeping dry and began to flash it around. Taking the incredible situation for granted, the first order of the day that logic suggested was to get more lights on. The control board defeated that thought at once – but Richard decided to refer it to Murphy the instant the engineer arrived. If Alexei could translate some of the Cyrillic, then Murphy would be sure to come up with something.

But of course Alexei had other fish to fry. 'Captain Mariner,' he called quietly, and Richard crossed at once to his side. 'Look at these control panels,' he continued. 'They are computerized. You see these display panels here? These screens should all be showing digital readouts. But the computers are shut down, so they are blank.'

'That's what you would expect, under the circumstances,' temporized Richard. 'Imagine what a drain all this would be on the boat's batteries if it was up and running. The same as leaving the headlights on in a parked car. You'd need to be very careful what you switched on here before the motors were running again and the alternators providing power for this lot.'

'So,' said Alexei, nodding in agreement. 'Maybe we look for the engine controls first? Or at least the alternators. Leave everything else alone until we get that all sorted out?'

'That is not satisfactory, Lieutenant,' growled Yagula from just behind them.

That was the third time, thought Richard. For such a big man, Yagula was light on his feet. He moved like a rugby player or an American footballer – fast, quiet and never quite where you expected him to be.

'When your engineer comes aboard I will have him start up the power. Switch on these computers. They will tell us all we need to know. I do not care about batteries and so forth.'

'You may want to think about what you do start up,' warned Richard. 'It was those computers that controlled the sub and brought it here. While they are down they can't do anything more. But if we wake them up, they could take control again. Literally. Take control and sail away again, with us all trapped aboard. And God knows where we could end up then.'

'Is he serious?' Yagula asked Maria Ivanova.

'The computers on *Prometheus 4* controlled her approach to the buoy out there,' she answered. 'I was aboard and saw. The officers needed do nothing – touch no controls, give no orders. It was all automatic. Max Asov says the computer systems could control everything in that vessel and in this one. And they are Max Asov's computers.'

'Perhaps Captain Mariner has a point, then. But will we be able to start up the lading computers independently of the others? Independently of the control computers, at least. And that would use up less battery power, would it not?'

'We'll have to ask Murphy when he arrives,' suggested Richard. 'In the meantime, there is an alternative. On most of my ships, we try to keep hard copy of readouts and records. Especially of records as crucial as what state your cargo is in.'

As Richard talked, he looked back past Yagula. The forensic team had arrived. One of them had begun a search already while the other painstakingly began to set up his equipment. The pair of them were going to be in Murphy's way, thought Richard. So they'd better not bank on the Engineer's immediate arrival.

'Hard copy,' repeated Yagula. 'You mean printouts?'

'Yes. An automatic log. And any system remotely similar to mine will produce print-outs automatically. When we're certain we have the lading controls then we'll look for printers nearby and see if there are records in the printers. They should still be here some-where...'

'Unless someone has taken them away,' sneered Yagula. 'Taken them and hidden or destroyed them.'

'But there's supposed to have been no one aboard to do that, has there, Regional Pro-secutor Yagula?' said Richard gently. 'If the boat has really been controlled by computer then the printouts will still be there. If they're *not* there, then there must be someone hiding aboard after all...'

'So, there's a great deal of information to be gleaned from those printouts, I think, Lav-renty Michaelovitch,' added Maria Ivanova, with a great deal of relish in her voice. 'Perhaps we'd better start to look for them...'

But no sooner had she said this than one of the forensics team called out the Russian word that Richard would soon come to recognize as *'Boss!'* And he was also quick to learn that it was always a sure sign of trouble.

CHAPTER FIFTEEN

The Final Expert

The forensics men were kneeling at the head of the companionway leading down to the next level. Under the brightness of their torches it was possible to see much more than had been obvious under the dull security lighting. But even then, thought Richard, he would probably have dismissed the brown stains on the metal steps as rust. Maria Ivanova's eyes narrowed as she glanced from the stain to the kneeling forensic man to Yagula. 'Blood?' she whispered.

A curt nod of the head in reply. The second forensic scientist shone his torch's bright halogen beam around the area at the head of the steep little stairway – but all that emerged from the shadows beneath the questing finger of light was a cupboard, set back out of the way, its door slid half open and its contents obviously long gone. Only half of the cupboard door was visible, but it was enough to give Richard pause, and fold his forehead into a frown as the beam moved on and darkness returned. On the next step down, however, the pool of brightness discovered a puddle of rust. Then he was off like a bloodhound, following a rusty trail.

Murphy appeared on the access ladder, reaching up to swing the inner hatchway shut, then stepped down into the thoughtful silence. Richard and Alexei took him aft immediately, and out of the corner of his eye, Richard saw a curt jerk of Yagula's head direct Maria Ivanova to follow them.

'Where will these records be?' she asked.

'It varies,' said Richard. 'We'll have to poke around, unless Murphy here can get any information up on the screens themselves.'

'Whether I can get them on depends on how they were switched off,' said Murphy thoughtfully.

'Meaning?' demanded Maria Ivanova.

'We have to assume that they were working up until the time the sub surfaced. She came up evenly and under control. Something – computers perhaps – was taking care of pumping out ballast, balancing the tanks, avoiding the shear, maintaining trim and so forth.'

'So the computers were working while she surfaced. And then they stopped.'

'Yes. But why? Were they working on a timer, which had been set or programmed earlier? Or were they working on some kind of environmental sensors that registered that the boat had surfaced and then closed everything down?'

'Or,' added Richard, completing Murphy's

thought as the Irishman paused, apparently searching for words, 'were they closed down by a signal? Because, now that the sub was on the surface, she was as wide open to incoming signals as *Prometheus 4*, or any other surface vessel is.'

And, as if to emphasize his very words, the alarm that warned of incoming radio traffic sounded and made them jump. Alexei went to answer it and then called back from the communications console, 'It's for the Regional Prosecutor. Routed via *Prometheus 4*.'

Yagula came back almost casually, as though he was used to receiving personal radio calls on deserted nuclear submarines in the middle of the Barents Sea. 'In the meantime,' he said pointedly as he passed them, 'you will be searching for the lading records, will you not?' The words were overtly addressed to Investigator Rusanova, but clearly embraced them all. And they were given further emphasis by the way in which he crouched beneath the lowering bulkhead with the radio headset pressed to the side of his face as he talked, looking out at them as though confident that the rapid Russian of his conversation would guarantee privacy enough.

'OK,' said Murphy. 'Lieutenant Skylerov, can you help me, please? Every control section I can see is labelled and colour-coded. The coding seems to be similar to that used on *Prometheus 4*, but the labels are in

Cyrillic. So can you look for one that says "Lading" or something like that? It may be coded orange or yellow.'

'There's one down there that says "Cargo Control",' supplied Maria Ivanova at once. 'That's yellow.' Richard followed her pointing arm, walking carefully, but with his eyes fastened on the Cyrillic label, burning the unfamiliar characters into his memory. But then he stopped. For there on the bulkhead above the computer, so faint that he had hardly noticed, was another piece of Cyrillic writing: *TK-20*' it said. And there was a bar above the *K*.

'There's what looks like a bank of printers down there too,' said Murphy, arriving at the lading section and looking around. 'It shouldn't be too difficult to find after all. Is there one with a yellow mark or tag? This isn't a secret nuclear attack sub anymore. It's just a glorified tanker. And the guys who put the computer stuff on *Prometheus 4* weren't subtle. They were logical, practical and masters of the obvious.'

'And they were the same guys that put the same stuff on here,' said Richard. 'So let's start with the obvious...'

They started there and finished there almost immediately. 'Bingo,' said Richard. 'Coded yellow. Headed with those same words in Cyrillic, what are they? "Cargo Control"? This looks like it, then. Alexei...'

The Russian Lading Officer took the records and carried them to the light, frown-

154

ing over the figures. 'Yes,' he confirmed. 'This is it.'

'According to this, *Titan 10* is fully laden.' He flipped over page after page after page. 'Ten thousand metric tonnes of cargo in the holds...'

Even Yagula came aft now, frowning with concentration as he followed Alexei's words. 'So,' he began, 'the cargo is—'

'Wait!' snapped Richard. He had been a lading officer in more tankers than he cared to remember. And he knew there was more. One final, vital fact. 'How full are the tanks, Alexei?' he whispered.

Alexei stopped flipping through the lading record and, frowning, held the sheets close to his eyes. Then he nodded, fatalistically. Lowered the papers and looked up at Richard. 'You were right to ask,' he said. 'Oh, how right you were to ask.'

'What?' snarled Yagula, frustrated beyond measure by the novelty of not being in charge of the situation – of standing ignorant of what these men so obviously knew.

'What are they, eighty per cent?' asked Richard.

'A little more,' said Alexei. 'But hardly enough to count.'

'How can this be?' howled Yagula. 'You said the tanks are fully laden. And yet they are only eighty per cent full. How can this be?' He turned from Alexei to Richard like a bear being baited by mastiffs.

'Because the weight of the cargo is one

hundred per cent of capacity,' said Richard. 'But its volume is only eighty per cent.'

'How can this be?' demanded Yagula again. He turned on Alexei but the Lading Officer looked across at Richard silently. Until Yagula turned back. 'Well?'

'Because water weighs more than oil. Because it takes a lesser volume of water to attain the same weight as a greater volume of oil. Especially if, for instance, the water is icy and heavy from somewhere in the Arctic Ocean while the oil is supposed to be hot and light, straight out of the well.' He fastened his most penetrating stare on the District Prosecutor. 'Because there is no oil at all in the tanks – just thousands of tonnes of nearly frozen brine from the bottom of the Kara Sea.'

Yagula stood there for a moment, bowed beneath the low deck-head, his eyes narrow and his mouth working. Then, 'Just as I suspected!' he said. 'It is the very thing that I supposed. Crew gone and cargo gone. Millions and millions of roubles – *gone!* Where is the importance of one nameless man found frozen in the water when compared with this?'

'Indeed,' said Maria Ivanova. 'Where is the importance of seventy-five missing men when compared with the millions of missing roubles?'

Richard suspected that this was a dangerous game and so he joined it at once. 'The importance of the missing men,' he said to

156

her quietly, 'is that they may be close to the missing roubles. Or even if they no longer are, then they might have some idea where the roubles are. Or who has them now. They are a small key, perhaps, to a much larger puzzle.'

Yagula heard his own words being thrown back at him and clearly he did not relish the experience. But the words had been true of Captain Birdseye – and they were true of *Titan 10*'s missing crew. The heart of the matter here for him was not the lives – lost or at risk – but the money. With all his accustomed insight, Richard saw at least a part of the man's complex motivations. He was a bureaucrat – perhaps not pure and certainly not simple – but an *apparatchik*. Richard had met them at every level of government – national and local – and in every public service and big business on the face of the globe. Men for whom the theory meant more than its application or effect. Men for whom the common good was more important than individual welfare. Men who saw no real difference between efficiency returns and accidental-death statistics; popularity ratings and crime figures – between MORI polls and murder rates.

Finding out who Captain Birdseye was or how he died or why was likely to be an inefficient use of time and resources – especially if it became complex. Discovering the whereabouts of seventy-five crew would be important only as part of the larger picture. But recovering millions and millions of roubles in lost or stolen oil – that was an enterprise well worth a huge investment of time and resource. And, as if to prove Richard's cynical suspicions, Yagula called to his forensics men, 'Get a sample of that to the pathologist. He has the equipment to identify it almost down to DNA. That would be better than wasting time on some flotsam from under an iceberg.'

'Sir!' said Maria Ivanova, her voice shocked.

'You examined him, did you not, Special Investigator? With the expert eyes of both the Doctor and the Captain here who so much impressed you. And did you find any hint as to his identity? Any of you?'

'No—'

'Then we have no proof that he is important. And until we have such proof let us assume that he is not important.'

'But, sir—'

'That is enough, Rusanova!'

'No, but—'

'One word more and there will be a disciplinary hearing over this. Without proof—'

Rusanova opened her mouth again. And it was clear to Richard, at least, that she had no intention of obeying. Hearing or no hearing.

'I have proof,' he interrupted. And even as he opened his mouth he regretted it. A feeling more than compounded by the look of utter horror Alexei shot him behind Yagula's back. Scuppered, he thought.

'Do you indeed?' spat the Regional Prosecutor. 'And what is that?'

'I can't show you here,' answered Richard.

'And why not?' demanded Yagula roughly, his hands automatically closing to fists. His Spetsnaz foot soldiers squared up in turn.

But Richard was suddenly in motion. Every bit as swiftly and unstoppably as a rugby forward heading for touchdown, he slipped past them all and crossed to the now-deserted head of the blood-spattered stairwell. 'Here's why,' he said, pushing the door of the recessed cupboard there wide.

'An empty cupboard,' spat Yagula. 'So what?'

'What does the sign on the door say?' Richard asked Alexei, sliding it shut over the empty shelves again. 'In English, what does it say?'

Alexei cleared his throat. 'It says, "Emergency Life Jackets. Submarine TK-20".'

'And it is empty,' said Yagula.

'But there was no marking on his lifebelt,' whispered Maria Ivanova. 'I looked. No marking on anything.'

'Not on him, no,' Richard acknowledged wearily. 'But floating not too far away. The emergency beacon from one of those missing life jackets, marked as plainly as you like *"TK-20"* in Cyrillic. Exactly the same as that cupboard door. *Bob* brought it aboard just the moment that you landed...'

'But you did not hand such a vital piece of evidence to the Special Investigator,' purred Yagula. 'Clearly this will have to be weighed carefully in our deliberations as we decide

159

how this investigation will proceed. And who will be most fully investigated. Where is this vital piece of evidence now?'

'It is aboard *Prometheus 4*. I will give it to the Special Investigator as soon as we return.'

'Indeed?' mused Yagula, softly and dangerously. 'To the Special Investigator. Well, we shall see. But in the meantime, I still choose to put a higher priority on discovering as much as I can about the blood upon the floor. And I will use the pathologist and his equipment to do it in spite of what either of you says. The matter is closed. As is this excursion. The blood was an added bonus. The blood and Captain Mariner's new evidence. But we have confirmed what we came aboard to confirm – that the cargo as well as the crew has vanished. What we must do now is to return to *Prometheus 4* and await events.'

'Events? What events?' demanded Richard, angered by his own stupidity and the danger he might well have put himself in – and Morgan, Murphy, Nancy and Alexei.

'I have one final expert flying out to help us. The radio message I received just now confirmed that he is in transit and expected soon. He is, I believe, just the perfect man for the job. Now, Engineer Murphy, as we have torches and as we have been warned about the danger that lights present to the batteries of parked vehicles, can you please contrive to switch everything off as we leave?'

The main piece of contrivance that Richard

160

managed immediately upon their arrival back aboard *Prometheus 4* was to get the emergency beacon off Murphy unobserved. Then he took it to the cabin the Chief Steward had assigned to Maria Ivanova Rusanova. He knocked gently on the door and she opened it to him at once.

She was wearing a blouse he had not seen her wearing before and she had answered the door clearly, halfway through tucking it into her severely tailored skirt. Her hair was dishevelled. She was clearly in the middle of dressing – or undressing and had been interrupted. Over her shoulder her laptop glowed, in e-mail mode. He saw the letters 'KARAK' in Cyrillic.

'Oh,' she said, as though she had been expecting someone else entirely.

'I have the missing evidence,' he told her, stiffly; more formally than he meant to. He held it out.

'So I see. Well, you had better come in.'

She stood back, holding the door wide, and he entered, forced to stoop under the lintel and coming, perforce, much closer to her than he would have liked in the confines of the little cabin. She stepped away, still holding the door. They would have to crush together quite intimately in order for her to close it behind him. Even with it still ajar, he was uncomfortably close to her. She smelt of that same perfume. It was heavy, sweet yet spicy.

The material of her blouse was so fine that

161

he could see lace through it. And what the lace contained. He focused on the emergency beacon and held it out to her almost at arm's length.

She reached for it, at last. 'This was under the ice,' she said. 'Quite close to the body.'

'Yes,' he said as she took it.

She turned it over, one-handed, and looked at the identification marks, nodding to herself. There was an air of satisfaction, almost of fulfilment, about the gesture.

'You knew about it, didn't you?' he asked.

Her black eyes came up, their gaze measuring him. It was impossible for him to read in them anything but that. 'What makes you think that?'

'And Yagula. He knew. Or knew that you knew. You were both just waiting for me to make it official.'

'We work together,' she explained. 'He is my superior. In the absence of the husband we discussed, he is my only hope of a better life. How should I not tell him the things my investigations make me suspect?'

'Of course,' he said. He turned to go.

And there was Yagula, filling the doorway behind him, far more absolutely and effectively than the half-open doorway itself. He too had changed his clothes, but this suit was almost as formal as the other. His head gleamed in the light of the corridor.

'You were prompt, Captain,' he said, his voice giving away no more than Rusanova's eyes.

162

'You were pretty quick yourself, Regional Prosecutor. Was it me you were looking for? Or the Special Investigator?'

'Either,' he growled. 'Or both. The helicopter is about to land. Our final expert will be on the bridge in ten minutes. You would do well to meet him there. Whatever we do next, he will play an important part.'

Richard stepped out and passed him. Maria Ivanova closed her laptop and followed him until she was standing in the doorway. He turned back at the foot of the companionway and glanced down the corridor towards them. They were still standing together looking at him, side by side, separated only by the thinness of the bedroom door. And they made a striking pair, he thought, as he climbed towards his new quarters. A striking pair indeed: Beauty and the Beast.

Richard arrived on the bridge ten minutes later, just as the hard-working Kamov was lifting away outside the clearview. He looked around to see who was there. Almost everybody, he noticed. And all of them sharing that hungry look of a crew whose dinner has been held back. He waved at Murphy, who grinned with relief – at last – over the worry of hiding the incriminating beacon. Nancy, too, grinned weakly.

Only Alexei was still frowning, warning Richard of the trouble he might still be in.

Richard shrugged and crossed to stand by Morgan Hand, who was waiting by the ship's helm. 'Do you know who he's expecting?' she asked.

'' Fraid not. Just an "expert", he said. The final one.'

The lift bell rang and the doors hissed open. Yagula strode out with Maria Ivanova at his side and his foot soldiers in close attendance as always. And between them walked a stooping, pallid, sick-looking man in a baggy business suit.

'My God!' said Morgan, thunderstruck.

Richard looked at her askance, for the stranger – only vaguely familiar to him – was clearly better known to her. Better known and utterly unexpected. She was white with simple shock.

'Peter,' she said, her face riven with surprise and concern. She took a step forward but Yagula, clearly enjoying himself, forestalled her.

'Captain Mariner. You see? You are not the only one with a sense of humour who keeps little surprises up his sleeves and close to his chest. Yes? I see Captain Hand has recognized my friend. But you have not yet met him, I believe.

'In that case may I formally introduce to you, not to Captain Birdseye of *Prometheus* the fire-bringer, but Captain Peter Korsakov, the commander of *Titan 10*.'

CHAPTER SIXTEEN

Korsakov

Richard immediately led them down to the officers' ward room. It was nowhere near Pour Out, so they could get some peace there. Both the Regional Prosecutor and his surprise guest clearly had some explaining to do – and seemed quite ready to do it. Yagula, ebulliently, promised every interested party access to his surprise expert. Maria Ivanova, apparently as wrong-footed as the others, followed Richard at his right shoulder while Morgan Hand, thunderstruck, followed at his left. Max and Tucker joined the little group, worried and suspicious.

Richard's mind raced as he strode down to A Deck, and by the time he ushered the women into the little room, he was certain he was beginning to pull things together. He turned and scanned Korsakov again as Yagula rushed him through the door, then followed, sliding it shut behind him. The Russian submarine Captain was white – paler even that was normal amongst these sunless men. He had clearly been unwell – seriously so. Perhaps even hospitalized, thought Richard as he watched the Captain fold himself into a chair as though suddenly elderly and frail. That would explain a lot, of course. And the possible reason wasn't too hard to imagine either – that stomach ache so casually mentioned to Morgan in the last communication. Appendicitis – at the very least.

Appendicitis was a lively horror amongst submariners, for appendicitis arrived unannounced – unsuspected – and raged through peritonitis to death with terrifying rapidity, long before the surface could be reached or help be summoned in some secret missions. In the old days, submariners would have healthy appendixes removed to set the worry of it aside. And in Russia, of course, 'the old days' were always dangerously close at hand.

Korsakov's first words, delivered in a voice just a little stronger than silence, confirmed Richard's deductions. 'I was taken off *Titan 10* a week ago, and have been in hospital since. I underwent emergency surgery five days ago for peritonitis and I am told I was fortunate to survive.'

'You were lucky to get off in the first place by the look of things,' probed Richard gently.

'Yes. We were in position to dive and fill the tanks when it struck. We were on the surface sending some last communications and updating the computer programs, though the weather was closing in and a severe storm was forecast. It was a sudden pain in my side – as though I had been stabbed...'

'You had to act quickly,' continued Richard. 'Hand over to your First Officer and summon aid from ... Where precisely?'

'There was a tug inbound for Port Dickson. Running at full speed to stay ahead of the storm. I went on that, but when the fever started they radioed ahead and an emergency helicopter came out.'

'You all seem very well equipped with helicopters up along this coast,' mused Richard. He glanced across at Tucker.

'Old military hardware coming down into general use, like the Titans,' answered Yagula, a little sharply. The questioning was not going precisely as he had planned.

'And they got you to hospital,' continued Morgan, still innocently solicitous.

'But there is no major hospital in Port Dickson,' Tucker pointed out, suspiciously.

'No.' Korsakov glanced nervously across at Yagula.

'So, where'd they take you?' continued the American. 'It's pretty sparsely populated up there. I'd guess the nearest big town must be...'

'Norilsk,' said Richard, almost silently.

'I found the Captain in the Municipal Hospital at Norilsk,' said Yagula as though something would seem innocent if you said it loudly enough.

'It is the best in the area,' continued Korsakov. 'It is one of several sponsored by Norilsk Nickel, one of the greatest—'

'We need not go into any further medical details, need we?' demanded Yagula, loudly again. 'We would not wish to upset Mr Asov by singing the praises of Bashnev Power's greatest rival.'

'Their greatest rival now that Khordorkovsky is out of things and Yukos Oil is being split up,' said Tucker.

'And now that Abramovich has moved so much of his fortune into British football,' concluded Asov easily. 'Our greatest rival in power generation at any rate. We do not mine minerals and they do not make computers. Yet.'

'So,' persisted Richard gently, turning back to Korsakov, 'you handed over to your First Officer and went off aboard the tug to Port Dickson. That means you were about seventy-five degrees North and eighty degrees East?'

'About that. The computer records will be precise as to minutes and seconds according to the GPS.'

'And that was it as far as you were concerned? You just handed over.'

'To First Officer Smirnov. Yes.'

'You were that confident in him?'

'Yes. The programs were in place and should take care of everything. Even the coming storm would have been of little trouble to *Titan 10* once she was submerged. And in any case, even if something unexpected did come up, all he had to do was follow the computers' directions. Even then, everything was planned for and programmed in – our men would only get involved for basic tasks if some tiny piece of reality went beyond the programmed parameters.'

'And as far as you were aware, First Officer Smirnov was simply going to submerge, follow the computer programs, fill up with oil and return to the rendezvous?'

'Of course. And it was little enough to do with Smirnov – or the rest of them aboard. That's what *Titan 10* was programmed to do. What would surprise me is if any of them knew enough to change that simple program in any way at all.'

'But someone did,' said Maria Ivanova, entering the conversation at last.

'Either that,' added Richard, 'or there was an extra section to the program that you didn't know anything about.'

'An extra rendezvous programmed in somewhere along the line.' Max's voice was calculating, almost dreamy – his mind apparently far withdrawn from the officers' ward room into distant realms of fantastic possibility.

Richard frowned, wrapped in more immediate speculation. For if there was an extra section to the program then it seemed most likely that Max Asov or his acolytes must have put it there. But that was something to be settled in the future. There were more immediate matters to be cleared up here. Here and now, in fact. 'So,' he continued, turning back to Korsakov. 'You were happy to hand command to Smirnov – though to say you were *happy* is maybe overstating the case – in the certainty that he would follow the computers' orders. He had done so on earlier occasions.'

'Yes.'

'But you were confident – given the nature of the emergency, and the limited number of options it allowed you – that the computers could get your vessel and crew safely to the well heads and then back to the rendezvous. Even without you on board.'

'Yes. And, as I have said, Smirnov and the crew were well trained. They could handle anything.'

'There's a problem there obviously,' growled Maria Ivanova. 'Because they clearly came up against something that they could not handle.'

'Unless, of course,' said Richard gently, 'they had been trained and prepared to pirate the oil and abandon the ship.'

'If that were so,' boomed Yagula, 'then you would have to be part of the plan, would you not, Captain Korsakov?'

'Peter would,' said Morgan defensively. 'Or First Officer Smirnov would. If he was able to take command, he'd be able to pirate the oil.'

'Or, to come full circle,' added Maria Ivanova, 'Mister Asov would.'

'An oversimplification,' answered Max, still cheerfully dismissive. 'In a company the size of Bashnev Oil, there are complete echelons of management capable of organizing something as simple as this and I would never have any idea about it on a personal level. You think I take personal responsibility for every manager in every section right across Russia?'

'Perhaps not,' answered Maria Ivanova, with a hard edge creeping into her tone. 'But I believe that a man such as yourself would be keeping the closest possible eye on a project such as this one. Richard. What is the name of your senior shipping manager in Europoort?'

'Finlayson,' said Richard immediately and without a second thought. 'Sam Finlayson.'

'Which of his deputies would be in charge of the trans-shipment of any oil from *Prometheus 4*?'

'Amanda Van—'

'You see my point, Mr Asov?' purred Maria Ivanova, interrupting an equally prompt answer. 'I am sure Mr Roanoake would be able to furnish me with the names of his relevant management teams equally quickly. Are you a lesser businessman than your partners here? Of course not. So you will know your people too, will you not?'

'But this is not a matter we can resolve immediately,' said Richard. 'We need to return to the central point. Captain Korsakov, have you any idea what happened to your crew or your cargo?'

'No.'

'Of course not,' said Morgan protectively.

Richard glanced across at Yagula, who was still smiling and nodding along, as though he were puppet-master here, pulling all their strings. 'Then have you any idea how we can

171

discover what happened to them?'

'Yes,' said Peter Korsakov. 'I have two.'

'What are they?' demanded Maria Ivanova when the Captain paused, summoning up the energy needed for a lengthier speech.

'Well, we can either tow *Titan 10* to port and get Mr Asov's computer experts to go aboard and check all the programming and the records to see what has been done and when...'

He stopped there, gasping.

'Or?' snapped Maria Ivanova. 'Or?'

'Or we can go aboard her ourselves, I would guess,' supplied Richard as Korsakov fought to get his breath. 'Wake up the computers, reverse the programs and take her back along every inch of the course she has just sailed along.'

CHAPTER SEVENTEEN

Plans

'Are you mad?' demanded Morgan, shocked into indiscretion by Richard's words. But her own words were drowned out by others.

'Could we do that?' whispered Maria Ivanova.

'What an idea!' boomed Yagula.

'Well, it's some kind of notion,' said Tucker, almost as surprised as Morgan.

'How would you crew it?' wondered Morgan practically, weakening to the others' enthusiasm. 'What about engineering? We have no nuclear motor men—'

'Brilliant!' decided Yagula, loudly overriding her concerns. 'Get the computers to reverse the course! How do we go about it?'

All of this was addressed to Richard, but Richard was looking at Korsakov. 'Could we do it, Peter?'

The submariner nodded, moving his head as though it weighed too much for his neck to bear. 'I believe we could. I have a good deal of knowledge and if I could borrow a competent officer who understands computing and programming, then it would not be an impossible task. Because, remember, the computers control everything.'

Korsakov's eyes were on Asov, and Max's eyes were narrow – his mind still seemingly lost in distant speculation.

But when Max spoke, he answered all of them. 'Yes,' he decided. 'It would be a risk, but it would not be madness. It might be difficult, but I believe it could be done. With a minimum crew – what do you call it? A skeleton? – and relying on the computers to oversee the engines and reactor. And it is a brilliant thought.'

'It would only be worth the risk if it will allow us to discover what has been done to *Titan 10* and her crew,' emphasized Richard

173

coolly – suddenly less than impressed by the alacrity with which his speculation had found favour. He felt like a politician who has tested a suggestion he finds faintly outrageous on a couple of parliamentary colleagues – only to see it taken as party policy at once.

'And the oil,' said Yagula, his tone of enthusiastic agreement showing his priorities pretty clearly.

'We would need Captain Korsakov to reassume command,' said Max, running with the idea like a wolfhound. 'And Pugin, who is familiar with the vessels. If you could spare First Officer Skylerov and Engineer Murphy, then a skeleton command crew could easily be assembled, with all the strength and experience that Captain Korsakov required. Richard. You would be a welcome addition of course, with so much practical knowledge and experience.'

'I would come with my team,' added Yagula. 'Thus we could at once provide security and continue the investigation. Rusanova would assist us, of course.' He laughed almost cruelly. 'And should she be worried about her own investigation we could even invite Captain Birdseye aboard, could we not? Now that Captain Mariner has proved the association between the dead man and the submarine.'

'Let's go, then,' decided Max.

'Wait!' called Richard. 'We need further thought, planning and time spent on research. It needn't take for ever – but we must invest a little more time in simply staying alive!' They all looked at him as though he was mad – all except Morgan and Peter, who were experienced enough to know what he was warning them about. 'In ensuring our safety at least,' he temporized.

'Look. We have searched through *Titan 10* for crew and oil – and found neither,' he persisted, calmly but still forcefully. 'But before we actually set out aboard her we must be sure we have adequate safeguards and supplies of everything else. Is the reactor safe and functioning correctly? Are the engines on-line OK? Is there food? Is there water? How is the situation with regard to fresh air?

'I understand there are shortages of many items that we would take for granted in some areas of Russia and the Republics – and they have barter value higher than oil. Toilet paper. Soap. Light bulbs. Are the security lights on only because they are in sealed lamps and can't have their bulbs stolen?'

They gaped at him in silence. Even Morgan and Alexei seemed nonplussed by the speed and detail of his thinking. It had simply not occurred to any of the rest of them at this stage that the whole vessel might have been stripped, even though the only cupboard they had looked in closely – the lifebelt store – had been empty. Even though only relatively worthless personal trash had been left in the cabins they had searched.

And yet it was a logical thought – if one admitted the possibility of a crew complicit in whatever crime had been perpetrated here.

175

Richard looked around them, and saw Maria Ivanova's black eyes catch fire as her mind leaped ahead down the path of reasoning he had opened for her.

Given a guilty crew, what they managed to pilfer as they committed the greater crime might tell an insightful investigator much about the conditions under which the thing was done. And that knowledge, of course, would put her out of the sideshow that Captain Birdseye threatened to become and into the main stream of the investigation, shoulder to shoulder with Yagula.

'Why don't I take Pugin and Alexei over with me one last time and see what we're dealing with?' Richard suggested. 'There's no way we can check the reactors or the engines until we get the computers up and running. That would all be the last thing to look at in any case. But in the meantime we can count light bulbs and check a quick manifest. Start raiding *Prometheus 4*'s stores if need be. That'll get the first stage under way at least. And that would be it for today, I think. A good night's sleep for all – especially Captain Korsakov here – and we'll see how things look in the morning.'

The Chief Steward emphasized his words at once by appearing at the doorway and asking, 'May I prepare for Pour Out now, Captain? Dinner will be served within the hour.'

Neither Alexei nor Pugin appreciated being dragged back aboard *Titan 10* in the freezing

176

overcast twilight that would last until tomorrow's icy dawn. But if Richard found himself making enemies of these two, nearly an hour later when they set out for *Titan 10* rather than sitting down to dinner, he made more of a friend of Maria Ivanova because he had let her come too. On his part it was a calculated move, and he did not at first consider that it might be calculated on her part too – calculated far beyond the spark of revelation he had lit in her eyes.

On the one hand he really did want to make a rough manifest. Only a genuine madman would set out on such an expedition without doing so. But on the other hand he wanted to try to keep a good long step ahead of the game. So he had supplied himself with two practical if resentful seafaring men capable of making the list and one bright detective capable of sharing with him its obscurer implications.

As the lifeboat pitched over towards the massive submarine, however, his stomach gave a growl and he suddenly found himself thinking back across a busy afternoon to the sandwich lunch he had neglected in the face of *Titan 10*'s appearance. Had he really been one step ahead, he would have brought soup and sandwiches as well as his back-up teams, he thought, ruefully. He glanced back from his position in the bow along the length of the craft to Pugin at the tiller. Two scowls and one brief grin. He was torn for a moment as to which expression he should be wearing himself.

Needing his hands free, he had put in a backpack all the bits and pieces designed to make the completion of their task easier and more efficient. Most important among these was a clipboard with a printout from *Prometheus 4*'s main supply record, listing everything aboard in sparse detail under main headings, with tick boxes. This was designed to be a ready reckoner for Alexei and Pugin as they checked what was – and was not – aboard *Titan 10*.

As soon as Pugin brought the lifeboat alongside, Richard was off, familiar with routine and route alike, now he was boarding *Titan 10* for the third time. He jogged along the foredeck and up on to the whale hump. Then on up the aqua-dynamic ladder without a second thought, his mind ranging speculatively ahead.

Up in the tiny bridge atop the conning tower he reached unerringly for the slide-down cover of the hatch control, pushing it up as he had seen Pugin do. His fingers seemed to know which was the right button of their own accord. Up popped the hatch, halving the floor space, just as Maria Ivanova arrived – and for the second time that afternoon he found himself crushed against her. Through the bulky wet-weather gear, their bodies seemed to touch almost sensuously. He felt for a fleeting but vivid instant the softness of her breasts and the firmness of her thighs against him. And the thought of her lacy underwear rose distractingly to his mind.

Richard swung down into the hatchway and, pausing only to ensure his backpack did not snag on anything, he climbed on down. Maria Ivanova followed immediately above him; so close, indeed, that as he turned in the darkness ten rungs down, seeking the switch to the inner hatch, he found her lithe body crushed against him once again. Distantly and with almost Puritan disapproval, he noted the senses' ability to make such contacts vividly intimate – even through eight or so layers of clothing. It was as though his chilled skin could feel the simple heat of her. He dismissed his distracting flesh and turned to the business in hand.

He automatically assumed that the contacts had been accidental. And even were they not – were Maria Ivanova seeking to extend their relationship from professional to personal for some reason – he was a happily married man – husband to a loving wife and beloved father of promising teenage twins; warden of his church at home. Predatory, casual or opportunistic sexual encounters had never been his style. It simply never occurred to him that the increasing physical intimacy that seemed to be growing between them was something that Maria Ivanova was stage-managing, for darker, more complicated purposes of her own.

He hit the button and the hatch hissed open. Down he went again without a second thought.

CHAPTER EIGHTEEN

Preparations

The air aboard *Titan 10* was worse than
Richard remembered. Even since earlier this
afternoon it seemed to have become fouler,
denser; more difficult and unpleasant to
breathe. The oilskin smell of his wet gear
made things worse. Only the sudden fra-
grance of Maria Ivanova's scent made the
atmosphere bearable. The security lighting
seemed to be dimmer too, setting her fathom-
less eyes at the depth of great shadowy pools
contained only by the pale ridges of her
cheekbones. Alexei and Pugin looked skeletal.

'Where should we begin?' asked Alexei as
Richard handed out supply lists and torches
from yesterday.

'In the nearest storeroom. Pugin, where
would that be?'

'On a Titan? I'm not sure.'

'On a Typhoon, then. The men at the shipyard don't seem to have changed anything
too much during refitting.'

'Down here,' he said readily enough, leading them down off the command bridge, along the corridor past the cabins, then down and down again into the Stygian darkness of the sub's main areas.

As Pugin led them deeper and darker, the four of them flashed the bright beams of their torches apparently randomly around. But Richard, for one, was looking carefully at the lights first of all. As soon as they got beyond the realm of the security lighting, he began to search the low bulkhead just above, counting the pearly gleam of light bulbs, white as blind eyes.

But then he remembered hearing stories of a market in Moscow where dead bulbs were offered for sale. You bought a dead bulb, took it to work and swapped it for a live one there – thus you were able to bring light to your home at least, and your employer had the funds and the clout to replace the dead ones in the office. Probably an exaggeration, he thought. And anyway – if they were able to sell dead bulbs as well as live ones, wouldn't all these bulbs be gone?

Richard had just arrived at this conclusion when Pugin stopped. 'Here,' he said, pointing with his torch beam to a doorway. Richard crossed towards it and pulled the handle back. He did this forcefully but casually, expecting the door to slide back. Instead, he staggered forward, a tearing pain in his shoulder.

'Locked,' he said, shrugging to ease the pain. 'Is that usual?'

'Standard practice. Unless the boat's been pirated,' said Pugin, grimly. Richard began to understand that perhaps both of these men had an unexpected stake in what was going on here – even if it was just in the reputation of their colleagues and shipmates. A reputation being so casually trampled underfoot by foreigners and investigators.

'Especially if the boat is being pirated,' opined Alexei. There was some amusement in his voice. 'The Captain would hold the keys as routine, unless the supplies officer and his men needed access. Not, of course, that there would be anything really worth pilfering.'

'No vodka on Typhoons,' confirmed Pugin, a long service of regret echoing in his voice.

'But what about Titans?' asked Richard gently.

'Looks like we'll never know,' said Alexei.

Side by side with Pugin he began to lead the way back. Richard and Maria Ivanova walked shoulder to shoulder, silently at first. Then, conversationally, apparently *a propos* of nothing, she observed, 'When Peter Korsakov felt the pain like a knife in his side a week ago, he had time to hand over his command to First Officer Smirnov before he went aboard the tug bound for Port Dickson.'

'His command and his keys?' said Richard, gently.

'How else would the crew stay stocked with supplies until they had filled up and begun the return journey?' she enquired, though the

182

question was rhetorical and needed no answer.

'Indeed,' responded Richard. 'So Smirnov had the keys. And should the recently vacated quarters next to the Captain's tidy and long-deserted cabin belong to the First Officer...'

'Then the bunch of keys left lying on the bedside table could well be the keys we need,' she concluded.

Richard swung the torch beam into the second cabin Maria Ivanova and he had searched instead of responding to Yagula's first call. And there, beside the picture of the bikini-clad blonde, lay the bunch of keys they sought.

Richard caught them up and looked at them, frowning. 'If these are what we're looking for,' he said quietly, 'then what do they tell us?'

'That Smirnov was not part of the plan?' hazarded Maria Ivanova. She was rifling through the cabin with more abandon now – her main objective no longer forensic – rather to confirm whose quarters these were.

'That the plan did not include pilferage – merely piracy?' Richard countered, putting the keys in his torch hand and sliding open a drawer. There were letters there, envelopes addressed in Cyrillic. But the surname seemed vaguely familiar – from a vodka label maybe?

'Or that he was actually taken as much by surprise as he seemed to be?' she wondered. He held up the envelopes for her to see and

183

she nodded decisively, grinning with childish delight at their simple cleverness. Then she frowned, looking at the sender's name on the back. 'These are nothing,' she said. 'Just from his brother.'

'Hmmm. Too much speculation and not enough hard fact, even if we have been proved right so far,' he concluded, putting the letters back and swapping the keys into his right hand again.

'But we know where to get hard facts, do we not?' she laughed. 'Back where you tore your shoulder.'

She turned and called, 'Pugin! We have some keys. Take us back to the storeroom!'

The third key Richard tried turned in the lock and he was able to slide the door wide. A treasure trove of simple, everyday supplies met their gaze. Simple items hardly worth a second glance – the sorts of things a London housewife bought weekly and a ship's chandler delivered every voyage. The kinds of items that made the household run and that kept the family – and the rooms they occupied – clean, comfortable, sweet-smelling. Everything from rubbish bags to rat poison, by the look of things. And brightly lit.

'No pilferage here after all,' said Maria Ivanova, disappointed.

'Perhaps no piracy either,' said Alexei. 'At least, not by *Titan 10*'s crew.'

'But you know that is so unlikely,' persisted the Special Investigator. 'How would you remove seventy unwilling men from the submarine? And all that oil? Where would you put them? Where would you store it?'

'Even if they were involved, the same questions must be asked, must they not?' he shot back angrily. 'Where is it? Where are they? And remember, there is blood on the stairs. You have a dead man wearing *Titan 10*'s equipment. What do these things say to you? To me they tell of people forced at gunpoint, hit and bleeding. Of desperate attempts to escape,' spat Alexei.

'Perhaps,' said Richard. 'But the dead man did not try to escape while the oil was being taken, did he? He came up from deep and froze. The oil transfer must have happened on the surface. The crew could only have been taken off on the surface. There is no way this could all have been done at the bottom of the sea.'

'*Where* then? And *why* did your Captain Birdseye die?'

'I can't tell you why as yet,' admitted Richard slowly. 'But one of us will know, in time. As to where? The Kara Sea is full of islands. There's a whole archipelago of them along the line of the undersea oil wells. Some of them are inhabited. Many more have simple docking and storage facilities. Two huge rivers drain into the Kara Basin – there has been trade of all sorts since the beginning of time, you know that. And things have only got busier recently. And then there's Novaya Zemlya.'

Alexei swung around to face him, apparently more enraged still. 'Let us hope then that they are neither foolish nor desperate enough to go ashore voluntarily in such places; let us pray that they have not been forced ashore and imprisoned there – for almost all the islands that you mention are contaminated with radiation at the very least. Because things have been so much busier recently, as you so glibly observe. And you know that it is years – mere years, not even decades – since the last full atom bomb test on Novaya Zemlya.'

The other three looked at the outraged man. Maria Ivanova spoke at last. 'You know, Alexei, that logic dictates that the cargo and the crew are in the same place – or were in the same place at least to begin with. And that makes the more dangerous islands most unlikely, does it not? Either way you look at it. For, even on the black market, who would want to buy radioactive oil?'

As brutal truths went, that one seemed to Richard peculiarly Russian. The safety of seventy sailors reliant upon maintaining the purity of the oil they had been shipping. Certainly, it was a conversation-stopper. In near silence, then, the four of them searched the rest of the submarine's main areas. They worked through keys and storerooms, discovering – to Maria Ivanova's disappointment – that everything had been left aboard. What was missing from the groaning shelves seemed consistent with a week or so's consumption as the submarine filled up beneath the Kara Sea and came west and south towards the rendezvous.

If the reactors were safe and the engines responsive, there seemed no reason that *Titan 10* could not set sail in the morning with a skeleton crew and *Prometheus 4* as surface escort – the gods of computers willing.

And, thought Richard – as he followed Maria Ivanova up the ladders and tried not to notice the way in which her lower body filled her wet-weather trousers with hardly a wrinkle except for the outlines of her underwear – if the gods of the weather and even the Fates themselves were willing.

CHAPTER NINETEEN

In

Richard was calculatingly content to take a back seat in the main debriefing when they got back aboard *Prometheus 4*. Both Alexei and Maria Ivanova had axes to grind, while it suited Richard – and Pugin, it seemed – to sit quiet and let them get on with it. But there was never any doubt that the long and the short of it all was that the skeleton crew would be over to *Titan 10* first thing in the morning. And in as soon as could be arranged.

The morning dawned as grey and threatening as yesterday. 'Dawn' was actually the wrong word, thought Richard as he shaved. There was little more than a sluggish lightening of the wearying glimmer of the Arctic summer's night. They were in the realms of the midnight sun here after all – were there ever to be any sun. 'The realm of the bright midnight overcast' seemed to describe the Barents Sea at this season better. Even with the strange unsettling atmosphere and the prospect of mystery and danger, Richard had slept well. A sandwich and a mug of cocoa warmed and settled him. A long call home had relaxed him. Even the disasters his teenage twins got involved in, and the heartache these caused their poor mother, seemed tinged with a golden glow when compared to his current situation and immediate future.

And now, he thought, that future was at hand. He finished scraping the bristles off his chin and dashed warm water over his face, straightening to grope for a towel. At that precise moment there came a tapping at his cabin door. He swung the towel round his neck and called, 'Come in,' as he reached for his shirt. He was expecting the Steward with his early morning tea or he would have been more hesitant, perhaps.

The door slid open and Maria Ivanova slipped in, glancing round the cramped quarters he now enjoyed, looking for a place to deposit the tray she carried. She wore a white cotton blouse and a black business skirt. Still dressed for the offices of some great fashion house rather than the command bridge of a mysterious submarine.

'Early morning tea, I believe,' she said breathlessly. 'I took it from a steward down the corridor.' She reached behind one tailored hip and slid the door shut again. Then she put the tray on his little bedside cupboard. Her eyes, having taken in his quarters, settled on his torso, raking lingeringly up and down.

Silently thanking God that at least he had his trousers on, Richard continued his easy gesture, grasping the neat rectangle of a shirt so perfectly laundered, ironed and starched that it might have been new.

'Good morning, Investigator. And what may I do for you?' he demanded formally. But his voice was icier than he had meant it to be and so he moderated his tone. 'Besides offering *you* a cup of English Breakfast...'

'I have come to beg your help and protection of course.'

She sank a little dramatically on to the white jumble of his unmade bunk. She leaned back across it as though seeking to rest her shoulders against the wall behind – but the bed was too wide. Instead, the depth of her bosom strained the already tight-stretched fabric of her blouse. Buttons pulled dangerously in buttonholes. Breasts pushed up into pale pink prominence, presenting a considerable cleavage. The tailored business skirt she wore slid up silken thighs to reveal, for an accidental instant, black lace stocking-tops astride a mysterious, beckoning shadow. The thighs stirred in the tiny, frozen instant, seeming to fall apart rather than to close. The whole of the tiny cabin filled with the musky scent of her.

But the gesture, like his earlier tone, seemed slightly different to what she had intended and so she switched from wanton mode to domestic, sliding demurely forward again, reaching for the teapot. Nevertheless she left him with a much more explicit and intimate version of the vision that had been haunting him of late.

He pulled off the towel with a force that burned the skin of his neck then he shook out the shirt like a bullfighter with a cape. Swung it over his shoulders and rammed his fists into the cool, smooth length of the sleeves. 'Protection,' he rasped. 'Against what?'

'Against Yagula and the others of course. It must have occurred to you that within an hour or two I shall be trapped aboard *Titan 10* with them. Without you, I shall be scuppered.' She lifted a brimming cup of golden tea towards him. The way she was sitting made the gesture intimately subservient. Her eyes were wide, their pupils huge in the gloom.

'You have that cup,' he said brusquely, reaching for a clean tooth mug.

She took the mug without a second thought, continuing, with a little more

190

emphasis: 'The only woman, forced into inescapable intimacy with so many men.' She looked down to pour the tea, her voice became almost a whisper as though she feared eavesdroppers everywhere. 'Men who might like to see me humiliated. Perhaps even hurt. Perhaps even worse.'

Up came the fragrantly steaming mug. Up came the wide, wide eyes.

Up came Richard's sense of probability. 'That's ridiculous,' he said, taking the mug. 'I agree there is the potential for embarrassment in such close and confined circumstances. There always is for single women aboard vessels crewed by men. But it really is pushing the bounds of probability to take things any further than that.'

She sipped her tea and he gulped a mouthful of his, burning his lips a little. 'You are trying to put my mind at rest. This is kind,' she said.

'It wasn't meant to be – particularly. Have you any reason for more precise suspicions?'

'Perhaps.' She put the teacup down and stood. When she brushed against him he realized he had not buttoned his shirt. 'But you are right. I need fear nothing, need I? And even if I have my suspicions, they are better kept locked within my breast. They would poison an already tense atmosphere, would they not? An atmosphere that is likely to become strained to say the least, when *Titan 10* goes down.'

There was a rap on the door, followed by

191

the immediate turning of the handle. The little doorway slid wide to reveal most of Yagula. 'I was seeking Inspector Rusanova,' he rumbled. 'And see! I have discovered her. Come, Maria Ivanova. There is no more time to take tea with the Captain. We must go aboard *Titan 10*. And you must also take your other boyfriend with you. Remember. It is better to sleep with the devil you know than to screw with the devil you don't...'

Richard was in two minds as to the real necessity of taking the dead sailor with them. But Yagula's reasoning was persuasive. Captain Birdseye was a clue. There was no gainsaying that. The whole matter seemed to have started with him. And the possibility that this might simply have been a strange coincidence had been weakened by *Bob*'s discovery of the second emergency beacon, marked with the submarine's ID.

Whoever the dead man was and however he had come to die – and why he had been found – might well be the source of more clues. Or the proof of more theories. Moreover, he was Maria Ivanova's case. Where she was, there should he be – as the focus for her investigation. That point of course was politically expedient. Richard and all the rest of them could see it clearly enough although it was never an explicit part of Yagula's reasoning. The Special Investigator was responsible for investigating an apparently unimportant, un-newsworthy, low-profile

192

death. The Regional Prosecutor was responsible for solving the massive, politically sensitive, high-profile disappearance of millions of roubles' worth of oil. Captain Birdseye's continued presence aboard emphasized these points. That pecking order.

Small surprise then that he went in first after Pugin, wrapped in plastic and strapped to a stretcher, slung between Yagula's minders. Then the rest of Yagula's team went in, followed by the Prosecutor himself. Alexei and Murphy followed, then Max, helping the still-frail Korsakov. Richard brought up the rear with Maria Ivanova. But, after the incident in his cabin, there was a calculated distance between them – though Richard was frankly not quite sure whether it originated with her or with himself. But, to be fair, the situation glimmered briefly at the edge of his thinking and then was dismissed like the daylight, when the main hatch closed above him.

Richard had never sailed in a submarine before. In spite of the fact that this adventure had originated with him, he remained sceptical as to whether he would sail in one now. Well supplied and apparently able though they were, the idea that they could simply wake up the computers, run whatever programs had most recently been in action backwards and sail – submerged or on the surface – back along the course of *Titan 10*'s last voyage seemed such an outside chance.

Or it did until Peter Korsakov, Alexei Skylerov and Max Asov went to work. Nobody even bothered settling in until Peter looked over his computers. If he couldn't switch them on then they were all bound back to *Prometheus 4* in any case. So they all gathered in the command bridge like guests at a strange cocktail party – with Captain Birdseye flat out in the corner with the rest of the baggage – and watched in near silence.

Peter and Alexei moved across the front of the command console with Max and Murphy close behind. Neither Richard nor Yagula had to strain to see over their shoulders – both heads were nearly brushing the ceiling – but Richard for one never saw which switch was pulled to light the whole lot up. But abruptly – with almost shocking suddenness – the whole console went from dull death to bright life. The whole hull around them went from near silence to a powerful stirring.

The group broke up – shattered, scattered as though a grenade had been dropped in the midst of them. Even Richard started back, turned away. Found himself looking down the small companionway past the empty lifebelt store and away along the dark passage where the crew's quarters lay. What shocked Richard was the way the lights came on – one after another, bulb after bulb after bulb, kicking back the darkness, reaching brightly out and down along numberless, sinister labyrinths of corridors.

'It's alive! It's alive!' cried Max, his voice

high with excitement – sounding just like Dr Frankenstein.

As Max's exultant cry was echoing, Alexei called, 'Novgorod has the computers. They're looking at the programs now.'

Yagula called to his men something impenetrable to Richard that seemed to mean, 'Find a cold store for the body then stow your kit away,' because that's what they went off to do.

The 'Incoming Message' signal made them all jump. Murphy was closest, so he took it. '*Prometheus 4* says we're lit up like a Christmas tree,' he reported.

Richard turned to Maria Ivanova. 'We're in business,' he said. And as he spoke the whole hull shuddered as full power came on and both alternators and engines stirred.

CHAPTER TWENTY

Down

Richard was by no means the only one aboard surprised by the speed and completeness of *Titan 10*'s reawakening. All the bustle of the arrival stopped. Everyone aboard, it seemed, simply froze. Surprised; shocked – maybe more. As Richard looked back from the unsettling, expanding brightness of the crew corridor, his eyes met Yagula's and he seemed to see behind the District Prosecutor's bluff mask for an instant. Although Yagula cloaked his expression again in a twinkling, Richard would have sworn the man was frightened.

Yagula turned away immediately, bellowing orders to the forensics team, but it seemed to Richard that he suspected what the Englishman had seen. And that knowledge was likely to prove dangerous. Perhaps it was Richard rather than Maria Ivanova who could prove to be at risk here. A thought registered, recognized; dismissed.

But then Richard himself was further distracted – by Maria Ivanova herself. She was flushed and breathless with simple excitement, disquietingly as though she had just made love. 'It is working,' she whispered. 'Just as you said it would! Now we shall see...' And she was off, without a further word.

Richard strode back across to the command console, swerving at the last minute to save his head from cracking against the periscope housing. He would need to keep his height in mind. Nowhere aboard was really designed on a scale to suit men like Yagula and himself. Every ceiling, every corridor, every bulkhead doorway would pose a threat.

He hardly needed to scan the bright schematics with their half-familiar dispositions and foreign lettering. The whole of his body told him how alive the vessel was. The

196

submarine was speaking to him with every pulse and judder, every throb and rumble. It was as though he were magically trapped in the shaft of a fishing rod with a salmon or a sailfish fighting on the line. Everything he touched or trod on – even the very air around him – thrilled to the stirring of the mighty submarine. The only thing that disturbed him was the one sound he could not place – a distant, almost subliminal tapping, as though someone were trapped somewhere.

Dismissing the thought, he passed behind Max, Peter and Alexei, crossing to Murphy's more specialized area, where the solid little Irishman stood shoulder to shoulder with Pugin. 'Reactors?' he asked.

'Everything sitting safely in the green,' answered Murphy, cheerfully. 'You could hit them with a missile according to this and they'd still behave. Engines at optimum. Alternators purring. Power and life-support all A-OK. It looks to me like we're ready when the guidance computers are.'

'Good God,' breathed Richard. But perhaps the second word was less audible than the first. Certainly Murphy looked over his shoulder and beamed – as excited as Maria Ivanova seemed to be.

He nodded in lively agreement. 'Good,' he repeated.

Pugin glanced back as well, his face as closed as Yagula's but with something of the Prosecutor's fear lurking deep within his eyes.

Richard returned to Max. 'What does

Novgorod say?'

'They'll be advising us any minute now...' answered Peter, his voice tense and just strong enough to carry over the restlessness all around them

'Ah. There it is,' sang out Max, also, apparently, disturbingly excited. 'It looks like we're good to go.'

'What? Now?' asked Richard, awed by the speed of events.

'As soon as we confirm,' answered Alexei. 'They're waiting for our word. Captain Korsakov?'

'To go where?' asked Richard, intensely. He leaned forward, lowering his voice. 'Max. Where? Back along the whole voyage? The last bit of it? As far as the point where things went wrong? How far? *Where?*'

'Here,' said Peter, gesturing to a screen similar to the main navigation screen aboard *Prometheus 4.*

There, in the midst of red figures, and half-familiar schematics varying from green to purple, the line of their course stretched out.

Richard looked at it blankly for a moment, and then it all fell into place under the wisdom of his experienced, seafarer's eyes. Stretching out behind them, the headings after a 180 degree turn were clear. Their course lay at 95 degrees – a little south of Due East – along the straight line of a trench in the bed of the Barents Sea between 90 and 100 metres deep, the soundings written both in square Cyrillic numbers and in familiar figures.

Then on, through the Kara Strait south of Novaya Zemlya between soundings marked 100 and 120 metres deep. Then away and away into the mysterious, storm-lashed, ice-bound fastnesses of the Kara Sea itself, where the course and the schematics, the depths and destinations were so much more difficult to read.

Richard's eyes narrowed as his mind raced. 'The soundings are very precise, to begin with, at least. Does that mean what I think it means?'

'Indeed,' answered Peter, surprise in his voice at his companion's unexpected acuity.

'Meaning?' probed Alexei, the mariner.

'We are programmed to run submerged,' confirmed Peter, the submariner. 'As far as the Kara Strait at least.'

'And through it as well,' added Richard grimly, pointing to the tell-tale figures on the screen. 'Into the Kara Sea.'

'Well,' said Max, excitement beginning to drain away again, 'perhaps we should alert everyone to that fact. We may need to settle in. Acclimatize in any case.' He looked at Peter, then glanced back at Richard.

'There's a certain amount of clearance to be done,' insisted Alexei. *Prometheus 4* may be cleared for the Barents Sea, for instance, but not for the Kara Sea. As far as the authorities are concerned, she's completed her voyage and will be turning around any moment now. And of course, we have to alert the coastguards all along our route that we will be returning. This is no longer a naval vessel, free to roam in secret wherever she is ordered. As I'm sure Captain Mariner and Mr Asov will confirm, commercial enterprises like ours have public, legal responsibilities. If we haven't crossed every *t* and dotted every *i* then we could be liable for who knows what lawsuits?'

Richard himself was nonplussed. The legal aspect was important of course – but seemed so insignificant beside the Health and Safety considerations. He did not relish the reality of the situation now that it had been so forcefully thrust upon him – or the immediate implications that it opened so vividly to his mind.

To voyage eastwards into the Kara Sea, submerged, simply at the command of the on-board computers, with little chance of overriding them, of even communicating with the outside world once they were running deep, seemed an extremely daunting prospect.

That was what Captain Birdseye had been trying to do in all likelihood, after all, he thought: communicate with the outside world when *Titan 10* was running deep. He felt sickened at the thought. Hesitant. Uncharacteristically, he would have advised them to wait. To see. To check and double-check.

But events overtook him in a way he might, indeed, have seen coming, had there not been so many distractions.

For the man with his finger on the 'Respond' button, of course, was the man who had commanded the vessel until a week ago. Who knew her and trusted her more than any of the rest of them. Who was desperate to discover what had happened to her. And to the cargo for which he had held himself responsible. And to the crew who were his friends.

Or who, at the very least, wished them to think that he felt all of these things.

So, even as Richard's mouth opened to advise inaction – caution – Captain Peter Korsakov acted, counting the cost no further.

He pushed the button down.

Just for an instant, nothing happened. The even tenor of the thrilling pulse remained unvaried. Yagula continued to shout at his forensics team. Maria Ivanova called, 'Where did you put him?' down to the returning Spetsnaz men.

Murphy shouted, 'Wait a minute, that's...'

And the alarms went off.

Richard was almost fooled into reaching for the radio but these were not the 'Incoming Message' alarms. They were the 'Dive' alarms.

Over the sound of their strident warning, the bolts on the inner hatch snapped shut like the cocking of massive pistols.

The trembling of the hull – of the very air – became more unsettlingly intense as a range of motors and pumps began to function in their pre-programmed sequence. Even the strange, distant tapping seemed to intensify, like an urgent warning. Then the engines began to beat, turning the massive screws behind them. The ballast pumps began to rumble, sucking in water as the hull began to gather way. The air recirculation equipment tripped as soon as the hatches were sealed.

The 'Incoming Message' alarm joined all the rest as *Prometheus 4* tried to ascertain what was going on.

'Email the course schematics to *Prometheus 4* before we dive,' ordered Richard. 'She needs to track us, remember. And under the circumstances I would really like to know that she is sitting right above us every inch of the way. Wherever the "way" might lead.'

Peter looked up. Even he seemed shaken by what the simple pushing of a button had unleashed. He nodded.

'Novgorod as well,' suggested Richard, his mind in overdrive, 'just in case. You can never be too careful ... Max, will your computers have registered all this automatically?'

'They should have.'

'Right. Peter, how long have we got before we lose outside contact?'

'Not long.'

'One last thing then. Prosecutor Yagula, can you come over here please? Good. Now who in Murmansk or Moscow – or wherever – can we alert about this situation? We have clearance to come and go, but *Prometheus 4* at least will need permission to enter the Kara Sea. If we don't get things organized before the communications go down, she'll be stopped at the Kara Strait. The quicker they can sort it out, the less alone we will be.'

CHAPTER TWENTY-ONE

Turn

Yagula was still speaking into the radio when *Titan 10* submerged and the shore-line went dead. The periscope was down. The whips of the radio antennae swept swiftly under the surface with the sail and all the rest. There was no communications buoy aloft. Yagula's half-finished sentence was the last message anyone would send for the time being. As soon as the surface surged, foaming, over them they were cut off. As utterly alone as Richard had predicted.

The Regional Prosecutor swung round the instant communication ceased, his face twisted with shock and simple outrage. He had never before been cut off in all his life – and that the ocean should have the temerity now ... 'I have not finished,' he snarled at Peter. 'Is there no way you can re-establish radio contact, at the least?'

'We have two radio buoys,' answered Peter steadily. 'One for emergencies and a back-up in case that one gets lost. Is your call an emergency, Mr Prosecutor?'

Yagula opened his mouth – no doubt to contend that his least little whim should count as an emergency. Then the reality of their situation struck him. His face, and the massive frame beneath it, both seemed to sag as he realized the full implications of the hissing silence. And it seemed to Richard that this, the final insult, really drove home to all of them their isolation and relative powerlessness. Had they actually been an experienced submarine crew none of this would have been novel, strange, disturbing. It was new to all of them except Peter and Pugin. New and terrifying.

What had seemed a vivid and thrilling environment only moments earlier, now seemed a dull and dangerous trap. The liveliness communicated in the throbbing barrel of the floating hull seemed to be soaked up by the massiveness of the water they were sailing through – no; *sinking* through. The hull, and everything in it, became as dead and echoing as a tomb. Where something still, so distantly, went *tap, tap, tap*. Richard decided he could not be the only one aboard to think – just for a fleeting moment – that all the great waters over the surface of the earth flowed into one another.

One might be isolated in the Australian Outback or in the Sahara Desert – or even in the Rocky Mountains or the Hindu Kush – but the scale of those experiences was contained by some kind of limit. The foothills of a range. The ending of an environment. The coasts of a continent.

But what was pressing down upon them now was every drop of water in all the seven seas of the world. And all the dreadful weight of it bore down on them relentlessly now, and would do so unremittingly from this moment until the instant that they surfaced. Richard was a brave man – though he had never really considered his bravery at all – but he saw at once that what they were experiencing now, and would experience through every second of the foreseeable future, would call upon a special kind of grit. A grit that had nothing at all to do with strength or power. Nothing at all to do with political connections or financial clout. This was a unique test – and all the more challenging for being so. He pulled in a juddering breath as he consciously tried to still the beating of his heart and calm the flutter of his nerves. As he did so, he glanced around. As far as he could see, only Peter Korsakov remained unmoved. Pugin continued to glower – but that had to be for reasons beyond the simple experience of the dive. Maria Ivanova remained almost ecstatically elated. But the rest of them, like Yagula, were pale and scared.

It was a situation that, on any of his personal commands, would have made Richard fearful of mutiny. And he reacted, as though against that very threat, by giving them all something to do. Something to take their minds off the fear until their bodies had made the adjustment. Something distracting – likely to keep them occupied through the immediate future while the long hull settled and tilted into the turn, reversing her course exactly before she headed for the Kara Sea. It did not occur to him that this was not his command – that it was up to Peter to give the orders here – or Yagula in matters of law and perhaps precedent. It certainly did not occur to him that clear and decisive leadership might make him a target; present him, as Yagula had said, as the tallest tree in the forest and the most likely to get chopped down.

'Right,' he commanded. 'Let's get sorted out and stowed away. Then we can go through this vessel with a fine tooth comb and find out precisely what we have at our disposal.'

Peter Korsakov stowed his own kit in his own cabin, pleased no doubt to find it so perfectly ready to receive him. Alexei went into Smirnov's. According to Peter, the order of the cabins went Captain and four navigating officers first, then Chief and four engineers. Beyond those ten on this deck, the eleventh, twelfth and so on upon the deck beneath had belonged to the lesser mortals aboard.

The pecking order became crucial at once, therefore. Yagula wanted his complete team beside him – which meant the last cabins on the upper deck would berth the two Spetsnaz men and the first forensics expert – while

Maria Ivanova would be consigned to the lower regions, isolated and potentially at risk. Particularly if the fears she had expressed to Richard had any real foundation.

But Richard put his foot down, and the others, to his own surprise, obeyed. The upper deck cabinned, therefore, Korsakov, Skylerov, Asov, Pugin and Murphy; Richard, then Yagula and his Spetsnaz guards (one on either hand – security giving way to precedence). And finally Maria Ivanova.

The rest went down below.

With *Titan 10*'s computers in control, there was little for them to do, and so, having agreed their accommodation, they all spent some time moving their kit into it, unpacking and tidying up. If any of them was fastidious about sleeping in used sheets, then that was just bad luck. This was the sort of adventure where creature comforts came low on the list. A fact that would really come home to some of them, thought Richard wryly, when they began to work out the galley rota and the cookhouse duties.

The cabin Richard moved into was smaller than the one he had just vacated on *Prometheus 4* – but not by much. The back wall curved strangely – a fact he had not noticed before – but the bunk was fitted to allow for this. There was no porthole, but instead there was a print of the icebreaker *Baikal* at work on the lake of the same name. It was a poster-sized print, battered and faded but still quite clear. It was stuck to the curving wall at the foot of the bunk and gave an illusion at least of vast space and cold, clear air. And Richard abruptly felt the need for both as the tightly confining surfaces all around him all tilted. *Titan 10* was turning.

There were few personal effects and therefore plenty of room for the basic necessities he had brought along himself. Unpacking, storage, tidying and bunk-making took him ten minutes. Then he was off, planning to do a little exploring. Were this vessel his command, he would begin with a tour of inspection – and then call Emergency Stations. The routine was in his bones and he answered it without further thought. Particularly as he was still keen to stay ahead of the game – and knowledge of *Titan 10*'s layout was likely to prove vital in a whole range of scenarios that he could think of.

No sooner did he begin than he found he was not alone. As he passed Peter Korsakov's door, the frail Captain stepped out and joined him, jingling his security keys thoughtfully. 'Tour of inspection?' asked Richard.

'Smirnov had his own way of doing things and a week to make changes. If he has done this I need to know. And there is the question of the vanished crew.' Peter paused. He glanced up at Richard, frowning. 'It is as though *Titan 10* is no longer mine. I must treat her like a new command. Get to know her once again.'

'That could be vitally important,' agreed Richard. 'Mind if I join you?'

'I'd be glad of the company.' As he spoke, Peter led the way out of the main command and accommodation area – and Richard started banging his head. Even when he remembered to keep clear of the low ceilings and the series of bulkhead doorways, lower still and requiring a distracting step up, the continued just-off-vertical tilt of everything would catch him out.

'*Titan 10* is a huge vessel, of course,' said Peter as they started their tour, 'but the quarters and work areas are all cramped. The only spacious areas are the tanks – and even those are strutted and strengthened. The original Typhoon twin-hull design has been retained, you see, but the twin pressure hulls are now the tanks. You are familiar with the concept? The old Typhoons were effectively two submarines lying side by side within the same huge hull, each one with its own weapon and propulsion system – and its own crew. They only communicated in a third section, a shared command area. Where we are now. We are going forward, so below us lies what were once the missile storage areas of both separate hulls. These are now just tanks. Tanks that stretch right back to the propulsion areas well aft. The propulsion areas, like the tanks of course, are sealed except for emergency access.'

'So we don't go there.'

'Not today. We have higher priorities as long as the computers keep telling us all is well down there. Under normal circumstances we would remain within this small, third area. Like your own supertankers – you largely remain on the bridge, yes? You visit the engineering sections during the day but they run unmanned at night. And hardly ever go into the tanks.'

'OK. I get the picture,' said Richard, stooping lower and following physically as well as intellectually. 'So how big is the bridge section?'

'It is a pressure chamber shaped like one of those tubes one used to find round expensive Cuban cigars and it is largely contained in the whale hump beneath the fin. It is a little over six metres in circumference and some thirty metres long. Within it there are three decks two metres in height, though under the fin itself the headroom rises, as you have observed I am sure, to two and a half metres. Each of the three decks is split into corridors between rooms designed for storage and accommodation. One can tell when one comes to the outer walls of the section because they are curved.'

'Like the wall at the back of my cabin.'

'Precisely. And at the end of the section, here, there is a spiral stair down to the next level. I will go first. Watch your head.'

The spiral stair – one of the most cramped Richard had ever negotiated – issued on to the next deck down, then wound on down to the third deck below. Feeling his back and shoulders beginning to cramp, he followed Peter on to the second deck, distantly aware that the tapping sounded louder here. He must ask about it – but Peter proceeded unconcerned and so he followed, thrusting the question aside.

The layout seemed the same on each deck. A central corridor a little more than three feet wide – just room for a couple of bodies to squeeze past one another. Rooms on either side behind sliding doors. Rooms that were little more than boxes a couple of metres deep and three or so long. Roomier store-rooms were made simply by missing out partition walls and creating areas six metres long – but still only two metres deep. Still and all, these were bigger rooms than the cabins on the deck above – Richard reckoned that the forensics team may have fallen on their feet. This thought was extended immediately after they squeezed round the periscope housing that stabbed through the middle of the passage and plunged right to the bottom of the boat. Under the main command area, towards the stern – where the main power-sources were located, a couple of sickrooms, the galley and ward room had been fitted. The galley itself was a boxroom two sections long with a similar-sized food store and ice compartment opposite, but the ward room opened out into the corridor and spread the whole width of the deck, making a decent-sized room with a table in the middle and cupboards down either side. Right at the rear was another spiral stair.

The lowest deck seemed more cramped

still. There was no living accommodation here – there were simply more storerooms and work-cum-maintenance areas. Like any other tanker likely to be at sea for considerable periods, *Titan 10* had to remain self-sufficient as far as possible and so the lowest deck was equipped to maintain, fix or replace almost everything aboard. But not, Richard noticed, the computers. Or, he assumed, the reactors.

'Where next?' he asked.

Peter gave a tight grin. 'The most important place of all,' he said. He set off up the spiral staircase with Richard on his heels. Up and up and up they went through all three decks – and then up again, round half a turn, into a cramped area that Richard had neither noticed nor suspected. The corridor aft of the command area stretched forward from his ankles, which must seem to a casual observer to be hanging from the ceiling.

Richard looked around, reckoning that Peter's crouching body and his own head and torso must be in the after housing of the great conning tower – or immediately behind it. Here was a tiny room giving on to a further compartment through a tightly closed bulkhead door.

This door was unusual in that there was a thick glass section in it, illuminated by a weird mixture of dim lighting both here and within the tiny chamber itself. And, looking through the thick glass, Richard was suddenly struck by something unexpected. The tiny room was full of water.

Peter didn't seem to have noticed. 'It's the main escape chamber,' he was explaining. 'I think we should bring them all up here and show it to them so that they know there's a way out if we have real trouble. Even my most experienced submariners would come and check in here when things got rough. It should help the amateurs we have aboard with us now.'

'I wouldn't do that yet,' said Richard grimly. 'I'd empty it first – and see if there's any way of checking who used it last.'

'What? My God you're right! It's been left open. Someone must have used it and then...' His voice trailed off as his mind whirled into speculation. 'Someone must have *used* it...' he repeated, then fell silent once again.

'But why?' he continued after a moment. 'And in God's name *who*?'

Richard looked up at the pallid, crouching man with his confused frown and his lost eyes. 'I don't think you've met our Captain Birdseye yet, have you?' he asked quietly.

CHAPTER TWENTY-TWO

Back

'I thought I knew all of my crew,' said Peter, ten minutes later. 'But I'm certain I've never seen this man before. Mind, the state of his face makes it harder – so blackened and swollen. It was a new crew put together specially. And there were a couple of men who came aboard just as we set sail. I wouldn't necessarily have met all of the crew before I fell ill.'

He looked up at Maria Ivanova standing beside Richard on the far side of Captain Birdseye. 'You're certain he was from *Titan 10*?'

'We have this,' said Maria Ivanova, showing him the emergency beacon with the tell-tale ID mark.

'And you have a flooded escape chamber,' added Richard. 'That makes it seem more likely.'

Peter nodded thoughtfully. 'But you don't know who the poor fellow is?' He glanced up and then down again at once.

'No name. No nationality, even,' admitted

the Special Investigator. 'No finger or toe-ends either, so no prints...' She warmed to her explanation and Richard stood back a little, physically as well as metaphorically. They were back on the lower deck in one of the big chilled storerooms – with what looked like far too little meat to feed the men they had aboard, let alone the full crew Peter had commanded. This was where the Spetsnaz men had left Birdseye on Yagula's orders. No doubt they had checked with Peter too, or they would never have found the place.

Richard stepped out through the heavy door and stood in the corridor, watching the chilled air come out into the warmer atmosphere like fog. The corridor was filling with white mist up to the depth of his knees. The first thing that struck him was that the surface of the fog, restless though it was, lay square-on to the walls. The deck below it was level too. He lingered there a moment longer, making his observations quite automatically as his mind dwelt on other things – distracted anew by the number of hiding places that seemed to be available even in the contained little pressure hull below the command bridge. Once again he was struck by how easy it would be for someone to be hiding down here. And, if there was access to the rest of the massive hull, one could probably hide an army down here. But would one want to? Were his suspicions just a blind alley leading out of a simple reluctance to believe that Max's computers could really have sailed this submarine alone, without any on-board human aid? He listened for the tapping that had half-convinced him there might be someone hiding aboard – but he could hear nothing. He stepped right out, resisting the automatic urge to close the door behind him – for that would trap the others inside with the corpse. This was the after end of the lower deck corridor, he thought. The end that he and Peter had hardly glanced at as they made their way straight up to the escape hatch three and a bit decks up. Now he looked more closely, tempted, perhaps, by the way the fog was flowing along the corridor and past the foot of the spiral staircase.

For the corridor did not end at the staircase, he realized abruptly. It went onwards beyond the light for another unexpected couple of metres. Lost in a brown study, his mind far away, deep in speculation as to whether someone could last aboard here alone without going mad and heading for the escape hatch, he let his feet guide him. Along the corridor and past the spiral stair. Into the gloomy little passage. And, for a wonder, the unexpected end of it was not curved. But then the end of it was not a wall.

It was a door.

Richard remembered what Peter had said. 'Not today...'

This must be the door that led down into the huge engineering sections below. And, of course, to the nuclear reactor itself.

'Captain Mariner!' Peter's voice was strong.

216

Penetrating. Commanding. Surprisingly formal, all of a sudden. Suspiciously so? Richard turned.

'Yes, Captain Korsakov?'

'Not that way. We will go back up to the command centre now. I wish to check our course.'

'Certainly. *Titan 10* has been running upright again for the last few minutes I should calculate so she must have settled on to her new course of ninety-five degrees. Is Inspector Rusanova finished?'

'Just coming, Richard. I have to cover the poor man's face and tidy him away. He deserves a little respect after all. There, I am ready now.'

'Good. Then lead on, please, Captain Korsakov.'

The others were waiting in the command area, restless and suspicious. Richard and Peter had been away for more than half an hour – and then Maria Ivanova had joined them for a further fifteen minutes. It must have been nearly an hour since anyone had seen them, Richard realized. Enough to make the hardiest of them nervous. But a carefully chosen word or two soon put their mind at rest. It was logical, after all, that the Captain would want to patrol his command – and understandable that he might want to show it off to a widely experienced colleague. And of course it was inevitable that, when he wondered about the corpse in the cold store, the Special Investigator should be summoned to explain it to him.

And, thought Richard, with a secret shrug, there was no point in telling them about the flooded escape chamber now. Luckily, not even Pugin seemed to have noticed the extra noise the pumps had made as they emptied the little room and prepared it for emergency use again.

After the discussion, Pugin stayed on watch and Peter took the rest of them on a quick guided tour of the major facilities, orientating them as to the whereabouts of toilet facilities, showers – both spacious but unisex of course, designed for seventy-five men. They had been placed just aft of the cabins on the top deck, and immediately above the sickrooms and the galley – where the water pipes and waste pipes ran. Another, smaller set lay below, between the galley itself and the ward room. Again the forensics team seemed to have fallen on their feet, thought Richard. Bigger cabins and private facilities. And the kitchen and the ward room close at hand. Perhaps Maria Ivanova and he should move down there after all.

They got no further than the galley, in fact, for the first sight of the cookers seemed to remind them all at once that it was lunch-time, and none of them had breakfasted before coming over to *Titan 10* that morning. A swift search revealed that there were tubs of dried milk, dried eggs and flour. There were no fresh salads or any fruit, but sacks of beets, cabbages, potatoes and onions. Tins of everything imaginable.

For most of them, their first meal aboard consisted of tinned ham. As they ate, and a sense of normality returned – strengthened by a cup of tea to wash the basic meal down – they discussed the more mundane plans. Time would pass; they would grow hungry again. Even in their strange and unsettling situation, they would need to eat and drink, sleep and entertain themselves in some way. Even trapped aboard as they were, even powerless to do much about their situation as they were, even looking to the future as it would be revealed by the programs that controlled everything around them – they would still need to get on with living.

Richard announced that he for one would be happy to prepare something more substantial for dinner. He could bake bread, boil potatoes, rice, pasta, lentils or any of the various dried beans aboard – and any of the other root vegetables on offer. He was hesitant to offer himself as anything other than a well-practised basic cook, but there was some chilled beef down by Captain Birdseye. He could guarantee some kind of a stew at least. His offer was hungrily accepted. Ham and tea had filled few stomachs – and those belonged to men like Yagula, who – according to Rusanova – could not even be imagined in a kitchen. Maria Ivanova, challenged – unexpectedly – and abruptly on her mettle, offered to help him. He in turn accepted with a quiet smile, suspecting that had she been told to do

219

the cooking, as the only woman aboard, she would probably have refused. As it was, she removed her executive jacket, rolled up her expensive cotton sleeves and fell to work beside him – even refusing the apron he discovered in the dry-goods store cupboard.

The afternoon began to pass, therefore, in unexpected domesticity. They made dough to Richard's mother's recipe – blessedly there was white flour and yeast as well as dried milk, salt and sugar. They kneaded it while the big electric oven came to heat, then she oversaw the baking of it while he went below to get the meat he needed for the stew.

He knew at once that someone had recently been in the cold store, for he stepped down off the spiral staircase into a puddle of milky mist. His suspicions all too swiftly aroused, he tested the door before opening it – but it had been closed. Even so, he tore it open abruptly so as to surprise any interloper foolish enough to have trapped himself in there. But the room was empty. Ever careful – especially given the suspicions he had just harboured, he secured the door so that it could not shut on him before he turned to work. As he did so, he glanced down. Yes. There was the tiniest tell-tale mark that showed where the door had been wedged – apparently shut but open just enough to stop the latch from catching. Someone had been very careful indeed. Had the mist not alerted him, he would likely never have suspected a thing. But now his suspicions had been aroused...

Before he crossed to the pile of meat he had come down here to get, he went over to the corpse on the stretcher. Yes. Someone had been examining it. He had watched Maria Ivanova tucking it away after showing it to Peter Korsakov. Her neat work was all un-done, but – again – by no means obviously. Someone had been looking at the face – and indeed, the chest below. He sat back on his heels and looked down the length of the body. All the way down to the feet, the wrap-pings seemed disturbed – as though, section by section they had been pulled apart by someone searching for something. Beside the body, on the floor, lay the sack that contained the corpse's clothing. That too seemed to have been opened and rifled.

Frowning, Richard stood up again and crossed to the shelf where the meat was piled. Preoccupied with his thoughts, he began to sort it out.

Korsakov was the most likely suspect, of course. The others had probably had the chance to search the corpse and its clothing before. But wait a moment – Yagula and his men might not have – certainly not in private; in secret. And Richard trusted none of them. Not Yagula; not his Spetsnaz men, who he was certain did speak English, nor his patho-logist or forensics men – likewise.

Nor did he trust Korsakov. His sickness was just too convenient. His absence at the vital time – and his reappearance – too pat. And his recovery beginning to look too rapid into the bargain. But then he didn't trust Maria Ivanova either. Morgan Hand had warned him not to trust Alexei – and Pugin was Alexei's henchman. That left Max and Murphy – and he wasn't too sure about Max. Perhaps he had better keep doing the cooking until the whole affair was done and dusted. It would certainly be safer that way. With one last look down at the corpse, he stepped out into the corridor and released the door. He began to climb back up the spiral stair. Why would anyone be searching the body? he wondered. Bringing the poor chap back aboard certainly seemed to have raised someone's hackles. And that made it seem even more likely that he had been aboard here before at some time. That it was in fact he who had exited through the escape chamber.

But then, thought Richard, if Captain Birdseye had done all that and the chamber had remained flooded, then he must have been the last person to use it. The last person to exit an empty sub, deep under water, being guided by soulless computers to a distant, pointless rendezvous with her tanks empty of oil and the rest of her crew long gone.

As he came past the end of the ward room, he wandered inwards a few steps, put the meat on the table, then returned and resumed his climb. He paused on the command deck, looking down the corridor to the bridge area – but no one was watching him. On he went, therefore, half a deck further up, into the cramped little room with that glass-sectioned door into the escape chamber. The escape chamber, whose outer hatch had automatically closed after Captain Birdseye's exit – or they would have noticed it the first time they came aboard. Whose inner room was now pumped dry. It was just about the last place the poor man had been alive and under some kind of control of his actions. Richard reached forward and closed his hands around the handles on the solid doorway. They turned surprisingly easily, and the door swung silently open.

Richard looked up first, his action dictated by that bone-deep feeling of the weight of the waters pressing down on *Titan 10* but the hatch in the roof was tight and secure. And then he looked down.

Had you asked him if he expected to find anything he would probably have said, 'No.' But there was that part of his mind that weighed possibilities and sometimes guided his actions from far below his consciousness. Perhaps deep down there he had suspected – perhaps even reasoned. For he did find something there. Two things. And they were things he might well have expected to find, had he sat down as he had not done – and worked it through. As, again, he had not done.

And yet, when he saw them, lying on the floor of the pumped-out chamber, lying on their sides on top of the grille on the main drain, he was not surprised to see them. The logic of their existence broke upon him in the instant that he saw them and he knew them for what they were as surely as if he has seen them arriving there himself.

Captain Birdseye's boots.

CHAPTER TWENTY-THREE

Strait

'A penny for your thoughts.'

'What?'

'This is correct, yes? *A penny for your thoughts?* Like Scuppered?'

'Yes. Very idiomatic. Like *Better to sleep with the devil you know...*'

'That is Yagula's idiom. Perhaps he would like to be the devil I know ... But you are very preoccupied, Richard. Surely frying some cubes of meat cannot occupy all of an intellect such as yours?'

'No. Indeed. I was just thinking. It doesn't matter. How are those onions coming?'

'Like old lovers. I have reduced them to mush. They have reduced me to tears.' She looked up at him, the expression on her face made almost tragic by the shine of her wet cheeks and the marks of running mascara. She saw surprise in his eyes. 'You think I have hard heart?'

'On the contrary,' he smiled, his mind beginning to engage with the present situation.

'Ha! You flatter. You flirt with me!'

'Not at all. Are those onions ready?'

'Yes, these onions are ready. You may add them to the meat now and I will seek potatoes in a moment. You Englishmen have the reputation for truthfulness. You do not flatter or deceive, so they say. All Englishmen are gentlemen, yes? Knights with armour?'

'Knights with armour. Knights without armour. No, of course not. We are the same as everyone else.'

'Ha! So you say! But this is not true. You are not the same as Yagula. He is the devil I know in all truth, whether I sleep with him or not. You are not the same as Russian men. Or Cossacks. Or Uzbecks. Or Kazaks. Or Latvians. Or Lithuanians. Or Chechyens...'

'Or Frenchmen. Or Italians. Or Greeks. Point made. What are Englishmen like, then?'

'Honest. No – more: *honourable*. Your word is your bond. No? Open. Shy but charming. Reliable. You stand by maidens in distress, do you not? Have you not stood by me? Kept me safe from the brute Yagula, even as I asked? Kept me indeed from being scuppered?'

Fortunately Richard was stirring the onions into his browning meat during all of this, so his blushes were spared. And he felt like blushing, because of course he was being anything but open and honest with her. As he

225

had kept the second beacon from her, so he was now hiding the boots from the escape chamber, waiting for an opportunity to sneak off and examine them more closely, whether his duplicity scuppered her or not.

'That bread smells done,' he said. 'And what do you think we should put in this stew? Other than potatoes. Beets? Beans? Cabbage? Is there red cabbage or only white?'

He turned when she did not answer, and there was Yagula, more than filling the door frame, staring in at them, narrow eyed.

'What do you think, Regional Prosecutor? Beets?' he asked equably, hoping the shock did not show.

'Beans and cabbage,' rumbled Yagula. 'And dumplings?'

'For you, Boss, anything,' said Maria Ivanova, suddenly finding her voice. Richard abruptly suspected that Yagula had been at the door for some time. She would have to watch out for reprisals from the devil she knew, he thought. And sooner rather than later.

Yagula shrugged himself under the lintel and entered. Richard was pleased to notice several welts across his shaven cranium. At least he wasn't the only one aboard regularly beating his brains out, he thought. But Yagula's visit was short. Maria Ivanova was right about him – he might be confident with his orders in a restaurant, but he was out of place in a kitchen. He picked and poked, treating the preparations much as though they were a crime scene. And that idea proved apt enough, for as he fussed and fiddled, so the forensics team made their first report. Maria Ivanova translated in a near-whisper, 'It is impossible to be specific about the blood they say – anxiously – because it seems to be a mixture. What? He demands – of sheep's blood and chicken's blood? Is this a leak from some butcher's delivery? Oh no, they say. It is all human. It has just come from more than one person. And this is true of all the bloodstains they have found...'

Yagula remained after the forensics men had left, moodily thoughtful. But the instant Maria Ivanova recalled him to himself by suggesting he wash some potatoes, however, he was off.

But the smell of the frying was beginning to fill the command area. Max was the next to follow his nose and come prowling into the kitchen. He was more amenable than Yagula. At least he was willing to wash the potatoes and put them in a pot to boil. But then his good nature also ran out – and he was supplanted by Alexei.

'I think they have all been in now,' said Maria Ivanova half an hour later, as they put the stew into a casserole and placed the doughy dumpling mix on top of it. 'It was nice of Captain Korsakov to warn us that he would not be eating any of this. Do you think we've cooked too much? No. It'll keep. But he was the last one I can think of. They've all been through.'

227

'I think you're right,' answered Richard. 'Except Pugin. And Murphy.'

'Murphy came in to make sure we were cooking the potatoes correctly.'

'So he did. Just Pugin, then. D'you think any of them are likely to come back, though? We seem to have made a lot of washing-up.'

'Now that is something all men share, regardless of colour, creed or race. It's a kind of gender-specific psychic genius. We won't see hide nor hair of any of them until after the washing-up is done.'

They ate when the food was ready. It was earlier, perhaps, than the normal routine would have dictated, but the cooks were merely gifted amateurs and unwilling to risk the perfection of what they had done. Nor, indeed, was there any need to do so, for the computers kept the watch and the humans, it seemed, were supercargoes.

There was plenty of room for them all around the ward-room table. There were thirteen of them, but it was designed to sit twenty. In a fully crewed *Titan 10* the meal would have been served in sittings – three or four depending on the watch situation – but as things were it all came at once.

And it was immediately obvious that they had not cooked anywhere near enough. The mashed potatoes seemed to disappear in an instant and the beef stew with cabbage, beans and herb dumplings was just as swiftly gone, the last of it soaked up with massive slices of the white bread they had baked. Richard's mother would have been proud. So, as is usually the case, the cooks ended up with nothing because their guests had taken it all. When the ravening hordes were gone, Richard and Maria Ivanova sat down with Peter Korsakov to view the empty ruin of all their work. They opened a tin of chicken and the three of them ate it cold on slices of the last loaf, which Richard had been wise enough to hide. There was butter – brought out of the cold store to enrich the mashed potatoes – but nothing else. It was providential, therefore, that Richard's mother's recipe had guaranteed outstandingly tasty bread. 'I think there's some cheese down in the store where I found this butter,' he said when they had finished the chicken but not the loaf. 'I'll go down and see if I can lay my hands on it.'

'Good idea,' said Maria Ivanova. 'Captain Korsakov and I can start the washing-up while we're waiting for you.'

'Call me Peter, please,' said Korsakov. 'But I'm afraid I cannot help you any more. I must send up the radio buoy and make sure *Prometheus 4* is just behind us. We'll be entering the Kara Straits later tonight, and I'll rest easier knowing she's there.'

When Richard returned with the cheese, he found Maria Ivanova alone, still eyeing the washing-up askance. But as he entered, she whirled to face him, her eyes a-sparkle with cunning. 'I have it!' she said, and disappeared into the dry goods cupboard. A moment or two later she emerged with a huge tin covered

229

with familiar markings – but unfamiliar writing. 'You can tell this is an American-sponsored project,' she said. 'Not only meat but good coffee too! I will brew some at once and when they smell it they'll be back. They only get to drink it when the washing-up is done!' The plan worked like a charm. As the aroma of the coffee wafted out, so the men came back in, and soon the most amenable – most desperate for caffeine – were up to their elbows in the sink. Even Yagula was drying up.

As the pile of dirty dishes dwindled, so Maria Ivanova began to serve out great, steaming mugs of coffee. Having dried a plate or two, Yagula was first in line, but the instant he reached out for his cup Peter Korsakov returned. 'I have good news and I have bad,' he announced.

Yagula put his cup down as he turned and all of them listened to the Captain while Maria Ivanova continued to fill the others.

'I put up the buoy and have contacted *Prometheus 4*,' he said. 'We are just about to enter the Kara Strait, and this was the last chance before we go deeper into the trench there. *Prometheus 4* is following us and has been cleared to come with us into the Kara Sea. But she is far behind and will take more than a day to catch up with us.' He took a deep breath and plunged onwards, a little desperately; aware, perhaps, that he was singly and solely responsible for this, for his finger – and his alone – had pressed the

'Return' button and started the voyage. 'Once we pass the Strait we will be out of contact for a while. Novaya Zemlya will form an effective barrier against radio contact and in any case, there is a high level of interference ... Nuclear pollution ... And we will have to be careful how we use any surface equipment. The weather is deteriorating rapidly with a northerly storm blowing straight off the Pole. There are ice warnings out for the whole of the Kara Sea.'

There was a silence, as they all looked at each other, spirits falling and tension rising. Richard stepped forward with a smile. 'Come and have a cup of coffee, Captain. And then you can tell us the bad news,' he said.

The coffee and the tension hyped them up. The evening stretched out before them, dangerously empty, ripe for trouble to start brewing. 'What do you do for entertainment on *Titan 10?*' asked Richard. 'We have film shows on *Prometheus 4.* Anything like that here?'

'We have a video projector,' said Peter, his voice betraying the fact that such minor considerations as entertainment had utterly slipped his mind. But he was right; they did. And they even had a screen. As *Titan 10* began to settle almost imperceptibly into the deeper waters of the Kara Strait, therefore, they all settled down to watch *The Hunt for Red October* in English, with Russian subtitles.

Richard slipped away as soon as he could, for he had not been absolutely honest when

231

he said that all he wanted to do was ensure the crew were entertained. He wanted to give himself some privacy, to look at Birdseye's boots. Even so, it took him the best part of an hour to assure himself that no one was watching him any longer. The first thing he needed to establish, if he could, of course, was whether or not they really did belong to the corpse in the meat-locker. But he decided it would be best to wait until the end of the film to perform the simplest and most obvious test. Through the ward room was the quickest and shortest route down. The alternative was to carry the boots the length of the command accommodation – four times. Twice going and twice coming back; passing twice through the open command section itself, under the eyes of any watch-keeper that Peter would be bound to set up there. Better to see what the footwear itself could tell him through close observation and guesswork while he waited for the others to finish up and settle down for the night.

He had put the boots in the bottom of the wardrobe quite openly between his own footwear and that of his cabin's previous occupant. It looked to him to be quite innocent and unremarkable there. Only quite a close inspection would reveal that the boots were sopping wet. When he picked them up to examine them more closely at last, they left quite a considerable puddle behind. They were waterlogged in fact, and so swollen as to be pulling apart at the seams. He carried them over to the bedside table where the light was strongest and fell to work.

They were standard lace-up working-men's boots. Size ten in English measure – looking the right size for Birdseye. They were sand-colour with thick soles made of rubber moulded like tractor tyres. The laces went through lace holes across the instep but then were secured in metal hooks up to the ankle. They had been unlaced in a desperate hurry – hooks on both sides were twisted and flattened. One was missing altogether. And they had been unlaced with desperate force – trapped under a swollen lace, tangled like a fishing-hook in the bushy fibres was half a fingernail torn bodily free. Richard remembered Birdseye's fingertips and shuddered. He tried not to imagine the panicky realization – as the water flooded into the little escape chamber – that survival techniques dictated removal of footwear.

Richard sat as though frozen for some time, trying not to empathize with the cramped, drowning, desperate fingers tearing to get the weighty, sopping, soaking boots off before they began to weigh as much as the concrete favoured by the Mafia of old. He remembered how battered the poor man's elbows and knees had been. And he felt every bit of it, relived every horrific second like some medium granted spiritual contact through the items he was holding. Such was his concentration that he did not even hear the stirring of the others beginning to bed down for the night, the film over and done with, the fictional submarine and crew in safe haven.

After a while, Richard put them down and began to pull the laces gently free. When they were lying on the table top he pushed the boot wings wide and pulled the tongues forward for a closer look inside. A combination of the water-logged swelling and the movement of the tongue caused the inner surfaces to move in a way that struck him as odd. He reached in one after the other to pull a pair of insoles free.

And under the right insole, held flat against the sole itself until that moment, he found a card. It was a corporate ID card made of plastic and covered with solid laminate. Waterproof. Damn near indestructible.

It had a picture of a square-faced, serious man upon it. Beside the picture was a Social Security number, an employee record number, a job title, a name and an address for both employee and employer.

The man's name was Joseph Bronowski.

The home address was in Austin, Texas.

The job title described him as a Field Engineer.

The employer was Texas Oil.

'Tucker Roanoake, you devious...' hissed Richard under his breath.

And his cabin door slid wide. He whirled, knocking everything into the well between the bunk and the bedside cupboard where he had been working. He needn't have bothered. Maria Ivanova stood there wrapped in a coat.

As he looked up at her she reached for the door frame and the coat fell open. She was stark naked underneath it.

Richard lurched to his feet. Even as he did so, she collapsed inwards, falling dramatically into his arms. Her eyes looked up at him, so wide it was impossible to say where the iris ended and the pupil began. Her lips moved in the most intimate of whispers. He lowered his face to hers and she whispered again.

'I've been poisoned. I think I'm dying.'

And the whole of her body convulsed.

CHAPTER TWENTY-FOUR

Death

Richard's first thought was *Yagula's pathologist.* Not as suspect – he was a long way from reasoning as yet – but as the nearest thing to a doctor they had aboard. He didn't know the man's name; had never spoken to him – even via Yagula himself. But he knew where to find him. And he knew where to collect Yagula along the way.

Stepping forward with the fainting woman in his arms, Richard came out of his cabin into the corridor. Mercifully he was quick-thinking enough to decide against a fireman's carry – that would have smashed her head on the ceiling. So he swung her across his chest and carried her as though she were a bride going over the threshold. She was gasping for breath and twitching. Her eyes were flooded with tears. She convulsed and dry-heaved helplessly, looking as weak as a baby.

On his way past Yagula's cabin Richard kicked the door. 'Up and out, Lavrenty Michaelovitch,' he called. 'We got trouble.' Then he moved on just fast enough to be clear of the next door when the Spetsnaz security men slammed out of it, alarmed by the disturbance.

By the time he was at the steps leading from the command area down on to the next level, Yagula was up and out behind him, the Spetsnaz men both in tow. 'It's Maria Ivanova,' called Richard over his shoulder. 'She says she's been poisoned. May be dying. Has your pathologist any current medical qualifications?'

'Yes.'

'Good. Then we'll need him. And you'd better ask your forensics team to join us as well.'

This conversation was enough to get them back along to the galley area, aft of which was the sickroom. Richard's burden had now stopped twitching and heaving and had relaxed into sinister stillness. She seemed to have got a good deal heavier into the bargain. As Richard swung the inert Maria Ivanova round into the corridor that led back towards the pale painted tree trunk of the periscope housing, he glanced across into the ward room. No one had bothered to pack anything away, of course. At least they seemed to have switched it all off; even the lights. One figure was still sitting there, alone, apparently still watching the dark, blank screen. Probably fallen asleep in the film and left there by his shipmates. It was the sort of humour popular in some of his old commands, thought Richard as he slid the door wide and stooped under the lintel, just managing to squeeze himself and his flaccid burden through together. There was a dull security light in here and he could see well enough to get Maria Ivanova on to a sick-bed before Yagula hit the light switch. The stark brightness of the glare when he did, however, emphasized the frail nudity of Maria Ivanova's body spread out upon the blackness of her coat. Richard ripped the sheet out from under her and spread it over her. Then he turned to find himself facing Yagula's pathologist.

'She thinks she's been poisoned. She says she's dying,' said Richard.

'Poisoned with what?' asked Yagula. Richard noted that he did not bother with any translation.

'I don't know. We'd better look. We can do that while the doctor is examining her. Doctor, she was gasping for breath, twitching. She fainted into my arms but she must have been dizzy first – she needed to hold herself up against my cabin door. Oh. And there's something the matter with her eyes...'

'Knowing what the poison was can make all the difference,' said Yagula. 'You do well to describe the symptoms but having the stuff would be better.'

'I know. But in the meantime he can begin to make informed decisions – does he need to induce vomiting, use a stomach pump or whatever. Does he have an antidote?'

'It's a bit late to induce vomiting,' said Yagula. 'You should see the state of her room.'

'Been up there have you? That was quick.' As Richard spoke, he stepped back to let the doctor look more closely at Maria Ivanova.

'Delegation. I sent one of my men.'

Peter Korsakov arrived. 'What's going on?' he demanded.

Yagula explained.

'Better get everyone up,' said Richard. 'In case it was something we all ate. I can't think of an infection that would work this quickly. Food poisoning's most likely. Poisoning of one sort or another.' There was a moment of silence as his words sank in.

'At least, if we've all been murdered,' Yagula observed grimly, 'we have just the team we'd need to solve the case before we die.'

'So let's get on,' said Richard. 'And leave the doctor to his work.'

'I'll send everyone down to the ward room,' said Peter.

'I'll go down to the galley,' said Richard. 'It's the logical place to start. It could have been anything from the beef to the beans. Or it could have been foul play, like Maria Ivanova seemed to think.'

He was in motion as he spoke, almost tearing himself out through the doorway as the pathologist stripped the sheet back again and leant forward for a closer examination of the seemingly stone-dead woman on the bed. Half a dozen strides and a careful stoop took him back to the galley. He paused for a moment and turned to switch on the lights again. He was just about to swing on into the galley itself when he stopped. The lone figure still sat there, staring up at the blankness of the screen.

And the strangeness of it struck Richard at last. He used the door-jamb as a solid base and swung himself bodily round. Five more strides brought him up beside the figure. It was Pugin. He took the little submariner by the shoulder. 'Pugin,' he said forcefully. 'Pugin. Wake up!' Pugin simply toppled forward and crashed lifelessly on to the floor. Only when he slid on to his side did Richard realize he was frozen in position, like a statue.

Yagula decided on an investigation at once – but Richard insisted on a head-count first. A finger at Pugin's throat had confirmed the man was dead – though the pathologist, suddenly far too busy, took him off to make certain. Richard didn't want anyone else lying silent and still in their berths, all too quietly dying while the rest of them faffed around.

But once they were all there, Yagula took command. He had risen through the rank of Investigator to the dizzy heights of Prosecutor. And even though his proposed path led ever upward towards National Officialdom at the Central Prosecutor's Office in Moscow, and then on to the gravy train of national politics, he remembered the old days well enough. The old skills.

'You have one hour to give me your first report,' he snarled at the forensics men. 'Tell Uncle Vanya he has the same,' he ordered one of the Spetsnaz men, then remembering, he repeated the order in Russian.

Uncle Vanya turned out to be the pathologist and he was less nervous of Yagula than the forensics team. He came out with the Spetsnaz man to discuss priorities with Yagula in person. 'I can tell you what killed the seaman within the hour,' he announced, in serviceable English. 'Or I can stop the woman dying. It should take the same time. Which one do you want?'

Yagula actually hesitated. 'Save the woman,' he said at last.

Uncle Vanya nodded. 'Then you may have to wait to learn exactly what killed this man Pugin,' he warned.

'Not if forensics do their job properly,' snarled Yagula.

'Indeed. Then let me do mine.' Uncle Vanya turned on his heel.

Is Uncle Vanya his real name or a literary reference? wondered Richard. The patholo-

240

gist had long, thin, sheep-like features with high cheekbones and huge eyes lurking behind gold-rimmed spectacles. With a grey fleece of hair at one end and a wispy goatee at the other, his face was that of any Russian uncle. His name seemed too good to be true – unless it was a reference to Chekhov's famous play. But Yagula and his men did not seem to be the kind who would waste their time in theatres. They'd be happier in the burgeoning strip joints the Mafia ran in all the popular tourist resorts. Undressing Anya – yes; Uncle Vanya – no. It was another question filed away to ask, like what could make the tapping sound?

In the meantime, Peter Korsakov, Max Asov, Alexei Skylerov, Murphy and Richard went through their most recent movements with Yagula. One of the Spetsnaz made notes while the other sat and glowered. Supposing, no doubt, like the KGB and the Spanish Inquisition before it, that truth was a function of fear. Yagula translated all the English into Russian but Richard noticed that the notes usually started before the translation began.

The situation allowed him to characterize the pair of them, however. His secretary in London was called Audrey – and that name suited the one that wrote the notes. 'Audrey' the secretary. And the other was 'Tom', for Tomas de Torquemada, founder of the Spanish Inquisition itself. He might have called him Lavrenty, after L. P. Beria, founder of the KGB – but Lavrenty Yagula's parents had taken care of that one already.

'It was the meal, then,' confirmed Yagula the better part of an excruciating hour later.

'Sure I could have told him that,' whispered Murphy. 'When else could we have been exposed to any poison?'

Richard agreed – on one level at least. There seemed no other time that the men and women aboard could have been poisoned since they all had come on to *Titan 10*. Though, of course, it seemed that only two of them actually had been poisoned then.

But he was also aware that they could all have been exposed to any poison in almost any place at almost any time during the last few days. Pugin especially – for he had been immersed in the water and beside that strange black iceberg for some time. All around the edges of the Barents Sea, ancient Russian factories and facilities held stockpiles of poisons, rotting in nothing more solid than plastic containers and paper sacks. DDT, paraquat, Agent Orange – God alone knew what. And their mining concerns, open-cast and inefficient by Western standards, generated wastelands full of cyanide, strychnine and arsenic, by-products of their relentless work. All of it swept down into polluted rivers and on into the festering seas. Which seas, of course, were filled with ancient, leaky shipping – especially at this time of year. Shipping for the most part moving chemicals like the poisons on the shore; and others. And oil, that leaked either from their holds or their bunkerage or when they cleaned their tanks out. The spray from a wave, the condensation from a cloud, a breath of apparently fresh air could have done the damage, let alone extended immersion in the poisonous stuff.

And, as if that wasn't enough, as *Titan 10* entered the Kara Sea – the waters the Soviets had never dreamed would ever be accessed by the West – they also had the radioactive legacy of the rotting nuclear fleets, which Tucker Roanoake had described in such horrific and impressively intimate detail. Described with such uncanny accuracy, thought Richard. And then he remembered who the source of at least some of that information had been. And he was jolted by the realization of what lay half under his unattended bunk within his open and available cabin.

'Hey, Richard,' said Max quietly. 'You OK?'

'Yes, fine. But, look. I just want to pop up to my cabin for a sec...'

Too late. The forensics team had run out of time. They came back quietly – a little nervously, looking not at Yagula but at 'Audrey' the note-taker and 'Tom' the hard man.

'What have you to report?' demanded Yagula.

Nothing at this point, apparently; at least not according to Yagula's ironic, increasingly insulting translation. All the pots and pans, plates and cutlery had been washed up as part of the price of the coffee. There was no trace of anything noxious on any of them.

Even the coffee cups, miraculously, had been cleared away and cleaned until they gleamed as though new. All the food and all the condiments seemed innocent and were likewise squared away tidily. All forensics could find on them was soap.

'That was Rusanova,' said Alexei quietly to Richard. 'She washed it all.'

Uncle Vanya arrived at that instant and saved the face of Yagula's team. 'It was cyanide,' he said.

Actually he said more than that but 'cyanide' was the bit that Richard understood. 'The woman's symptoms, as well described by the man who carried her down here, were consistent with medium-dose cyanide poisoning,' Uncle Vanya continued, as though addressing a bunch of trainee pathologists. 'Fast breathing, rapid pulse, faintness, eye irritation – nausea and vomiting as confirmed by the Regional Prosecutor. I have proceeded on that assumption and administered an antidote. She has responded well – and that in itself is proof. I see no reason to suppose at this stage that Pugin died any other way – but his dose must have been massive. He has convulsed. Locked, passed immediately into a coma – too swiftly even to raise an alarm, apparently, and died on the spot. When he relaxes from his spasm, I will be in a position to open his stomach for a full autopsy. I will be able to give you further details then.'

'But who'd want to kill poor Pugin?' demanded Alexei.

'Poison is a notoriously inaccurate weapon,' observed Richard quietly. 'Perhaps it wasn't supposed to be Pugin that died at all.'

CHAPTER TWENTY-FIVE

Suspicion

'Well,' said Uncle Vanya drily, 'if you're getting into that game you'd better all be very careful. Cyanide is one of the deadliest substances in nature. Outside of plants such as apples, apricots, potatoes and rhubarb, where it is found in abundance, it comes in a range of preparations. It is easy to get hold of because it is so widely used in the production of paper, paints, plastics and cloths of all sorts as well as in photography, mining and a range of electrical activities. It is vital in so many areas that it is not unusual for fire-fighters to face smoke full of cyanide gas when buildings catch alight. And not just commercial premises – ordinary houses. It can be eaten, drunk, breathed in or rubbed on. It can be injected, but it passes through the skin so readily that injection is a waste of time. It is traditionally supposed to smell of almonds but doesn't always do so. It is supposed to taste bitter but doesn't always do so.

And even were someone to be using the bitter crystalline variety, mixing it with, say, sugar, will make it almost undetectable to the victim, although, to be fair, it looks more like salt. It would be almost impossible to detect, now I think of it, in almost any granulated artificial sweetener. On the other hand it will be equally hard to detect in a bitter medium, like black unsweetened coffee, for instance. Impossible to detect until after the victim has taken it, of course. By which time it is usually too late. In that it seems to have been administered orally to both of the current victims, it seems either that there has been random contamination or, as Captain Mariner has suggested, someone is using it more surgically. Surgically if not necessarily very accurately.'

'So if it is cyanide,' said Yagula. 'Where has it come from?'

'I have said,' answered Uncle Vanya. 'Almost anywhere!'

'But where? Where aboard this vessel?'

'Haven't you noticed how clean everything is?' asked Richard.

'What?' Yagula was not used to Richard's leaps of reason. He was confused and angered by the Englishman's irrelevant question.

'It's an old ship. Been in service for years, in and out of ports. Hundreds of men aboard. But where are the mice? The rats?'

'You're right!' said Uncle Vanya, shaking his head. 'Someone has been through this ship with poison.'

'At Severodvinsk, I should imagine,' said Richard. 'But I bet it's still aboard. In one of the storerooms. A box labelled something like "All Kill Pest Repellent. Handle with care. Dangerous to pets and humans. Contains cyanide." And, now I think of it, there is a box in the biggest storeroom...'

Ten minutes later the box was sitting on the ward-room table wrapped in a plastic bag, to preserve the unlikely possibility of finger-prints. The box was half full. 'Or half empty,' said Uncle Vanya. 'And we need to ask, was this the only box? And where is the rest of the contents?' But nobody had an answer. Or, if they did then they weren't saying anything.

'So, we come back to the first question,' said Richard. 'Was Pugin the target? And if so, why? *And if not, then who?*'

'We will move him next door so that I can get to work on him,' said Uncle Vanya. 'I can begin to confirm matters I believe with a simple blood sample. It is the oxyhaemoglobin that the poison attacks after all...'

'The same is true of Investigator Rusanova, surely,' observed Yagula silkily, as they came out of the second sickroom, having laid Pugin on the basic operating table there. 'Was she a target? And if so, then why?'

'I agree,' acknowledged Richard. Then he frowned. 'But the outcome of the question must be different for each, must it not?'

'Meaning?' Now it was Yagula's turn to frown.

'Meaning that if Pugin was the target, then

247

the attack has succeeded and our best way forward is to investigate Pugin himself – hoping to find out why he was killed. This should give us some idea who would want to kill him. With Maria Ivanova things are different. If she was the target, then the attacker missed. She may have her own suspicions and these will be the best place for us to start. We must wait till she wakes up, therefore. On the other hand, having missed, the murderer may try again. Especially if he thinks like us – in which case he has a vested interest in making sure she never wakes up. So we must investigate Pugin and guard Maria Ivanova,' Richard concluded.

Then he glanced across at Yagula and added, 'But I believe I am trying to teach my grandmother to suck eggs.'

'I know this saying,' crowed Yagula, mightily pleased with himself. 'I am your grandmother, am I not? It is my eggs we suck. Indeed, you but echo my thoughts. Your observations are very logical, however. We must investigate Pugin and protect Maria Ivanova. But who can we trust to do this – if we do not know who is trying to kill her?'

'She came to me as soon as she realized what was happening to her.'

'True, Captain Mariner,' admitted Yagula. 'But did she come to ask for help or to accuse you to your face?'

'She came for help. If I had wanted her dead, I would not have been so quick to get her to Uncle Vanya. That must prove something.'

'Well. Let us admit to that, Captain Mariner.'

'And the same is true of Uncle Vanya himself, is it not?' insisted Richard. 'Had he wanted her dead, she would be dead now, with not a shadow of suspicion pointing to him. So one or other of us can watch her. And the rest of you can investigate poor Pugin.'

'That will do,' decided Yagula. 'What an amusing way to pass a night.'

So Richard was in many ways the author of his own misfortune. He had certainly talked himself out of all hope of returning to his cabin and hiding what was there. As Murphy went past, therefore, Richard whispered to him, 'Do me a favour, would you, Murphy...'

Moments later Richard was in the doorway of the sickroom, on watch. A lesser man might have been content to go right inside and guard his subject closely, but that would have isolated guardian as well as victim. And Richard was far too interested in what else was going on aboard to stay isolated for long. He took a chair, therefore, and put it athwart the doorway, half in the room and half in the corridor, facing aft. Here he could look down into the ward room – or up towards the command area over his shoulder. And at the same time he could glance in at the still form of the sleeping woman. It was a perfect defensive position, too. No one could creep up on him. The only problem with it was that the door held open by the chair-back throbbed and juddered between his shoulders. Every now and then it touched the back of his head, pushing the relentless rhythm of the submarine's movement straight into his brain. No matter how distracting the bustling investigation proved, the strangeness and the sheer danger of the situation remained there, only just beneath the surface, like the tapping he could hear once more when the door hit the back of his skull.

The ward room claimed his attention because it was here that Yagula remained centred, just as Peter had resumed formal control of the command area, with Alexei – now that sleep was no longer an option – alertly at his side. Richard soon found that there was a good deal to be learned from the simple observation of what the Regional Prosecutor got up to. There was the coming and going of the forensics team – with the sugar first, then with a range of commercially available granulated saccharines. Then the coffee.

Then the Spetsnaz men passed through – both 'Audrey' and 'Tom' were active, while Yagula himself made notes. It was easy enough for Richard to guess what they were up to – for he had sewn the seed of the idea himself. The forensics men continued to search the kitchen for cyanide. 'Audrey' and 'Tom' searched Pugin's quarters, bringing down to Yagula anything they found suspicious – or even interesting. Pugin had hardly been in the room and had died down here –

the chairs remained scattered around the place where he had fallen, all awaiting the forensics men's examination next.

There was no need for Yagula to bother with Pugin's cabin personally, of course. It was his effects that were of interest. A backpack came down – like the one Richard had worn across with everything he possessed in the way of warm clothing and footwear. Pugin, too, seemed to have brought extra clothing in his. And, from what Richard could see, little more.

Things proceeded in this vein for some time, with Richard on watch and Yagula's teams at work. Then Murphy returned. 'I've tidied up your room,' he whispered. 'Everything's stowed away.' And Richard nodded.

'I'll take a turn on the command area,' said Murphy. 'It's where the other real sailors are.'

Richard nodded again. And the night settled into a routine.

But then 'Audrey' returned with a bundle wrapped in plastic. His head went low to Yagula's and both of them glanced up at Richard. So chillingly suspicious were their glances that Richard, feeling his conscience pricking, got up and went in for a closer look at Maria Ivanova.

She seemed to be resting safely. She was on some kind of drip – he checked the needle taped in her arm. Then, lost in thought, he tucked in the sheet and smoothed the pillow with fatherly fingers, as he would do for Mary his daughter when she slept.

'*What are you doing?!*' Yagula's voice snapped from the doorway.

Richard swung round, forcing himself to look calm, in control. 'Actually,' he said, at his most icily, unassailably British, 'I was giving you and your henchman a little privacy to examine whatever came down from Pugin's cabin wrapped in that plastic bag.'

'Ah.' Yagula sounded sceptical. He paused. The eyes just beneath the lintel narrowed as he thought. Then relaxed. 'You mean this,' he said, pushing something in through the door.

Richard took a step across the little room, holding out his hand. Lost in Yagula's great bear-paw was a Geiger counter. Modern, neat, one of the smallest he had ever seen. He froze, his hand hovering just above it. He looked up through the doorway at those level, speculative eyes.

'This was Pugin's?' he asked.

'It was in his quarters,' confirmed Yagula. 'In his stuff.'

Not part of the previous occupant's kit then, thought Richard, picking up on Yagula's emphasis. Something Pugin had brought. On purpose. Suspecting danger. And Pugin was the most experienced man amongst them. The only one who had served on Titans or Typhoons.

'Have you switched it on?' asked Richard. His mouth was suddenly dry.

Yagula shook his head, silently.

'We'd better. If Pugin was scared of radiation, then maybe we should be as well.'

252

Yagula's thumb hesitated. 'But what would we do?'

'If that thing reads into the red, then we override the computers, surface and get the hell off. If we can – which, to be fair, I doubt.'

'Sit in the middle of the Kara Sea in the middle of the night in the middle of a storm with a murderer in a life raft – if there is one – and wait for *Prometheus 4*? Which isn't even through the Strait yet and doesn't know where we are?'

'If we have to. She has our projected course. She'll be up with us soon. What else do you suggest?'

'On *K-19*, they drank red wine to ward off the radiation, after the reactor went critical on them. They brought her home in the end.'

'This is a dry ship, Lavrenty Michaelovitch. There's no wine here unless you brought it aboard.'

Yagula shook his head. 'Then we would have no choice, would we?' He pushed the button, and both men jumped at the noise the little radiation meter made.

Richard leaned forward, gasping in shock. 'What's it set for?'

'It says "Rems" here on the LCD. You know what that means?'

'Roentgen Equivalent in Man. A standard measure of alpha and gamma particles. Broadband. One rem is about the equivalent of having an X-ray taken. Most standard radiation is measured in millirems. If you work in a nuclear power station you might experience one rem on a regular basis. If you smoke a pack of cigarettes a day, the same. On the other hand, if you go into high-radiation environments you really start damaging yourself. Over one rem for a long time will start to damage you – like cyanide, it will start to destroy your blood. If you go over about 120 you'll get sick. 300 you get very sick. 450 you die slowly. 600 and you die quickly. It varies on body mass so we'd last longer. What does it say?'

'It says 01.'

'Thank God. But thank God only if we don't stay being exposed to it for any great length of time. And, of course only if it says the same in all parts of the sub.'

'I guess maybe that's what Pugin came aboard to find out.'

'Right.' Richard paused for an instant, thinking. 'That kind of information could close this whole thing down in no time. If the subs were badly contaminated.'

'It could.' Yagula nodded.

'Costing your government, and several other people I could think of, an almost incalculable amount of money. Standing. Credibility. Power...'

'Incalculable. Certainly enough to be worth killing for.'

'At the very least it would be information worth millions...'

'Almost as much as your cargo of missing oil.'

'Enough, as you say, to be well worth killing

for.' Richard paused. Then added, 'Or killing to stop.'

Yagula nodded thoughtfully.

'So maybe Pugin was the target after all.'

'Maybe,' said Yagula, sounding surprised.

'But I thought you were the target, Regional Prosecutor.'

'So did I,' said Yagula. 'So did I.' And on his word, the floor tilted sideways strongly enough to send them both staggering. From the galley came the sound of something shattering and a confused shouting from the forensics team. Alexei appeared almost at once. His face was pale and his eyes a little hunted. 'All OK here?' he asked. His hunted eyes flicked down to the Geiger counter in Yagula's hand. Seemed hardly to notice its existence. Flicked up again.

'Yes,' said Richard. 'All OK here. What was that?'

'That was a ninety degree turn,' said Alexei. 'We're heading due north. And going flank speed. Due north, with nothing but the point of Mys Zhelaniya between us and the North Pole.'

CHAPTER TWENTY-SIX

Aft

'Who do you trust?' Richard asked.

'What?' Yagula swung back to face him, having watched Alexei run back up into the command area.

'Who do you really trust, Lavrenty Michaelovitch?'

'No one, of course!' The Regional Prosecutor, practising for the exercise of real power, laughed at such a naive question.

'Not even yourself?'

'Myself least of all, sometimes.' Was it the arrogance of power? Or had Richard tricked him into the admission.

'Who do you mistrust least, then, of the people we have aboard?' Richard probed, glancing back at the soundly sleeping woman.

'The people I can frighten. Control.' Dangerous honesty again; but a self-evident truth.

'The forensics team?'

'Yes. But only while I have them under my eye. They are not the Einstein brothers.' Another self-evident truth.

'The Spetsnaz men?'

'Ha! You think they are Spetsnaz, do you? That is very funny. But yes; again. I trust them if I can see them.'

'Captain Korsakov?'

'I think not. There is too much about him that makes me wonder...'

'Me too. What about Max Asov?'

'Again. I think not.' Yagula glanced down at the Geiger counter, frowning, suddenly impatient. 'Why do you ask these questions?'

'Alexei Skylerov?'

'I would have trusted him and Pugin most, I think. Until Pugin got himself killed and Skylerov pretended he didn't recognize this Geiger counter just now. That mistake shows us that he knows what it is and, probably, why it is here. He was in league with the dead man, perhaps.'

'Perhaps. A worry in any case. High on our list of problems. Murphy?'

'I trust him to do what you tell him to do. If that is trust.'

'Me?'

'I trust you to do what you want; not to do what I want.'

'That trust is mutual, I assure you. Uncle Vanya?'

'Yes. Yes, I trust Uncle Vanya.'

'So do I. So, let's leave Uncle Vanya guarding Maria Ivanova and go exploring with Pugin's Geiger counter. We should take Captain Korsakov with us and leave Murphy to watch Alexei on the bridge. That way we'd hardly have to trust anyone at all.'

'Ah! Now I understand!'

'You can bring one Spetsnaz man to watch our backs and leave the other to keep an eye on the forensics team.'

'Very tempting, but—'

'I have torches in case we need to explore dark places. And we need to get on, don't we?' Richard suddenly came face to face with the Russian, looking almost directly into his eyes and speaking with powerful sincerity. 'We have no real idea where *Titan 10* is heading, or what to expect when we get there. Mys Zhelaniya is eighteen hours' fast sailing straight ahead, but it's nowhere near the well heads, and, if I remember correctly, the mention of it upset you almost as much as mentioning Norilsk. Apart from being one of the coldest places on earth, it also overlooks the biggest and most dangerous submarine arms dumping ground on earth. So I hope the hell we're not going there. Because now that we're moving at full speed, the exit hatch is never going to open. And we know what our chances of controlling the computers amount to. So we have no real hope of getting off this tub. And judging by the tilt of the floor we're powering down to more than a hundred metres deep. If we're going into the Kara Trench off Cape Gulla – which must be almost dead ahead, and so it seems quite likely – we'll need a deep-sea rescue vehicle to get at us in any case. Come on, Lavrenty Michaelovitch, we need to know what those radiation levels really are. And that's just the beginning of what we'll need to know – and soon!'

Fifteen minutes later, Peter Korsakov was hesitating by the door behind the aft spiral ladder's foot. 'Are you sure you want to go in here?'

'We just want to check it,' said Richard. 'We won't play with anything.'

'Open up,' snapped Yagula, made more impatient than usual by the strain of following somebody else's suggestions.

Peter obeyed and the bulkhead door swung towards them with a hiss. Automatically, he stepped forward over the raised metal jamb and led the way into the tunnel that stretched away down the after section of the boat. There was more than forty metres of tunnel in all, but after ten metres or so, it had more pressure doors designed to open into the major engineering sections on right and left.

Richard swung in after Peter, thinking that if he got the chance to return later, he would bring young Murphy down here. 'Going in now, Geiger still reading only a couple of rems,' said Yagula into a walkie-talkie. He was using 'Tom' as his back-up and reporting back to 'Audrey'. He was speaking in Russian but Peter was whispering a translation for Richard. The four of them moved in two pairs, Peter and Richard first – but they could almost have walked abreast. The passageway was low but wide. It was even more Spartan than the forward section and a combination of oily smell and intensive, unbaffled vibration made it seem very much an engineering area.

Yagula spoke almost constantly – sometimes to one minder, sometimes to the other. Peter kept up a running commentary into which Richard dropped every now and then, when his mind wasn't preoccupied with more immediate things.

'Yagula is surprised that the Geiger counter is now registering less than two rems again. Now it is back to one rem. And this place is so clean.'

Away to his right Richard saw the first great door. He crossed to it and swung it open. There was another immediately opposite. He opened that as well. The tunnel, which had felt so low buried as it was under the whale hump and the sail – almost underground, in relationship to the rest of the ship – was suddenly a gallery. High above cathedral spaces, it seemed to hang like a balcony as the engine rooms fell more than fifteen metres sheer to the great turbines driven by power from the water-cooled reactors beneath and forward. Turbines relentlessly driving the great propeller shafts that whirled at maximum revolutions now. Pounding them north along their strange new course.

Turning, Richard crossed to open two more doors and look down into an identical cavern on the left of the tunnel. Never until now had he really felt that there were two hulls within the great shell of the submarine. Two parallel submarines, in effect, with a tunnel here, following the cleavage of their close-snugged aft sections. There was no doubt left in his mind now. And the scale of this really helped him to imagine how huge the tanks in the forward sections must be, each hull, stripped of its weaponry, storage, individual guidance, extra crewing and all the rest, capable of containing more than 5,000 tonnes of Kara Sea crude oil in each. 10,000 tonnes in all.

Such was the enormousness of everything around him, that Richard nearly overlooked the next, vital clue because it was so small. Stairways led down from the doorways' sides, plunging like flying buttresses through the shadowy depths. At each turn of these there was a cage the size of a modest room. The sides of these were made of woven wire – like wire fences. The same material roofed them – though they were floored with patterned steel like the walkways and the steps. And in the cage nearest beneath Richard's feet was lying what looked like a headless body.

Richard gasped as though he had been punched. Winded by shock, he whirled and clattered away down the steps. Peter paused at the top and Yagula stood behind him w/t jammed against his cheek, yelling. But as he drew nearer, Richard's eyes cleared – particularly as his torch beam dispelled some of the gloom. The headless corpse was a sleeping bag, and beside it were the remains of a little camp. Clearly a little secret camp. In the floor of the cage there was a sizeable trap-door that opened down into a big tool compartment. The tools were long gone and a snug little hidey-hole had been put in there instead.

Richard looked up at Peter. 'Stowaway?' he hazarded.

But Peter shook his head. 'Impossible,' he said briefly. 'But someone certainly has been hiding here.'

'Birdseye?' wondered Richard. 'All this stuff would fit him, I guess. You had some really strange things happening aboard this boat, Peter.'

'*I* certainly did not! I assure you that if anything strange has happened then it was while I was sick ashore!'

'If?' called Yagula. '*If?* Where's your *crew*, Captain Korsakov? Where's your *cargo* gone? *"If anything strange has happened ..."'*

'There's nothing here,' said Richard after a few more minutes. 'This stuff could all have come from aboard – and probably did. Smuggled down here from galley and stores. The sleeping bag gives no clues. Nothing at all – except that it proves someone was hiding away sometime.'

'But not now?' asked Peter, looking around nervously. 'He's not still hiding somewhere nearby now?'

'No. This food is stale – though not yet mouldy, see? Everything's cold. Deserted. This hasn't been used in a week and more. It's no proof of anyone secretly running the programs. Controlling the computers in secret and hiding away from us. It may be proof of Captain Birdseye's whereabouts before he jumped ship. But that's about all, I'd guess.'

'You know the thing that really surprises me?' asked Yagula suddenly.

'No. What?'

'The fact that this box is sitting almost exactly on top of the nuclear generators...'

He stopped speaking for a moment, so Richard prompted, 'On top of the nuclear generators. Yes?'

Yagula held out the Geiger counter. 'And yet the reading on this thing is by far the lowest so far.'

Peter looked anxiously from one of them to the other. 'And that's a good thing? Yes?'

'What's the reading here?' asked Richard half an hour later.

'Going up,' answered Yagula.

'You want to stay in the command area, Regional Prosecutor?'

'You think I trust English people to crawl over Russian submarines unattended by responsible officialdom?'

'As you wish. Open up, please, Peter.'

Peter reached forward and loosened the bolts around a smaller doorway right at the top-forward level of the command capsule. When it hissed back, they all fell back a step in unison, but then Yagula stepped forward with the Geiger counter and Richard crouched down to get a good look at their next area for exploration.

Although Richard hadn't noticed the door at the forward end in his earlier visits here, logic dictated its existence. He had realized it would be here as he was considering the twin-hull layout of the stern. There must be a cleavage between the forward sections as well as the aft sections.

Access to the cargo tanks themselves must be from the outside – for loading and un-loading of cargo at least. Probably through some specially modified missile doors. But there must also be hatches accessible from the inside, designed to allow maintenance, cleaning and so forth. And, therefore, there must also be a tunnel reaching forward along the steel-sided valley that led to the bows.

But the pattern of radiation seemed to be the opposite of what logic might have dictated. It seemed to be much less intense at the stern beside the water-cooled nuclear reactors and the engines that they drove – and much more intense forward, beside the tanks, where there should have been nothing more radioactive than cargo – or sea water.

Richard looked past Yagula's stooping form into the long, narrow tunnel. There was much less space between the forward sections of the hulls than there was between the after sections. Where the aft tunnel had an air of spaciousness enhanced by the open galleries ten metres in, this tunnel seemed dangerously cramped.

It was a sensation exacerbated by the fact

that a narrow floor was flanked by forty-five degree angles instead of vertical walls reaching to a low, wide ceiling, thought Richard. Out of these strangely angled walls in series sprang the upward thrust of inspection hatches, and from the ceiling hung the protective equipment needed to carry out the work which the hatches were designed to facilitate. They looked substantial, were probably designed to be anti-static and had breathing equipment built into them. What good against high radiation levels they would be he was less certain. About as much use as cling film, he thought.

'If that thing gets anywhere near twenty-five rems we're coming out,' he said to Yagula.

'If it goes over twenty you're on your own,' answered Yagula. 'I still have plans for an active and productive sex life! If I ever see land again. Or a woman other than Maria Ivanova.' He turned and grinned mysteriously. 'Better to sleep with the devil you know than screw with the devil you don't,' he said. But Richard was distracted by a gentle, echoing *Thump!*

'What is that?' he asked. But when they listened, there was nothing.

They went in single file. Yagula went first because he would not give up the Geiger counter and it really needed to be in the lead. 'Tom' went in behind him, then Richard, and Peter last of all. It was an intensely strange and unpleasant experience. The suits were all in disorientatingly vibrant motion. The anti-static material clung to faces, hands and the backs of necks. Their touch was light but cold and slimy, like the clinging brush of weeds in foetid ponds. But a hand raised to push the creepy softness away would set the air-tanks swinging – with painful results to the next head behind. Yagula's minder seemed particularly active in this area and Richard soon found he had to pay careful attention if he didn't want canister after canister smacking him between the eyes. But this too had its price. The inspection hatches were covered in catches and bolts apparently designed to cripple ankles and trip unwary feet.

Were this all not bad enough, their entry into the tunnel seemed to coincide with the submarine's arrival at the trench Richard had referred to. And, as he had predicted, the long hull seemed to dive down into it at maximum rate, hugging the deep sea bottom. Because of this, they seemed to be walking down a considerable slope. And they were all too well aware that there was a tremendous weight of water gathering above their heads. An inch or two above their heads. They could even hear the thunderous hiss of it as it rushed across the same steel plates they could touch if they just reached up a little way. The water seemed to make more than a rushing hiss. Occasionally, with no discernible rhythm or reason, there would be that soft but distinct *bang!* into the bargain. But this was neither the time nor the place to stop and discuss it. The shaking hull was thrusting relentlessly deeper

– far beyond their power to control or hope to escape. The slope of the floor was such that even if Yagula's Geiger counter went over 20 rems – or 200 for that matter – they would have one hell of a job just turning round and getting back out into the command area.

'Eighteen,' called Yagula. 'Do you think we should go on?'

'Let's try for twenty,' called Richard. 'We're only thirty metres in. There's another sixty or so to go. Peter, what do you think is doing this? Is the Kara Sea so polluted it's actually registering this level of activity? I mean that's all there is in the tanks – the lading records proved that.'

'Twenty,' called the Russian. 'That's it. We turn round now.'

Peter obeyed at once, and faced with Tom's glowering countenance, Richard turned as well. They began to make their way back out again. This time, Richard's perspective was very different. He was walking uphill. Peter was much more careful with the canisters. He could take the time to watch his feet and spare his aching ankles.

Which is exactly what Richard was doing when he saw the bright-orange section of cloth. The cloth was striking for several reasons. To begin with, it was the same bright orange that Captain Birdseye had been wearing – and it likely belonged to another crewman, therefore. Secondly, it did not appear to be torn at all. It was the corner of a sleeve or trouser cuff, folded and neatly machined. Thirdly and most strangely of all, it was protruding from the bottom of one of the secured hatches.

Richard paused and 'Tom' crashed into the back of him.

'What's up?' called Yagula.

'Just a moment,' called Richard. 'There's something strange here in this hatch.' He reached down and tugged the cloth, but it remained immovably wedged where it was.

'Whatever it is, it's in the last hatch,' called Yagula. 'If it's that important, let us out and come back in.'

'Good idea,' said Richard amenably and moved forward. Yagula was right. To look at that piece of cloth more closely, Richard would have to open the hatch. To do that, he would have to get suited up because even opening the hatch an inch might release gases deadly enough to kill him on the spot and explosive enough to blow the front of the submarine open.

But he never doubted that he should risk doing it. He was suited up within ten minutes – even given that the space outside the door where he changed was almost as cramped as the tunnel itself. 'Close the door after me,' he ordered.

'Of course,' replied Peter. 'And I will switch on the fans. All standard safety procedures.'

'And I will wait also,' decided Yagula. 'Anything worth this much trouble is worth my attention also.'

'It's probably nothing,' said Richard, turning to step back in.

As he did so, the submarine levelled off. He paused, testing his breathing equipment. The air was strangely dry and dead-smelling. But it seemed breathable. He took a couple of little sips and then a deeper breath. The pressure gauge read low – but was still in the green. That was fine – he had no intention of being in the passageway for long.

He lingered over this routine, waiting for the hull to settle. When he was satisfied, he stepped up over the raised doorway into the passage. Peter eased the bulkhead door closed behind him and at least had the sensitivity to close it silently. No doom-laden, final *bang!* thought Richard. Crouching a little, he settled the headpiece in place and went to work. There were four catches like big levers. They were of white-paned metal and looked new. They worked easily, in pairs, and it took Richard only an instant to loosen them all.

Something went *thump!* quite close by. The sound seemed to echo down the fabric of the boat. He took the handle and, with his eye on the piece of cloth, he raised the hatch. Immediately, all the subtler sounds around him were drowned beneath the rumbling of the pumps. The strange suits began to dance like ghosts in the draught. But he was aware of this strange movement only in the outer periphery of his vision, because he was watching the piece of cloth.

And it simply disappeared. It did not fall to the floor. It did not remain wedged on the lip of the hatch. It simply jerked into the tank and vanished. Almost entranced, Richard raised the hatch to its fullest extent and looked into the tank. As with the dancing suits, the outer reaches of his vision fed him information about vast darkness filled with restless liquid crusted with tar-thick emulsified oil.

But there, in the all-too-clear and accurate centre of his vision, lay the cloth he had been seeking. The sleeve of an orange uniform. But the sleeve was attached to the rest of the clothing. And the clothing was being worn by a body that was floating face-down on the scum. As Richard watched, riven with horror, the body swung round a little and his boots struck the side of the tank. *Thump!*

Richard reached up and pulled the hatchway closed again, forcing it against the slow-close mechanism, until it was shut tight, ready to be bolted down.

In the time that it took him to do this, Richard counted ten more bodies floating face-down in the tank.

CHAPTER TWENTY-SEVEN

North

'Can we put up a buoy?' demanded Yagula.

'We can try,' answered Peter. 'But we're really too deep and we're still moving too fast.'

'Well, we can't do anything about either of those circumstances until we can reprogram the computers,' said Richard. 'Max? Alexei? Any luck?'

'No,' answered Max roundly. 'It's one of those self cancelling situations. We can't contact anyone until we sort out the computers...'

'...and you can't sort out the computers until after you've made contact with someone.' Richard completed Max's sentence. It was one of the few signs of stress apparent in him. Though, since he had stepped out of the forward tunnel he had been ruthlessly decisive, reducing even Yagula to relative subservience.

'Do you think it's the whole of the crew?' asked Peter, shaken and white. 'Are all of them in there?'

'I don't have any idea,' said Richard grimly. 'I only looked in one tank and I only saw the ones that were floating. To be certain, we'd have to drain the lot and then do a body count. It's utterly beyond anything we could consider at the moment. The best we can hope for is to count the ones we can see – get some kind of an idea.

'But of course it would be very dangerous indeed to let this new situation distract us too much, especially as we can't do much about it at this point except to try and alert the authorities. We are all still potentially at risk ourselves, remember. We have one dead man and another person lucky to be alive among our own number. If we don't stay on top of things that are closer to home, and the madman with the cyanide gets carried away, then we'll just end up being added to the list of bodies in the oil tanks.'

'What we need,' snarled Yagula, 'is help.'

'That's the one thing we won't get unless we reprogram the computers and find a way to send out a message,' said Richard. 'But those are the two things we don't seem able to do at the moment. As Max said, it's a self-cancelling situation. But let's give communication a go anyway. Alexei, what's our depth?'

'One hundred and seventy-five metres.'

'More than five hundred and twenty-five feet,' translated Richard. 'Peter, is the line to your radio buoy long enough to tackle that?'

'Perhaps.'

'Then let's go for it.'

'It's the speed, Richard. The speed at which *Titan 10* is moving will pull the buoy under the surface unless I put out thousands of feet of line – and keep feeding it out to compensate. And even then, live, real-time contact will be next to impossible, even if we get the buoy safely up and it stays afloat for long enough to reach anyone. Because the line the message comes down from the surface will be trembling like a violin string. A violin string about a thousand feet in length.'

'OK,' said Richard. 'So we go at it two ways. Does your buoy have a record and replay facility?'

'Well, yes...'

'Right. Then one way or another, we're in business.' He took a deep breath. 'All I need to do is to go back in and get as accurate a body count as possible.' He turned away, and then turned back. 'And all you need to do is make sure everyone out here stays alive until I get back. We'll worry about everything else then. OK?'

Because he knew what caused it, it was the gentle banging that disturbed Richard the most. The narrow corridor seemed to echo with it – though it seemed impossible that it should actually resonate above the combined thunders of the pulsing water outside and the air-pumps within.

Bang! it went, quite gently; seeming to echo in his head. Even the steady rhythmic hiss-roar of his breathing through the compressed

273

air system could not cover it. Slowly and methodically he opened each of the first three hatches on each side. That took him down to the point Yagula read more than 20 rems on the Geiger counter. And it let in quite enough light on both sides to allow Richard his grim calculations. In fact the first pair on each side would have been sufficient for the task. The bodies were grouped near the first one on each side – and had clearly just been dumped in through there. He counted ten bodies floating on each side.

How had they died? Richard wondered morbidly. Shot? Stabbed? Shoved in there alive to suffocate or drown? But then he gave himself a mental shake. For the present purposes it hardly mattered. What mattered was that they were dead. That whoever had interrupted *Titan 10*'s voyage to pirate her oil had chosen to murder half the crew. Half of them at least; maybe all of them. There could easily be another ten bodies in each hold, he supposed, all lying somewhere beneath the thick, black-scummed surface.

As he laboriously checked and double-checked his grim work, his mind ranged further and further away. In time – to what must have been happening here little more than a week ago. In speculation – as to the patterns that had led to these events and outcomes. Patterns that were still working themselves out amongst those left living here aboard. Patterns that might even threaten *Prometheus 4* and those souls still aboard her, who were coming steaming to the rescue – and sailing straight into the heart of unimaginable danger, all unknowing, as they did so. Yagula was right, he thought. They really needed to warn someone.

'...and our current heading is thirty degrees magnetic. I say again this is L. M. Yagula, Regional Prosecutor, Murmansk Region.' Yagula waited two beats, looking up from his notes to the second hand on his watch. As he did so, the recorder switched itself off.

'Perfect,' said Richard. 'All the information we need passed out in two minutes of Russian and two minutes of English. Now, if we can't get through in real time, we just need to release the beacon altogether and that will be broadcast automatically on a four-minute continuous loop through the emergency wavebands.'

'Just like the signal that started all this,' said Alexei. 'The ghost that Nancy Rider picked up that was coming from Captain Birdseye's beacon. It didn't do him much good, did it?'

'Let's hope we're luckier than he was, then,' said Richard bracingly. 'Max, we're all set to do this now, but it's in the middle of the night. I know there'll be someone on watch aboard *Prometheus 4* if we get through live. But will there be anyone at your computer centre?'

'Of course. We offer a 24/7 service. It's always daylight over some part of the Internet.'

275

'Right, then. Let's do it. Murphy, you know how this little recorder fits in the buoy – and how the buoy goes overboard. Peter. Lavrenty Michaelovitch, let's get to the radio shack.'

It was the strangest experience, thought Richard. Somewhere between sound and sensation. As though he were fishing with a radio antenna instead of a rod. The sound made by the radio was not static, somehow; it was a bubbling, rushing hissing, as though the buoy was broadcasting its own environment straight down the line to them. And what really surprised him was the fact that as the line to the buoy got longer, so the signal seemed to become more intense. The three of them sat in the cramped little three-sided radio shack listening to the sound from the speakers, all alike entranced. 'What would this sound like through headphones?' wondered Richard.

'Intense,' answered Peter. 'Like a spinal massage followed by a neck and head workout – all from the inside. It's strangely intimate – almost invasive. This is the word, yes? Invasive?'

'I would hate this,' said Yagula. 'I am content without headphones.'

They fell silent again, listening to the weird harmonics of it.

'How long will it take?' asked Yagula after a few moments more.

'Not much longer,' answered Peter. 'We should get something one way or another soon ... There!'

The radio gave a kind of a roar. The sound was immediately smothered in a keening howl, overlaid with a rumbling, relentless thundering.

Peter hit the 'Send' button and gave their call sign. '*Titan 10* calling *Prometheus 4* and Bashnev Computing,' he said. 'Come in either contact.'

He flicked to 'Receive' but only the thunder came back. Thunder with the strangest grinding cracking sound, as though the buoy had surfaced in the middle of a slowly collapsing tower block.

'I know that sound,' said Richard quietly.

Peter hit 'Send' again. '*Prometheus 4*, this is *Titan 10*. I say again ... Bashnev Computing. Come in Bashnev...'

He flicked to 'Receive'. '...Come in, *Titan 10*. This is *Prometheus 4*. We can route your message to Bashnev. Can your computers acquire ours?'

'Max?' called Richard, too relieved to show it. 'Alexei? Looks like we're in. Can you get an electronic link with *Prometheus 4* while we talk?'

'Yes! We're through!' called Alexei. 'Sending now. It'll only be a matter of seconds before...'

But even as he was speaking, Peter was gabbling, 'Morgan. We're running more than a hundred metres deep at full speed up the Kara Trench. We—'

And the buoy hit something. The contact was so intimate, so immediate, that they all

277

felt it. They all lurched backwards as though they had been slapped in the face. The speakers gave a strange kind of explosion – the sound equivalent of lightning, no sooner there than silenced.

And Richard was too wise to say that he now remembered what the strange collapsing-building sound had been. It was ice.

'That's that then,' he said fatalistically. 'Alexei, did you get anything back from the boys at Bashnev?'

'No. They were confirming link.'

'Peter. Well done. I'm sure Morgan will be able to guesstimate where we were when contact was made.'

'That's it?' shouted Yagula. 'That's *all*?'

' 'Fraid so. Unless the buoy is robust enough to have lived through whatever just happened. If it was, then at least it'll be sending our full prerecorded message out. Two minutes of Russian, two minutes of English, time after time. So, Lavrenty Michaelovitch, we're probably still relying on you. Now, Peter? Alexei? Is that all for the time being? If so, let's get back to the galley and the ward room, shall we? I would kill for a cup of coffee.'

'I'm afraid someone has beaten you to it, Captain Mariner,' came Uncle Vanya's dry, ascetic voice. 'The forensics boys have just confirmed that the coffee was where our murderer put the cyanide.'

CHAPTER TWENTY-EIGHT

Prints

Richard looked down at the steaming, fragrant cup of strong, black coffee, then up at the expectant faces of Uncle Vanya and the two forensics men. Yagula's words rang in his mind, *'Not the Einstein brothers.'* No, he thought. More like the *Darwin twins* – living proof at any rate of the Theory of Evolution. They smiled encouragingly and nodded in unison, raising their beetling brows like a couple of friendly gorillas.

'Quite safe?' he asked again.

They nodded. They smiled. They didn't understand English.

'Quite safe,' insisted Uncle Vanya. He was sitting on Richard's chair, half in and half out of the sickroom door, still guarding Maria Ivanova.

'The poison was on a spoon,' he continued. 'A wet spoon was put into the coffee tin and used to serve coffee. Instant coffee stuck to it quite thickly. Then it was used again to stir in the cyanide. This was done quickly, so that the coffee did not all dissolve. A residue was left on the spoon. Residue mixed with cyanide.'

'The spoon was then placed, apparently innocently, by the sink,' Yagula took up the story – which he had gleaned from his experts while Richard was boiling the kettle. He was standing massively in the doorway to the galley. He looked like a painted portrait too big for its paltry frame. 'It should have been washed up with the cups themselves no doubt but it fell down the side of the sink instead. There are minute traces on one part of the stainless-steel draining board – right at the edge. And more on the floor where the spoon landed. It seems to have slid out again when we performed that tight turn. Other than that, there is still no sign of the poison itself other than the pack from the storeroom. Your coffee is absolutely safe, however. They guarantee it.'

Richard took a sip. The Darwin Twins froze, their faces a twin picture of intense speculation. He swallowed. They sighed and continued to observe him with clinical intensity – as though there was a prize for the first one who spotted a symptom of cyanide poisoning. 'So, Regional Prosecutor Yagula,' he said, 'you are to be congratulated. You have coffee and cyanide intermixed at one end of this spoon. And at the other end, if you're careful, you have the murderer's fingerprints.'

'Indeed. We have begun to look into that.' He gestured at the spoon, lying wrapped in a plastic bag on the end of the table nearest the kitchen.

'You need my fingerprints?'

'Yes. We will be taking everybody's fingerprints as a matter of some urgency. Although haste may place the eventual prosecution of the guilty party at risk,' Yagula intoned virtuously, 'that is obviously a lower priority than detecting and stopping them here and now.'

Richard nodded. 'Good point,' he agreed. Then he took a less self-conscious swig of coffee. It was quite tasty. More importantly, he could feel the caffeine in the strong brew beginning to sharpen his fatigued and stress-dulled senses. The Darwin Twins were starting to look a little crestfallen. Uncle Vanya seemed highly amused.

Peter appeared. 'The beacon line's all in,' he announced. 'Alexei and Murphy have just attached the spare. We were lucky that whatever made the first beacon break away only took the top metre or so. We'd have been in big trouble if the line had broken off just outside the hull.'

Yagula looked at him askance. 'Big trouble,' he echoed. 'You really are a master of understatement. Here we are trapped in a runaway submarine full of dead people at the bottom of the Kara Sea, heading at full speed for the North Pole, with a murderer tying to wipe us all out before we get there. Trouble just doesn't get any bigger, Captain Korsakov!'

No sooner had he spat out the last two

words than all the lights went out.

'Wait!' called Richard immediately over the stirring of shock and panic. 'Stay still! Security lights should be on at any moment. Captain Korsakov, is this part of regular ship's routine?'

'It is if it's midnight.'

'Anyone got a digital watch with an LED? My Rolex is luminous but there hasn't been enough sunlight to wake it up.'

'Mine says two after midnight,' called Uncle Vanya.

The security lights came on. After the blaze of the full lighting, they were dull, filling the whole area with shadows. Making Richard, for one, suddenly very much aware that all of the areas they had been exploring earlier were effectively closed again now, unless they took the largest of their torches, and a great deal of fortitude, with them.

But at least, he thought, the pounding heartbeat of the engines never varied. Thank God for small mercies. 'What about the heating?' he asked.

'That will go down to night routine as well,' answered Peter.

'Then it's going to get cold. We'd better find a way to wrap up. What about the galley?'

'All non-essential power goes down.'

'I'm glad I had this coffee, then. Anyone else want to use up the last of the water in the kettle? Sounds like that's it until, what, eight o'clock, Peter? Peter, when can we expect the power back up?'

But Peter, like the others, had vanished into the galley after the last of the hot water and the rest of the unpoisoned coffee.

The next few hours passed in a strange sort of twilight, therefore. The security lighting was dull – it isolated each of them in a private cage of shadow. It made it hard to see who was nearby – and impossible to identify any-one except those within arm's length with any certainty. The energy-saving routine was predicated upon the assumption that the engines and engineering spaces could con-tinue their unmanned routine, that only the most important watch officers would be up, and everyone else would be asleep.

It was a business-standard routine, thought Richard uncomfortably, designed to save money for board members and shareholders at the expense of a little discomfort for the men actually working at the sharp end. Naturally, there was no allowance made for even a skeleton crew who wanted to remain awake, active, alert and on watch against each other in case a murderer should strike again.

The first thing to break down, of course, was Richard and Yagula's careful overlapping watch. With the coming of darkness no one could keep any kind of effective watch on anyone else. Uncle Vanya, disdaining the common rush for coffee, went off to get some warm clothing. Richard lingered in the sick-room doorway looking in at Maria Ivanova's still figure – though she was little more than a silent, shapeless lump of shadow, almost impossible to see.

When Uncle Vanya returned, it was Richard's turn to go back to his cabin – at long, long last. He pulled on the extra pullover he had brought and gave the shadowy little box of a room a thorough search. But Murphy had hidden the boots well. There was no sign of them at all. When Richard returned to the main area, Murphy himself had disappeared, so Richard went in search of Peter Korsakov. If he couldn't ask one set of questions, he could ask another set, he thought.

Richard found Peter up in the command area. 'Where's the night-setting override?' he asked quietly, reluctant to show the young Captain up; half-convinced he had just panicked and failed to see the obvious. 'There must be an override,' he continued quietly. 'What if there's an emergency? You can't hope to meet it by security light alone.'

'There is,' said Peter, wretchedly. 'I thought of it at once. But it's no good. It's not working. I keep putting in the override code, but like everything else, the computers simply refuse to respond. Beyond that, I really don't know what to do!'

This last humiliation, it seemed to Richard, was the straw likely to break the camel's back. He could hardly begin to imagine what it must be like for Peter Korsakov to be on the bridge of his own command – but unable to command her. Returning from a life-threatening illness only to find her at the heart of a murderous mystery. Discovering that she was headed who knew where and who knew why. Realizing her holds were full of murdered crew-mates. And not even being able to switch the lights back on.

'You could unplug all the bloody computers, I suppose,' said Richard, trying to face down the enormity of it all with a wisecrack and a wry grin. 'It seems to work for my PC at home.'

But Peter was not in a jocular mood. 'Are you mad? We'd die,' he said almost hysterically. 'Switch off power, guidance and life support here and now? We'd go straight to the bottom. We'd crash. We'd all die.'

'I don't suppose you know where the main plug is anyway,' concluded Richard, hearing the edge of hysteria in the young Captain's voice and determined not to get too serious.

'I do,' snapped Peter. 'It's at Bashnev Power in Novgorod!'

'Now, what's that supposed to mean?' demanded Max Asov, stepping out of the shadows.

'It means that none of this could be going on without your knowledge and complicity,' snarled Peter. 'The computers control everything. They take us off course – to places nowhere near the oil wells. For reasons no one seems to understand; no one aboard at least. They cannot even be accessed by any of us. And it is this, all of this, that has caused the murder of my crew and the desecration of my command.'

'Desecration?' snarled Max. 'What sort of a

word is that?'

'What else would you call it? It is as Prosecutor Yagula has said. Things could not be worse. And it is you, your acolytes and your computers that have caused this!'

'Don't be ridiculous!' snapped back Asov. 'Computers do not just hijack submarines and pump out oil into the sea without reason. Computers do not force people into holds full of water to drown and die. Men do that! *Men.* Can you not see that? Men have come and stolen the oil and put it in a ship or a facility and taken it away – on to the black market, as likely as not. Men have come and killed your crew-mates. Mafia men, if the ruthlessness and the body count are anything to go by. But men nevertheless. Men have come and changed the programs in my computers. If there has been desecration done it is to my computers, not your submarine!'

'No,' said Yagula, who stood leaning against the handrail at the top of the little companionway as though he had always been there. 'If anything has been desecrated it is the law. There has been conspiracy, deception, fraud, misappropriation, theft, hijacking, piracy, attempted murder, murder and mass murder at the least.

'If I find you have actually got any kind of control over these computers, Mr Asov, I might charge you with kidnapping into the bargain.'

Once again, Yagula's summation of the

situation was enough to quieten things down. The ill-tempered group split up. Peter and Alexei continued to stand the watch – by which they simply were there in the command area, making observations, quietly discussing them and recording anything they thought important. But they did so in the certainty that the machines that were really in control were making their own records too. And the machine log rather than the human one would be more likely to stand up in court.

Max came to Richard hoping to have his ruffled feathers smoothed. 'Did you hear that?' he huffed.

'Of course,' said Richard, still trying to keep the tone light. 'But hearing is not always believing, any more than seeing is.'

'But to accuse me...'

'Well, Max, they are your computers. We saw how well they controlled *Prometheus 4* right at the start of this. And how bolshie they got if their programs were overridden...'

'But that's my point. When they are properly installed, then they can be overridden – as we did to rescue Pugin. And then – with a little trouble, I admit – they set us back upon our course. What has happened here is very different. This must go right back to the refit. Right back to Shipyard No 402 at Severodvinsk.'

'But you were there to oversee all that,' said Richard, quietly. 'You or your people.'

'Not all of it, no. And not all the time either.

Tucker Roanoake was over for a good deal of it once the agreements were made and the deals were ready for signing. He had a number of his computer people with him – hangers-on, you know? And of course Alexei Skylerov was there – he needed training in the whole system for both vessels the same as Smirnov, his opposite number, did. And Morgan Hand was there towards the end – for the *Titan/ Prometheus* interface stuff. Where the computers actually talk to each other – in laymen's terms at least. That's where she met Peter Korsakov and Smirnov, his First Officer.'

'Sounds like quite a party,' said Richard thoughtfully. 'I hadn't realized. I'm sorry I missed it.'

'It was nothing much. Severodvinsk is not quite Paris, London or New York. Hell, it isn't even Norilsk, yet!'

With Max beginning to talk himself off his high horse, Richard went to see if Uncle Vanya wanted relieving. But he found the sickroom doorway unguarded. He was just on his way into the shadowy interior when Uncle Vanya came puffing up. 'No patience,' he complained, wringing his hands. 'No sense and no patience!'

Richard turned, smiling. 'What?'

'Yagula and those men of his. *"Time to be fingerprinted. Now! Forget the woman. She won't come to any harm..."'*

Richard looked down. The pathologist was not wringing his hands – he was wiping the ink off his fingers.

'Pah!' continued Uncle Vanya – Richard had never heard anyone actually say *Pah!* before. 'This mess will not come off. Stay here, please. I must go and wash my hands.'

He turned to go back into the sickbay next door, but the moment he slid the door to the shadowy little chamber wide, there was a scuffle that claimed Richard's attention. The Darwin Twins descended on him, each of them making vivid gestures that could only mean one thing. 'Time to be fingerprinted. Forget the woman. She won't come to any harm...' He shrugged and followed them. As they passed the end of the table he noticed that the spoon which had caused all this fuss was gone again.

They had set up their makeshift lab in the galley, where the inadequate security lighting was being supplemented by a couple of torches that Richard thought looked suspiciously like his. 'Audrey', the Spetsnaz secretary, was there to back them up, and as Richard entered, Yagula exited with 'Tom'. 'Are those my torches?' asked Richard, reaching for a closer look. 'Audrey' reached forward to check him and knocked a couple of pans off the draining rack. The clatter brought Yagula and his minder back again at once. 'Yes,' snapped the Prosecutor. 'They are your torches. We use them to keep everybody safe from cyanide poisoning. You have a problem?'

'No,' countered Richard. 'But it would have

'been nice to be asked.'

'Please may we use your torches, Captain Mariner?'

'Of course, Prosecutor Yagula.'

'Now may we please take your fingerprints, Captain Mariner?'

'Of course, Prosecutor Yagula.'

He nodded to the Darwin Twins and they went to work. 'Napravo pazhalsta,' said one of them taking his right hand.

Then, 'Nalyevo pazhalsta,' said the other one, taking his left.

When they had finished, he seemed to be wearing black gloves.

'Spasseeba,' they said in unison.

'Do svidanya,' he replied, getting up and taking the proffered toilet paper. 'And spasseeba to you too.'

When he stepped out of the door he saw the spoon at once. It was lying on the floor under the table. He reached down to pick it up but only succeeded in smearing the plastic bag with ink. He used the paper and tried again, but of course the paper was no more capable of taking the ink off his fingers than it had been off Uncle Vanya's. Without a second thought, Richard walked past the open doorway to the first sickbay and slid the door to the second one wide. He stepped over the low sill and immediately felt himself beginning to slip. He looked down. He seemed to be sliding through a huge puddle of oil. In the dimness, that's what it looked like, at least.

It was only when he saw Uncle Vanya, and

realized that the oil was leaking from all around the long steel scalpel sticking out of his throat, that he realized what was really going on.

CHAPTER TWENTY-NINE

Up

'Up,' screamed Yagula. 'Up and out, all of you!'

The murder of Uncle Vanya hit Yagula and his team much harder than that of Pugin – or even the massacre of Peter Korsakov's crew. Richard could see the inevitability of it. Those were professional. This was personal.

But Yagula still went almost literally insane.

'Up,' screamed Yagula. 'Up and out. I want every single one of you in the ward room, where I can see you!'

They all assembled there and the enraged Prosecutor did a savage headcount, checking whether they might have been able to have performed the murder, shining the accusing finger of Richard's torch beam into each face and shouting accusations. Peter Korsakov and Alexei Skylerov gave each other an alibi: they had been in the command area together. But Yagula hardly counted that.

'You could be working together,' he snarled. 'One of you could have slipped down the corridor. Or both of you. One to hold him and one to stab!' He made the gesture, all too accurately reflecting the way the long-bladed dissecting scalpel, fresh from Pugin's incomplete autopsy, must have been used. Sliding through the soft throat tissue just behind Uncle Vanya's Adam's apple, slicing through carotid arteries and jugular vein, releasing almost all of the blood going to and from his brain at once. A little jerk forward and the razor-sharp blade had opened his windpipe, letting the deluge of blood flood into his lungs and finish what shock had started.

And almost silently – a little strangled choking, that would have been all. And, until he fell to the floor and spasmed, almost no mess at all.

'You. Murphy. Where were you?'

'I was back double-checking the reserve radio buoy. Captain Korsakov told me. You check with him!'

'It's true...'

'Ha! Another self-serving alibi. If I do not believe you and Skylerov when you must have been watching each other, why should I believe your story for a man you couldn't even see?'

The Prosecutor swung round, in search of a new victim. Saw Max. Moderated his tone just a little. 'Asov, where were you?'

'I was in my berth, Yagula. I'd just had a conversation with Captain Mariner that had

292

given me a lot to chew over. I needed some privacy to think some things through.'

'So! You have no alibi at all!' The rage was returning.

'Like that makes a difference. Jesus! You'll be accusing Pugin next!'

'Pugin at least has an alibi that I believe. Though he is covered in Uncle Vanya's blood. As I would expect the murderer to be. And you, Captain Mariner? You, like Pugin, are covered in blood.'

'Oh, come on now! I slipped in the stuff. I was with you!'

'True,' allowed Yagula, grudgingly. And he opened his mouth and closed it again. As if to say that this alibi, too, was not quite good enough.

The Darwin Twins had worked out the modus operandi within ten minutes and explained it to Yagula while he was still raging around the place, calling everyone up and out. Richard was shaken, horrified, literally shocked. But also, ultimately, impressed with them. He mentally resolved to stop calling them Darwin Twins. Then he found he had no better name for them. Though, to be fair, he decided, as he began to think more clearly again, the diagnosis wasn't exactly rocket science. The scalpel was still in the wound: the handle protruding as he had seen it, from the right, and the deadly double-edged point emerging from just below the left jaw-point. It was a vision that had seared itself into Richard's memory with indelible precision.

They had taken Yagula in there and showed him. They had brought no camera equipment, so rather than trying to record the scene in any more detail, they closed the door and taped it shut with black and yellow crime scene tape that could have come from any Western cop show.

'And Rusanova!' added Yagula, madly. 'Get that bitch up and in here!' Then he realized he had been speaking in English and began again in Russian.

'Now wait a minute...' Richard snapped. 'There's no need for that.' He was up at once, using Yagula's mistake in order to grab the initiative – and one of the torches. He was at the sickroom door just ahead of 'Audrey'. 'Look,' he said and shone the torch into the little room. Maria Ivanova was lying on the bed exactly as she had done all evening. Her body lay corpse-like on its back, outlined by the sheet, which had settled intimately over her, outlining every curve and fold like mummy wrappings. The drip which Uncle Vanya had set up still led to the tape in the crook of her arm. 'Audrey' hesitated, looked back at Yagula.

Yagula gestured fiercely and 'Audrey' went to push past Richard for a closer inspection still. Richard, again, prevented him. He followed the torch beam across the room to the comatose woman, calling her name as he went. There was no reaction. Even under the glare of the torch beam, her eyes remained still behind their closed lids.

All too clearly aware of 'Audrey' hulking at his shoulder, Richard reached down and shook her, firmly. Her head flopped helplessly from side to side as though her neck were broken. Her upper body juddered. Her breasts shuddered like blancmange, graphically outlined by the clinging sheet. She made a tiny mewing sound, like a kitten in pain. He withdrew his hand from the crumpled cotton. Automatically went to smooth it out again. And froze.

There on the white cloth was a telltale trace of red. It was fresh blood. As vivid as a red rag. His heart seemed to flip over in his chest. He gasped with simple horror. But then his reason took over. Surely he would have noticed such a bright mark if it had been there before he reached down to shake her, he thought. He looked at his own trembling palm. Uncle Vanya's blood was still caked thickly between the fingers from where he had slipped in the mess. He had just put the incriminating little mark on her himself. Then he noticed yet another mark – black this time. He reached down and moved her hands. Her fingertips were black. The Darwin twins had fingerprinted her as well – and that fact really angered him.

He turned and ushered the big Spetsnaz man out of the crowded little room. As he stepped out of the doorway behind him, Richard called, 'She's still out cold. She hasn't moved a muscle. I just gave her a good shake and she's stayed asleep. I warn you, though, some of Uncle Vanya's blood went off my hand and on to her sheet, so don't get paranoid when you see it there!'

Richard's words were interrupted by one of the Darwin Twins with the spoon and a sheepish grin. He whispered in Yagula's ear but Max heard. 'The fingerprints on the spoon are Pugin's,' he called.

'Oh great,' laughed Richard bitterly. He faced Yagula down, every bit as angry as the Russian. 'If I were you, I'd go with the only person who has any actual proof against them. The poor bastard lying in there covered with Uncle Vanya's blood, with his prints all over the murder weapon! The murderer just has to be Pugin, Lavrenty Michaelovitch. Why don't you get the guys here to beat a confession out of him and have done with it?'

Yagula's mouth opened. A sound came out of it which might have been the beginning of a word – or which might have been something much more elemental than that. But they never found out just what he was going to utter because at that very moment the engines throttled back and the submarine's hull abruptly angled upwards.

It was a sign of the extra strain that all of them had been feeling while the submarine plunged faster and deeper into the abyss beneath the Kara Sea, that this simple change in her disposition stopped everything else in its tracks. Perhaps only the restoration of light and power – still hours away if Peter was right – could have had an equal impact.

Yagula raised no immediate objection when Peter and Alexei went straight up into the command area to check what their new disposition promised. The others sat, tense and silent, until they returned.

'If we can believe the schematics,' said Peter, 'we'll surface at dawn.'

'We're above the Arctic Circle in the middle of summer,' snarled Max. 'It's never fucking dark! When is "dawn", Korsakov?'

'Oh. Yes. I see.' Once again, the strain was showing on Peter, thought Richard. A week ago he had been at death's door. Five days ago, under the surgeon's knife. Four days ago still in intensive care. And things had gone downhill like an avalanche in the forty-eight hours since Yagula had dragged him out of hospital. No wonder he was looking so terrible. 'Well, about eight, then. When we get light and power back too,' he faltered.

'Peter, have you any idea where we will surface?' asked Richard gently.

'According to the schematics, just off Mys Zhelaniya.'

'Why there?' wondered Richard aloud. 'It's the back of beyond and dangerous into the bargain, and yet the name keeps coming up with the same relentless regularity as Norilsk. What's there? What's in either place?'

'A long-deserted weather station and a modern company hospital, respectively,' said Yagula dismissively. 'That's all that need concern us. We have other priorities. Back to the matter in hand, please. I would like each of

297

you to come to this table over here, where the forensics team will make an initial examination of hands and clothing, looking for traces of blood.'

As it was clearly a waste of time looking at Richard, he was excused. While the others acquiesced with varying degrees of reluctance, Richard wandered back to his guard post. But Maria Ivanova was still asleep. In the shadows she was all but invisible, and the little mewing sounds she made as she dreamed started to distract him in ways he did not welcome. There was a whole group of people out here, he thought; and most of them policemen of one sort or another – she would be safe without his continued watch.

He closed the door almost entirely and went hurrying past the closed and taped-up second door, with its two dead bodies safe inside, up to the vacant command area. Here he began to prowl around, sniffing into things restlessly. He had no theories to be tested, no real ideas formulated. He had no real priorities short of getting Murphy on his own for long enough to discover where Captain Birdseye's boots and ID were hidden.

He was exhausted but wired. Sleep was not an option – and would never have been even had he not drunk the coffee. He began by checking the course monitor because it was the brightest, most interesting-looking thing there. It was similar to the equivalent on *Prometheus*, except that the schematic seemed to pulse. The lines, lights, points and figures were defined in waves of brightness that spread outwards and ahead. With each bright wave, he noticed, everything shifted infinitesimally. But he had no trouble working out the way the seabed was hulking into valley sides on either hand. On the left, the valley reached up relentlessly above the line he guessed to be water level and became the hills of Novaya Zemlya's northernmost island. Ice-capped like Greenland through to the black cliffs of its northernmost point where the half-deserted weather station and the long-abandoned whaling huts were. And something else, apparently. But what? A rendezvous, perhaps? It was certainly out-of-the-way enough. No one in their right mind would want to go there unless they had to.

Richard had never been there. He had only read about it, as he said, in his Admiralty Pilots that described the waters here. It was a name to him and little more. A set of statistics about wind and weather, tides and currents. Most of them out of date, for the weather station, as Yagula had said, was long deserted. A drawing of an anchorage and a warning. A drawing – done in the 1930s – because no one with a camera had been allowed to photograph it more recently. That's how secret it was.

And the warning about the explosives dumping ground. The dumping ground had been there since the Second World War at least. Great piles of rotting weaponry lying rusting on the seabed. Everything from shells designed to defend Stalingrad to obsolete battleships scuttled and left. Out-of-date intercontinental ballistic missiles as likely as not. And the dead hulls of the submarines that had sailed the world in secret waiting to deliver them. Dead hulls in every regard except in radiation terms. Their engines still intact, so he had heard. Their nuclear power plants lying watercooled in ways their designers would never have dared to imagine. Even the water at Mys Zhelaniya was said to be radioactive, and anyone actually mad enough to drop an anchor there would be likely to blow the bottom off their boat.

With these thoughts darkening his mind, Richard stared at the bright display. As he did so, other patterns began to make themselves apparent to him. The surface level on the schematic registered as a thin blue line. But it was dotted with little lights of varying intensity and colour. Some had no real shape, but moved in slow, ghostly series. Others had shape but little more. One or two, the brightest and clearest, had shape and definition – tiny code words written under them.

Richard put aside his thoughts about Mys Zhelaniya and frowned. His fingers reached out and actually stroked the screen, as though touching the strange lights would help him understand them better. He sensed rather than saw someone coming up behind him. 'How does it do this?' he asked almost dreamily. 'On *Prometheus 4* we use satellite information, computer enhanced. How does *Titan 10* do it?'

'Computer-enhanced sonar,' said Alexei. 'That's why it pulses like that.'

'Must be pretty powerful to see that far – and to give us above-water schematics,' said Richard.

'It is powerful. But not that powerful. The above-water stuff is simple three-D mapping graphics from the memory designed to fit in with what the sonar reads.'

'I thought submarines were a bit careful about using sonar.'

'That's old thinking,' explained Alexei. 'It's only true of military subs on secret missions. We don't care who sees us, do we? Because we're a commercial vessel about our legitimate business.'

'Are we really?' said Richard. 'I'd have thought anything but, just at the moment. But tell me, what are these lights and shapes here?'

'The blue line is the surface, of course, and the lights are things that are on it.' Peter Korsakov took up the story, sounding more lively and positive now that he was showing off his amazing machines to someone who would appreciate them. Alexei began to check around in the background. 'This shapeless blue mass here...' continued Peter. 'That's ice. There's a fair amount of it because it's being blown south by a pretty vicious northerly gale. We were told that at our last contact with the surface, remember. The sonar doesn't do weather.'

'I'd be surprised to hear that it did. And these?'

'Those are ships. It registers any vessel within the radius of the schematic and monitors their course automatically.'

'Like the collision alarm radar on *Prometheus 4* that predicts courses and warns us if they are likely to cross ours?'

'It has a collision alarm function, yes. But it's more like a course-convergence warning, because we, of course, would be running far deeper than the keel of a surface vessel could reach.'

'OK. I see that. But why do some vessels have numbers too?'

'Identification. Some ships carry ID signals that work under water as well as on the surface. And, in some cases, if *Titan 10* has made prolonged contact with a ship the computers will recognize her, even from the sonar *ping*. Look! There's an excellent example! You see that tiny dot back there with those figures just below it? It's small because it's still far away, not because it's a tiny ship. That's *Prometheus 4*!'

'That's fantastic! But look. One of them has lit up. That one much closer than *Prometheus 4*. See? There's a red line...'

Richard squinted at the screen, eyes narrow. It was exactly as he had said. One of the dots nearby – one of the two or three that *Titan 10* apparently recognized alongside *Prometheus 4* – was flashing bright red. And a line was reaching out from her, like a bolt of straight lightning that came striking towards the red line of their own course, again and again.

'Ah,' said Peter Korsakov. 'There you are. That's just what I was describing. That ship, whoever she is, has set a course the computer predicts would intercept our own if we were running on the surface.'

'That's interesting,' said Richard. 'Can it tell us where or when?'

'Yes,' said Alexei suddenly close behind. 'At Mys Zhelaniya. At dawn.'

And, even as he spoke, the whole bright display before them froze and died. 'Don't panic,' said Peter, sounding a little wild again. 'Nothing to worry about. It's not broken. She's just switched to silent running.'

The three of them exchanged a long, frowning look. They were all familiar with the phrase. Silent running was what submarines used to do in the old days, with the old thinking, when they wanted to go undetected. Had anyone on the surface been tracking her, *Titan 10* would just have vanished from their screens.

'Now why would she want to do that?' mused Alexei.

'Because she wants to surface in secret, perhaps,' said Richard, grimly.

CHAPTER THIRTY

Out

Titan 10 slid silently on to the surface three hours later. Her motors had slowed and they reversed briefly as soon as the great sail slit the ice-speckled chop to bring the submarine to an absolute stop, leaving only the generators grumbling. Then they too stopped. No sooner did they do so than the lighting and heating all came on aboard, for it was 08:00 on the dot.

'Signal!' yelled Yagula at the hapless Peter Korsakov. His eyes were slitted against the sudden glare, which only made his face look more wildly enraged. 'Send my message at once.'

'There's an automatic message going out on a pre-set frequency,' explained Alexei grimly. 'Has been since we came to periscope depth. We can't do anything until it stops.'

'We can go out for a look-see,' said Richard. Because of the continued chill of the night, they all had raided even the old crews' clothing – so he was well prepared to go out as he stood. He was even wearing gloves. He turned to Murphy, who was almost as well bundled up. 'Murphy, can you help me open the hatches, please?' Such was Yagula's pre-occupation with his radio message that he let them go. Allowed them to be alone together, in fact, for the first time in over six hours. 'ID card?' asked Richard as he pulled down the ladders to the inner hatchway.

'Tucked behind a poster on your wall. Slipped it in safe and sound behind a poster of some ancient-looking ice-breaker. No one will ever find it. The boots are in Rusanova's wardrobe. I guessed she won't be going in there. Or even into her cabin, come to that. No one will. You've never seen so much vomit! You'd have thought she'd have tried to get it in the sink at least. And better her cabin than Pugin's. People might be looking for more Geiger counters in Pugin's kit, I thought. Good thing too, given the ransacking and raiding for warm clothes that went on later in the night. I think only Rusanova's remained untouched! Right then. After you, Captain!'

So it was Richard who stepped out into the grim, grey morning first. After the isolation, almost the sensory deprivation, of the last day, the simple scale of it all seemed absolutely overwhelming. It was the sound that hit him first. On his climb up the ladder towards the second, outer hatch, he had heard a gathering cacophony. Even though he realized it was being distorted by the metal all around him, he had no inkling of how much

305

it was also being muffled. The moment he flung the hatch back, he realized all too clearly, however. The clang of the hatch falling was lost beneath the whimper of the wind, the restless roaring of the sea and an enormous growling creaking – as though a huge beast were crunching bones nearby.

Then the cold gripped him – even after the chill within. The wind they had been warned of had died to a gentle, insidious and keenly penetrating breeze. As he pulled himself stiffly out through the hatchway, it grasped him as though the monstrous, growling, bone-crunching giant had closed a fist of purest ice about him.

But it was what he saw as he stepped fully out into the day that really took his breath away. The submarine was sitting about half a mile off what seemed to be a tall cliff-walled, ice-capped island. Only when he narrowed his streaming eyes against the pearly glare did he see that the island was joined by an isthmus to a low grey heave of land that gathered away southwards into the misty distance. At the northward high-point of it, shrouded in low-lying, breeze-stirring mist, he could see the skeletal outlines of a radio mast and the black crouch of the shacks that stood around it. Even at this distance, they had a desolate, deserted air.

Away northwards from the island stretched an almost unbroken ice field – some floes were massively aground, some restlessly afloat. It was this ice field that was making the noise. And the noise was so overpowering because the weirdly lacy, outer fringes of the field itself were stirring like strange weed in the oil-thick, oil-black water below, actually seeming to brush against *Titan 10*'s massive flanks, like the fingers of the Ice Queen.

Richard slipped across the instantly freezing, ice-thick decking and grabbed the forward safety rail. Immediately he thanked heaven for the gloves. He would have lost a layer or two of skin on the freezing rail. But the movement allowed his vision to widen further, along the eastward edge of the southward-drifting ice field. Allowed him to observe, away on the eastward horizon, the diamond-bright gleaming of a ship's navigation lights.

Richard narrowed his eyes, staring at the distant vessel for several moments. There was an air of bustle about it; a sense of purpose. Something disturbing that he did not quite like, though he could never have said what or explained why. It came battering along the edge of the ice-field, a fat black hull with high grimy-grey upper-works, topped by funnels belching thick black smoke. Richard felt a movement behind him and turned. Peter Korsakov was there, also staring uneasily eastward, frowning.

'Have we any binoculars aboard?' asked Richard. Murphy went to look.

'I wonder,' said Richard conversationally, 'whether that is one of the vessels *Titan 10*'s computers recognized.'

'It might even be the vessel she's sending the automatic signal to,' said Peter in a mournfully defeated voice. 'We've no way of knowing.'

'Then we'd better signal her ourselves, had we not? Just in case?'

'We can't get at the radio...'

'But surely we can get at a signal lamp. Or is Morse code too old-fashioned for you now?' So the minute Murphy appeared with the binoculars, he was sent back down again.

Richard would have been happy enough to let Peter have the field glasses first, but the submarine Captain still seemed so exhausted that he just stood there, overwhelmed by the enormity of it all. Richard pressed the icy rims of the glasses beneath the solid jut of his brows therefore and pushed the 'focus' button. The motors whirred, setting to infinity because the vessel was still far beyond the infra-red rangefinder.

What struck him first was the simple size of the approaching ship. It was coming head-on and so the beam was immediately obvious. As was the square-on height of the bridge houses: it seemed to have one fore and another one aft in the approved manner of Russian marine architecture. The ice along whose edge it was pounding, seemed to be like lily-pads beside it and it was only when Richard lowered the binoculars to let his eyes assess true proportion, that he realized just how thick the ice in fact was. How huge, therefore, the approaching vessel was. 'It looks like a factory ship,' he told Peter. 'And a pretty big one too. I can't get any real idea of her exact size from this angle but even so...'

He looked at it for a few moments longer, then he swung the binoculars in a long arc 170 degrees or so through north to almost due west. Here, up on top of the forbidding cliffs of Mys Zhelaniya, the forlorn shacks of the radio station looked even more depressingly deserted than ever. He hesitated on the sight, searching for signs of movement but there was none.

Then something that had flashed through his consciousness in the blur of that long sweep northwards and westwards, re-registered upon his conscious mind. More slowly, he reversed the movement, sweeping the widescreen digital view northwards once again. And there, wedged upon the very point of the long finger of grounded ice, was a bruise-dark fingernail. It was the cousin – perhaps the brother – of the black berg that had been there at the start of this. And Richard remembered what he and Morgan Hand had discussed, about the weather. A week of storms and easterly winds running at near-hurricane force, might well have moved the black berg into the southward currents, carrying it from here to where they had found it. Carrying Captain Birdseye along with it. This black piece of ice might be a twin to the other, therefore – perhaps even a Siamese twin.

'May I?' The brusque voice jogged Richard out of his reverie and he turned, surprised, to find Peter Korsakov gone below and Max standing in his place, hand held out for the binoculars. It was only after he had handed them over that Richard realized that Max had been holding out his left hand. A southpaw. Richard hadn't noticed that before. But then the thought settled away into the back of his mind as he stepped back to allow Max clear view of the approaching vessel.

'Any distinguishing signs?' he asked. 'I couldn't see a name from this angle – but I probably wouldn't be able to read it anyway.'

'Nothing other than the colour. Though there are plenty of black ships in the Kara Sea, God knows.'

'Looks like that would be a good enough name. The Black Ship,' said Richard. And that's how he began thinking of her. As the Black Ship.

But no sooner had he completed this brief conversation than he found himself turning to help Murphy up. And Murphy needed help because the signalling lantern he was carrying looked very heavy indeed. The Irishman saw the look on Richard's face. 'It says "Portable" on the case,' he said wryly. 'Portable by elephant maybe...' His Irish eyes crinkled at the edges and he gave a deep, infectious chuckle. It was the closest thing to a joke Richard had ever heard on *Titan 10* and so he was happy to join in the laughter.

Certainly it took two of them to clip it to the mounting and settle it into place. As soon as they had done this, Murphy was off back below. It was only then that the obvious struck Richard. They needed not just Morse code – but *Russian* Morse code, if such a thing existed. It seemed to him that Alexei would be a better bet than Peter, but either man would do – so down he went, hard on Murphy's heels.

At the foot of the inner ladder, Richard stepped into what seemed like a deep, foetid pool of stinking air. And into the fierce current of another confrontation. It was one he did not really understand – for Yagula and Alexei were yelling at each other in impenetrable Russian while Peter stood by, looking like a ghost in the midday sun. Richard crossed to the Captain's side, and nearly tripped over the signal lamp's case. He stooped, and lifted the obstacle, meaning to put it aside. 'What's this all about?'

'Lack of communications,' answered Peter.

'Failure of communications has been at the root of most of the trouble so far,' agreed Richard bracingly.

'No. Outside communications. Yagula wants to – what do you say? – *Call in the cavalry.* But the radio still will not let him. He believes this is Alexei's fault. But it is not. The radio is stuck on automatic. It is digital. There are no knobs to turn...'

'Still and all,' mused Richard. 'A man could manage a lot of isolation and confusion – and blame it on the computers.'

If Peter was going to reply to this, he lost his chance. For Alexei turned away and Richard stepped into the breach, literally. He stepped massively forward to hold the periscope housing. 'We can communicate,' he announced, loudly, apparently to no one in particular but actually to everybody there. 'The signal lamp is up and ready and a factory ship is heading our way. Shall I start sending an SOS? Or does anyone here have anything more complex to pass along – and the ability to do it in Morse code?'

There was a concerted rush towards the ladder. Richard stepped back, grimly amused, and let Yagula go first. Alexei followed hard upon his heels. Richard swung round to go next – then remembered he still held the case. He stepped back, looking for somewhere out of the way to put it. Peter pushed up next, therefore. Then Murphy himself bustled past with a message notebook and a pen.

Richard had to force himself on to the little bridge like the last sardine going into the tin. Max was still there, though he had relinquished the binoculars. Alexei crouched over the lamp, clicking away furiously. Yagula stood on one side of him, fuming. Peter stood on the other, the binoculars pushed hard against his eyes, with Murphy at his shoulder, poised and expectant. All of them, like Richard himself, were wrapped in many layers of clothing and so seemed even huger than usual. Yagula, in the merciless brightness of the sunlight, looked stranger still, for his cranium was grey with stubble. And so were his jowls and cheeks to the high, sharp ridges of cheekbone – almost up to his Asiatic eyes. Amid the clouds of his breath, it was almost possible to see the simple heat of frustration pouring off him as though his head were the head of a flaming match.

He snarled something in Russian as Richard arrived, and then repeated in English, with grudging courtesy, 'Have you made contact yet?'

'You will see as soon as I do. There will be a bright flashing light to answer our own. And Captain Korsakov will translate any message we get back. Murphy will write it down. All in English because Murphy speaks no Russian. So it will be a little laborious.' But even as Alexei finished speaking, a diamond bright gleam flashed out of the approaching bridge, reaching effortlessly and instantaneously across the intervening miles.

Two hours later Murphy's pad was only half full. Yagula had sent a series of laborious but cryptic messages to be retransmitted by the ship's radio. In between the Regional Prosecutor's almost paranoid missives to Murmansk and Max's equally careful orders for Novgorod, Alexei and Peter had taken care of the immediate priorities. They had won the agreement of the factory ship's captain that he would help them: the flash of the 'Yes' was just about the only signal other than 'Message received'.

The ship was close enough to have a name now, the *Karakov*. Richard was proud of the

313

fact that he could read it so well, it was almost familiar. The Cyrillic letters he had studied allowed him to understand the *K*, the *A*, the *R* that made up most of her name. But if her captain had a name, Richard for one had yet to hear it.

At last, the two huge vessels began to come massively together. *Titan 10* was lying facing east, exactly along the southern edge of the ice. She had no power available because the computers remained stubbornly silent – while the automatic broadcast went relentlessly on. The *Karakov*, therefore, came nestling in beside her, stem to stern. The near approach of the massive factory ship caused a good deal of action aboard the submarine. As they were all going aboard the providential vessel, they could actually now be rid of the computer system in exactly the way Richard had jocularly suggested to Peter all those weary hours ago. Peter and Alexei took Murphy below to find the main power cable linking the machines to the on-board batteries. It was their immediate plan simply to 'pull the plug'. What did it matter what else went down with the computers? They would all be off and away. Indeed, *Karakov*'s captain had insisted, in the face of Yagula's reports, that he would only take *Titan 10* in tow if her power was all down. And Richard could see the logic. The great factory ship had enormous power at her command by the look of things. But she also had a set of her own trawls rigged aft and, were *Titan 10* to start pulling away, the tow ropes would do enormous amounts of damage while they were attached – and even more when they parted and whipped back. No doubt the captain wanted *Titan 10* powerless, empty and closed up tight as a drum. And the only way to ensure all that was to pull the plug on those wretched machines.

But controlling the computers was only the beginning. There was a good number of people to be transferred, some of whom were unlikely to get there under their own steam – one invalid to begin with; and three corpses, if Peter had translated Yagula's orders correctly. Richard was keen to help and, as ever, he had his own priorities to ensure. He was by no means alone in this. Max preceded him down the ladders – so that the last sardine into the can was the last to leave it as well.

For the last twenty minutes of *Karakov's* approach, therefore, the bridge atop *Titan 10's* sail stood empty. But even had a watch-keeper lingered there, he would have had precious little to see, for as the factory ship's captain remained nameless, so he remained faceless. And so did his crew. So much so, that when Richard reappeared on the open bridge, he had an eerie sense of *déjà vu,* for it seemed that *Karakov,* like *Titan 10,* was going to come to rest without anyone actually aboard her at all. Excited, nevertheless, and looking forward to getting safely out of danger and back to normality, he looked upwards. He was using the binoculars, but that scarcely made things better – all he could see was pallid suggestions of movement behind the utter blackness of her windows and portholes. But then he was distracted even from that unnervingly arresting sight. A fresh wind had sprung up since he had been below. And although the wind was coming from the south-east, a new set to the sea was running counter to it, with waves coming south-west from under the complaining ice. It wasn't much, but it was enough to set the hulls chewing together like a pair of jaws.

There were no fenders out – fenders would have been useless in any case, for the hulls were so disproportionate that nothing could really have come between them. *Karakov* was longer – maybe seven hundred feet to *Titan 10*'s five-fifty. She was taller too, of course, towering over the submarine's sail. Richard stood nearly forty feet above the water. *Karakov*'s invisible captain must have stood at least the same again above Richard, up on his command bridge. Even the scuppers at the foot of the deck-rails stood more than ten feet higher than he did – and of course they were nearly forty feet to his right in any case. He could see nothing beyond their red-weeping edges.

Down out of the still sky settled the first fine dusting of black speckles from the funnel-fumes. Up out of the hatch at Richard's feet came Peter Korsakov. He glanced up, past Richard. 'She's bloody big,' he said. For the first time since coming aboard *Prometheus 4* he sounded cheerful. Like Richard and the rest he was excited by the prospect of rescue.

'She is,' agreed Richard, but his words were lost beneath a sudden thunder. A door in the side of the *Karakov* slammed open about three levels down from the scuppers, and a forty foot gangplank came rumbling down to crash on to *Titan 10*. The whole half-submerged hull seemed to shudder, shake and tilt a little.

The sound and movement brought Max up at the double. 'No luck with switching things off,' reported Max. 'Can we secure that somehow? There'll need to be a lot of coming and going and it looks as though it could slide right off.'

Peter seemed to shake himself into action. 'Yes,' he said. 'There are some hand-holds down there deep enough to take a securing rope.'

'Right,' said Max. 'Let's go.' Peter led the way, with Max close behind him. Already planning a quick call home, Richard stood and watched the two men climbing carefully down on to the deck. Once Peter and Max were safely on the flat, it was only a matter of a step or two before they were at the foot of the gangplank. There were ropes there, coiled around the hand-rails. Their importance was immediately made obvious, for even as Peter knelt to secure the first one, so the ice on *Titan 10*'s port side gave another heave. *Titan 10* herself stirred. *Karakov* too rolled slightly and the gangplank see-sawed. Peter rode the movement easily enough as he finished his work, but Max staggered. The situation was so trivial. Max caught the rail and steadied himself. He called something more – his voice lost under the stirring of the ice. Someone stepped out on to the gangplank from *Karakov*, as though answering. Then he stepped back once again.

Peter was crossing to Max, smiling and confident, every inch the Captain at last. At the movement from the other ship he turned, distracted. The hulls stirred once again. Max staggered forward, half-catching the rail with his right hand and reaching out with his left. Peter turned back and Max's hand caught him as he too staggered, looking shocked rather than unsteady. Max caught him but did not hold him. Even as Richard watched in dawning horror, Peter seemed to step back off *Titan 10*'s deck. His expression had altered again. From cheerful, confident expectancy it had changed to simple horror – as though something truly terrible stood waiting, hidden at the head of the gangplank. His feet went out from under him at once and he slammed down on to his face. His nose seemed to explode as it hit the black metal and he left a bright-red smear as he slid hopelessly over the rounded side of his command and slithered helplessly down between the restlessly champing jaws of the grinding iron hulls. It was over in an instant – like the fall of a guillotine blade or the impact of a speeding car. He was crushed out of sight even before the stricken spectators really registered that he was going down.

CHAPTER THIRTY-ONE

Black Ship

The two hulls stirred again, grinding together at the very point Peter had vanished. Max ran forward to the edge of the flat deck, holding on to the near rail of the gangplank as he looked down. 'He's gone,' he bellowed, his voice shaking with horror. He looked up, ashen-faced, at Richard, as though needing to lessen the horror by sharing it – like a trouble. 'He burst,' he added, straightening and banging his fists together, simulating the sides of the massive vessels. 'Burst like a grape.'

At the sound of his voice, as though in reaction to it, *Titan 10* began to scream. At least that's how it seemed to Richard, for an unsettlingly disorientating moment. The sound went on, rising in tone and volume, echoing up from the very bowels of the submarine. And then he realized.

Inspector Rusanova was awake.

Max's grim words made it all too plain there was nothing to be done for the Captain now. With a heavy heart he turned and went back down the hatchway.

As he stepped off the ladder, Richard found himself at the heart of a whirl of activity, most of it generated by Yagula. 'Now we can get off this cursed vessel,' the Regional Inspector told him, his voice rising over the falling sobs from the sickbay. 'We can continue the investigation in safer circumstances, especially when the resources I have summoned here arrive. But we must disconnect all the power before we go aboard the *Karakov*, must we not?'

'I don't think we can do that,' said Alexei suddenly. 'But I'm sure there'll be a chief engineer and an electrical officer aboard *Karakov* who will be competent. I think we just want to get up and out. But we'll need to confirm that with Captain Korsakov.'

'I agree,' nodded Yagula. 'Captain Mariner, can you find a way of shutting that bloody woman up?'

'In a moment. Alexei, I'm afraid I have some bad news. Peter's gone overboard. I'm pretty certain he's dead, from what Max just called up. So you're in command now, I'd say.'

Alexei accepted the news without missing a beat. 'Right. In that case we're off here as soon as we're able. Captain Mariner ... The Special Investigator...'

Maria Ivanova was sitting on the edge of her bed, huddled into the folds of her black coat. The darkness of the material – and of the wild hair above it – simply emphasized the utter pallor of her face. The only colour in it seemed to be the bruise-blue rings beneath her eyes. As Richard entered, so she seemed to get her hysterics under control but she sat there shivering and when she looked up it took a moment or two for recognition to stir within the desperate blankness of her eyes.

As soon as he was certain she knew who he was, Richard began to fill her in on the highlights of the last few hours. As he did so, interweaving instructions and suggestions into the story, he stood her up and supported her to the stinking wreckage of her cabin. Together they searched her kit for warm, clean clothing. When they found enough, he left her for a moment or two, ostensibly to allow her privacy to change. Actually to retrieve the ID card from behind the print of the ice-breaker. Then, taking a leaf out of the original owner's book, Richard slipped it into his own shoe before checking that his own papers were all safely in his pocket.

Within a surprisingly few moments they were both back in the command area – just in time to see a large, square stranger step down off the ladder, on the heels of Max Asov, who had clearly just guided him aboard. He look-ed around them and began to speak in rumb-ling Russian.

'He is asking, *Where is my brother?*' trans-lated Maria Ivanova quietly. *'I have received distress call from my brother's submarine and have hurried here to find him. Where is he?'*

'Who is his brother?' wondered Richard quietly to Maria Ivanova. 'He certainly looks nothing like Peter Korsakov.'

The stranger heard and understood, it seemed, for he turned and fixed Richard with a cold stare. 'I am Captain Boris Smirnov of factory ship *Karakov*,' he said. 'I seek my brother Ivan Smirnov. He is Captain Lieutenant here. How you would say, *First Mate*, yes?'

Yagula stepped into the instant of silence born of this revelation. As Captain Smirnov had switched to English, Yagula continued in the same language, allowing Richard at least to marvel at his suitability for political office – at least in the areas of half-truth and spin. 'I am Yagula, Regional Prosecutor for Murmansk. You find us in the middle of an investigation – as my messages will have made clear. Some of the crew of this vessel have unfortunately gone missing and it may be that your brother is amongst them. We cannot be certain. A computer malfunction has brought us here as Mr Asov's messages may have explained. And the loss of poor Captain Korsakov at the very moment of rescue has shocked us all. But if you will take our vessel in tow, then everything will be resolved, I am certain.'

'So. My brother is not aboard after all. Then there will be the question of salvage,' observed Captain Smirnov, slowly.

'The hull is owned by a Russian holding company which I can represent and sails under the flag of the Russian Federation,' said Max.

'It is leased to an International Consortium for whom I can speak,' added Richard. 'And, like my own hulls, it is fully insured at Lloyd's of London. Any salvage would be under standard Lloyd's Open Form. Though how that would be affected by the work the Regional Prosecutor still has to do aboard I cannot say.'

'Well, I am happy to undertake humanitarian work,' said Captain Smirnov more expansively. 'And I will do my best to bring you and your ... ah *crime scene* ... safely to port. But not at the risk of my own ship. Can you override your malfunctioning computer systems?'

'No,' answered Alexei shortly.

'Well, perhaps I have men who can. Let us get you all off and get them on. And swiftly, for the weather is worsening. There is another storm predicted to arrive within the next twelve hours. You need bring only essentials. We can supply much – and you will be able to return aboard in due course. Now let us hurry!' He stepped back as though he had finished speaking. But then he had a second thought. 'You must be sure of course that you have all of your identity papers, passports and such things with you.'

With little more than the clothes they wore and the papers they habitually carried, the relieved survivors allowed themselves to be hurried from one vessel to the other. Yagula went first, with 'Audrey' and 'Tom' close behind, followed by the Darwin Twins. Richard helped Maria Ivanova next, glancing back to see a frowning Murphy hard on his heels. Max came on more slowly and Alexei lingered a little longer still, apparently discussing with Captain Smirnov the best way to disable the computers.

Down the side of the sail they went, and off the whale hump on to the flat decking. Here Captain Smirnov's men were lined up on either side, in what may have been designed as a welcoming committee. But to Richard they looked a little more like guards at the gate of a gulag. They studied the men and woman they had rescued in silence, guiding them along the tunnel between their tight-packed bodies with tiny gestures. There was nowhere else to go other than up the gang-plank in any case.

The gangplank led up into a wide corridor which stood empty apart from the others walking warily forward. There were no doors – and once again, nowhere else to go. There was a door at the end of the tunnel that opened into a larger assembly area with companionways leading up and down. Here, at least, there was a proper reception committee. Half a dozen men and women – almost indistinguishable in overalls and woollens – waited.

When they were all there, the tallest of them began to speak. 'I am Chef Petty Officer Gregor,' translated Maria Ivanova. 'And these are the members of my team. This is the

Ship's Doctor. He will examine you and then we will accommodate you. In these modern days we no longer have Political Officers aboard so I will collect your papers and keep them safely in the ship's secure facility. They will, of course, be returned to you as soon as you leave us to go ashore. This is a working vessel and not a cruise liner, so we must apologize at once that you will not be together. Nor will you be very comfortable. But we will do our best. We will feed you with the first shift of the crew at midday. We hope you enjoy fish. That is what we process and that is what we eat.'

'Fish!' whispered Richard. 'All I can smell is oil!'

'Fish oil perhaps?' suggested Maria Ivanova and Richard was relieved to see that she seemed to be getting better.

The processing began at once and it was gentler and more courteous than their initial reception had led Richard to expect. It was logical that Maria Ivanova should be led away first, by a woman, towards the Doctor. Yagula, too, was shown out early, followed by his guards and the Darwin Twins. Richard, Max and Murphy stuck together and Petty Officer Gregor seemed happy enough to keep them as a threesome, especially when he discovered that two of them needed the third to translate for them.

Richard did not like giving up his papers – nor did Murphy. But Max assured them it was just routine, and probably safer in the long run. 'Remember the black market,' he joked bracingly. 'If you can sell a used light bulb, just think what Western identity papers would fetch. And this is a factory ship, not a Girl Scout camp.'

As he spoke, Gregor was leading them down into a large canteen area, already packed. 'Late breakfast for the last of the night shift,' explained Max. 'We may eat now. Borscht and boiled fish. There is black bread also. And coffee that is not real – or vodka that is.'

But Richard had stopped listening. For there, at the table immediately in front of him, wearily spooning red soup dotted with pink spongy fish-islands into his mouth, was the man whose ID was stuck inside his shoe. The man whom he had thought to be Captain Birdseye, dead and frozen. Joe Bronowski, the Field Engineer from Austin, employed by Texas Oil; Tucker Roanoake's secret industrial espionage agent.

Richard was in action at once, even as his mind spun, trying to get a grip on the new situation. Mercifully, the seat opposite Bronowski was vacant. He sat in it immediately, glancing up at Murphy. 'Get me what he's having,' he ordered, gesturing at Bronowski's plate. Murphy frowned but nodded. Max shrugged and followed. 'Strastvitye,' said Richard as soon as the others were gone. He looked around cheerfully – a chatty patron in a crowded bar. Bronowski glanced up. He grunted.

'Menya zhovut Richard Mariner,' Richard persisted. 'CEO of Heritage Mariner, London.' He found he was fighting a very real urge to get the ID out of his shoe and double-check. The rollercoaster ride of the last few hours was beginning to tell on his nerves, he thought. Bronowski's eyes went from one side to the other. His nearest companions were finishing their thin soup and wiping out their bowls with chunks of coarse black bread.

'Strastvitye,' he answered guardedly. Relief swept through Richard at the simple contact – even though it proved next to nothing.

'Hurrasho?' enquired Richard, gesturing at the soup.

Bronowski gave a grunt of humourless laughter. 'Da.' He licked his lips and smacked his chops with glacial irony. He had one of those faces that seemed to be roughly carved from granite. The face of a Hun or a Cossack. Perhaps a Polish face, thought Richard. The perfect face for an American spy in the heart of a Soviet enterprise.

'Gahryacho?' asked Richard, gesturing to the steaming bowl.

'Da,' Bronowski allowed, shrugging. 'Gahryacho.' Hot but not much else.

This more or less exhausted Richard's conversational Russian, but it kept Bronowski there for a moment more. The two nearest diners departed. Max and Murphy arrived. Automatically, unremarkably, they sat in the vacant chairs on either side of him. Those numerous eyes watching them were simply studying strange faces – and that was all, thought Richard. 'This smells good,' he said conversationally, as Murphy slid the steaming slop towards him. 'I wonder what Tucker Roanoake would make of it? He seemed to enjoy the Russian food we had on *Prometheus 4*, didn't he, Max?'

The long, dark almost Asiatic eyes Bronowski shared with Yagula flickered up and down; side to side. The expression on his chiselled face didn't change. Unlike Richard's, when he tasted his first spoonful.

'Is this the sort of thing your chaps at Bashnev Power eat, or does the great Max Asov have his own chef?' Richard continued, pushing his plate away. 'I can't see it going down too well with the board of Texas Oil if Tucker tried it there. It's probably steak and mash for the boys in Austin. My people at Heritage Mariner would walk out *en masse* if I served this in London. They like their steak and kidney pudding. We must ask Regional Prosecutor Yagula how it would go down in Murmansk. He'll be through soon.'

Max was frowning at his friend. Richard smiled brightly and stopped talking. If Bronowski was who he thought, then enough of a message had been passed. If he wasn't, then proceeding would be pointless in any case. 'What shall we do after we've eaten?' asked Murphy. 'You think they'll let us explore a bit?'

'Unless they want half a dozen very bored passengers,' said Max.

'Maybe they'll put us on the production line,' suggested Richard. 'Make us earn our keep like stowaways.' Murphy looked worried at that; Max looked simply horrified. 'I was joking,' he continued. 'They look as though they've enough hands aboard here to run a pair of factory ships – and a couple of trawlers into the bargain.'

'It's strange,' agreed Max. 'And it's disturbing. There seems to be so many of them and so little room. I keep seeing faces I half-recognize.'

'I know what you mean...' Richard stopped talking and looked up at the sound of a sudden commotion. Yagula strode in with his all-too-familiar face like thunder. Seeing only three others he recognized, he strode towards them. Bronowski, who'd finished, stood up and the Regional Prosecutor threw himself into the briefly vacant seat – which creaked dangerously under his weight. 'Trouble?' asked Richard sympathetically.

'None of your business!'

Max glanced across at Richard. His eyebrows rose.

'Captain Smirnov has probably confiscated everybody's guns,' said Richard. He swung away from Yagula's purple countenance and looked across the canteen. Half-hidden by clouds of acrid cigarette smoke, Bronowski was slouching out of a door beside the servery. Halfway out, there was just the slightest hesitation; the merest gesture towards looking back. Had Bronowski been Lot's wife, thought Richard, his heart lightening still further, he'd never have turned to salt.

'Do svdanya, chaps,' Richard whispered and slid to his feet at once. He had no doubt that Captain Smirnov and Chief Petty Officer Gregor would both want an eye kept on their guests but he hoped that decisive – unexpected – action would at the very least split up any group assigned to follow him. He added to his simple plan almost without thought, joining a crowd of diners as they exited, stooping low and taking an instant to destroy the last vestiges of his last London haircut. The fact that he hadn't shaved since Rusanova's visit to his cabin on *Prometheus 4* also helped him fit in facelessly. Or so he fondly imagined.

He followed his new companions into a long dim corridor. Away ahead, Bronowski's shoulder hesitated at the third opening on the right. When Richard turned down that – alone for an instant – it was there again at the fourth on the left. Which proved not to be a passage, but the door into a huge stinking store-space. It was steel-sided, at least two decks deep, ill-lit, empty and far too large to be called a room. All Richard could see of Bronowski was the red point of a cigarette being smoked in the shadows nearby. But it was the stench of the place that was really arresting. A piercing acridity that burned in his throat and behind his nose, bringing tears to his eyes. At once intimately familiar and revoltingly strange. He dismissed it as easily as he dashed the tears from his eyes, crossing purposefully towards the cigarette. Even the bitter fumes of the Belmor were a relief. Unlike the words that issued from the clouds of them.

'Have you the slightest idea of what is going down here?'

'I knew there were a pair of Smirnov brothers from the letters aboard the sub. But I had no idea Tucker had sent two spies.'

'You'd better thank God fasting that he did.'

'It's that bad?'

'Worse than you can imagine. This is where they did it to the last lot. The guys they put back aboard? You found them? Can't you smell it?'

'Cordite!'

'Crap and cordite. Sure. Is that why you have a Regional Prosecutor with you? And back-up, I do hope and pray. More than the Special Forces pussies that'll be down here in a few moments, I'd guess, and back aboard with the rest in half an hour or so. Tell me you have called the Marines or whatever the hell the Russkies have instead.'

'No such luck, I'm afraid. One of my tankers will be here in a couple of hours if everything's going to plan.'

'That may not be quick enough. As soon as they've finished on *Titan 10* they'll finish with you-all. No more mistakes now they have a heaven-sent second chance. And I don't have poor Sam to fall back on this time.'

There was a tiny silence, then Bronowski said, 'Tell me what you know, Captain Mariner.' He dropped the long tube of the cigarette's so-called filter and ground it underfoot.

Richard took a deep breath. And instantly regretted it. 'It has to begin with the Smirnov brothers,' he said. 'If Boris is Captain, I'd guess Ivan is still here aboard somewhere? In spite of the charade Boris played out to trick us quietly aboard? Ivan and the rest who wanted in on the deal?'

'Those that didn't want in went back aboard her,' agreed Bronowski.

'In body-bags so to speak. There was blood on the companionways. Several people's all mixed together. But we were taken off and brought aboard here by a practised ruse as I said – the same trick that they used the last time. But I'm getting ahead of myself. The Smirnov brothers found themselves in a position to earn a little money on the black market selling my oil. To the Mafia, I'd guess. Ivan bribed or threatened – or poisoned – Captain Korsakov into leaving his command. Or maybe Lady Luck smiled and it really was appendicitis. Then he took command and sailed to the oilfields. Fully laden, *Titan 10* turned for home – but the computers had been tampered with. And instead of heading for the Kara Strait she went hell-for-leather towards the most desolate, unfrequented spot in the Kara Sea – Mys Zhelaniya. General consternation, fomented to panic by those that were in the know. After a couple of days well out of control, up she pops right here. Great relief on all sides – especially when the good ship *Karakov* heaves into view and her captain comes aboard in answer to his little brother's distress call. The weather was closing in, so things were getting desperate. They all put on their life jackets and came on board here. And were shown into these quarters – unless they were in the know already. Which you were, Joe, weren't you? You and Sam had come aboard right at the last minute, deep undercover. The moment things went wrong, you went bad – or seemed to do so – and Sam went missing. And Sam, well hidden, safely and secretly, took your ID just in case. I should have seen that at once. But he stayed aboard *Titan 10* alone while they transferred the oil to the tanks they have below here, where half the factory facilities and a good deal of the accommodation ought to be.'

He shrugged. 'OK, I'm guessing about the facilities – but not the accommodation. Three shifts to breakfast? Not since Gorbachev and Perestroika, surely? But anyway, as the oil came off, things started to go wrong. I'd guess from Yagula's experience that some-one was careless with the friendly body searches and a hero or two in here decided to fight back. Which led to a slaughter. But then Boris and Ivan got worried. What do you do with a pile of corpses like that? Twenty or more? That's not murder – it's massacre. You

333

certainly can't just dump them overboard – not twenty or more ... I'd guess Ivan thought of putting them back aboard – he'd know how to do it. And *Titan 10* was due to go down anyway, wasn't she? Lost with all hands, like the *Kursk* and all the others.

'And that's where Sam came in. He saw what was going on. Shocked, sickened, panicked perhaps, he came out of hiding and tripped the automatic switch when *Karakov*'s crew had come back here for a breather. Ivan had even left his keys on the table by his bunk. *Titan 10* dived and there was nothing they could do to stop her. Off she went with all that evidence. But Sam couldn't stand the idea of being aboard with all those dead people, so he ran for the escape hatch and up he came – wearing the last life jacket.

'But of course you chaps are oil men, not submariners. I know he panicked in the escape hatch. He tore his fingernails off getting his boots free at the last moment. He came up too fast from too deep. He was probably dead when he came through the surface. But his beacon was on so they found him no trouble. Brought him aboard. Dumped him somewhere while they had a think.'

'In the freezer,' said Bronowski.

'Of course. In the freezer. Where he froze solid. And his clothing froze to the floor – the back of it ripped off; its probably still there. But in the end they decided he'd better go over the side. They'd flushed out their bilges and they reckoned that if they dumped him in the toxic soup of crude oil and cargo there wouldn't be much of him left. Fair chance he'd be eaten with the fish-parts anyway. But then, to make assurance double sure they took a sander to his fingers and his toe-tips. And, close to, they maybe thought his dental work was just a little distinctive so they took some superglue to that. Then over he went into the middle of the mess she left behind, and off went *Karakov* to deliver the oil.'

'I put a second emergency beacon over with him,' said Bronowski. 'Thought it would keep broadcasting if his ran out.'

'It didn't,' said Richard shortly. 'But it proved useful nevertheless. Yours ran out but his kept going as he became stuck to the underside of a berg infected by their noxious soup. A berg blown round the north end of the island and then south into the middle of the Barents Sea by the storm you were battened down to run through. Took him nearly as far as North Cape, and that's where we found him. Though we didn't have any idea *what* we had found at that stage, of course. Still. That's the first, major section of it well in place. But there's more. Something I haven't covered yet. Something that led on to the next phase. Gave the Smirnov brothers their second bite at the cherry...'

'Something like that?' whispered Bronowski, gesturing over Richard's shoulder with his chin.

Richard whirled. Froze. There in the doorway, framed in the light, with two hulking shadows just behind her, stood Special Investigator Rusanova. And Richard remembered where he had seen *Karakov*'s oddly familiar name before – on the screen of her laptop.

Richard turned back, going down on one knee as though searching for something on the deck at his feet as he looked vainly for some escape route. 'Joe?' he whispered. 'Is there any way out of here?'

But Bronowski had vanished without trace.

CHAPTER THIRTY-TWO

The Devil You Know

At school and university Richard had been the backbone of the drama societies and he had taken the lead in many a play and on-board entertainment since. His pretence of pleasurable surprise rang pretty true therefore. His air of vague confusion that he had become so lost and isolated when simply looking for the toilet might have flattered a professional actor. His double relief at not only being found, but being found by Maria Ivanova, was almost worthy of Hollywood.

Of course it cut no ice with the grim-faced Special Investigator or with her massive escorts. And the fact that they led him back to the canteen instead of clapping him in irons or heaving him over the side simply made him wonder what further plans they actually had in mind for him. But the fact that she left him with his escorts at the door without even bothering to come up with a covering fiction to explain her abrupt recovery seemed to Richard to mean that the plans – whatever they were – probably did not include either immediate freedom or long life. And that thought set his heart pounding – and his brain racing. For it was by no means the first time in his long life that he had harboured it.

Yagula, Max and Murphy were still sitting where he had left them – and the seat he had vacated was waiting still untenanted, in spite of the continuing bustle. It was here that Rusanova's heavies deposited him – which made him more suspicious still. As soon as he sat, therefore, Richard started to speak in quiet, insistent English, just as he had done when Joe Bronowski was seated opposite him. 'This ship really is a shit-bucket,' he observed, his uncharacteristic coarseness raising his companions' eyebrows. 'Still,' he continued relentlessly, 'in a pigsty of a country like this it's hardly surprising. Even under the Communists it was far more backward than we in the West supposed. And since the Communist Empire collapsed it's really gone down the toilet, hasn't it? Corruption and scandal all over the place. The only people capable of organizing anything seem to be the Mafia. Talk about Third World! Buying and selling used light bulbs. I ask you. And I've been to villages in the depths of Equatorial Africa where the food was better than this. Villages on the verge of civil war, of course, being ravaged by armies equipped with cheap Kalashnikov automatic assault rifles, T80 main battle tanks and Hind D helicopter gunships all supplied by the Soviet arms industry – just another arm of the Communist imperialist state. Selling their wealth cut-price abroad for clapped-out political ends while their people at home suffered and starved. But even that fades into nothing compared with what is going on here...'

Yagula had gone past purple. His face was as white as Rusanova's had been before she came aboard. 'Just what the hell do you think...' he grated.

'What do I think I'm doing?' continued Richard smoothly. 'I think I'm checking whether any of our watchful companions here speak English, Regional Prosecutor. I'm sorry to be so crude and obvious. But as yours is the only reaction to my words we may guess that you were the only Russian to understand them, apart from Max here.'

'And what's the point of that?' demanded Max, quite put out himself.

'If no one understands what we are saying then we can say what we like. We can assess our situation and plan to escape from it.'

'Escape?' Yagula looked around, seeming to

dismiss the mere proletariat around him, secure in the powers given to him by the state.

'Before they kill us.'

'Who is going to do all this?' demanded Yagula. 'Who would dare?'

'The brothers Smirnov, Captain Boris and Captain-Lieutenant Ivan. But they are really only the local chapter of the Mafia, I think. As, indeed, in one way or another, is almost everyone aboard the *Karakov*. Except for us, and an undercover American engineer, supposedly doing a little industrial espionage but way, way out of his depth...' Richard quietly began to fill them in on the conversation he had had with Joe Bronowski.

And that led him on to the second part of his conjectures. 'Because of what Sam had done before he died, sending the sub back to the rendezvous point under automatic pilot, *Karakov* had to go home with her job only half done. They had the oil, but they had missed the rest. Not only that but they had a submarine full of corpses sailing away out of their control. It was a situation likely to generate exactly the kind of investigation they were desperate to avoid – which, to a limited extent, you have begun, Regional Prosecutor. Though what you have achieved so far is nothing compared to what you will do when you are fully in control again. And they know it. Which is why they will have taken careful note of all your messages – and sent none of them at all. But I digress. The disappearance

339

of *Titan 10*, therefore, would have been a major problem for them. Just like the unexpected – long-odds – problem of the discovery of Captain Birdseye. But these were exactly the kind of problems they had planned to cover if anything ever arose, because if everything had gone to plan, *Titan 10* would simply have disappeared and the scam could have continued – one more time at least, with any luck. Which is why they had to have someone planted aboard *Prometheus 4*. My bet would be Alexei Skylerov, for all sorts of reasons, but mostly because he was down at Severodvinsk, where all this must have been put together. Which is also where they recruited Special Investigator Rusanova to their side.

'As the records of her laptop will show, she emailed them on a regular basis from *Prometheus 4* and warned them how the investigations were proceeding – first into Sam's death, and then into the appearance of *Titan 10*. Her last message – which I saw her send – would have been to confirm that we were going to follow my plan and retrace the route recorded in *Titan 10*'s computers. We played right into their hands then. *Karakov* set sail once more, knowing she would meet her victim at the same point she had lost her. That they could complete their original scheme.'

'What scheme?' asked Max. 'They have the oil. What else is there?'

'We talked it through the moment we came

aboard her but I didn't see how right we were. In an economy where a used light bulb has a price? What else did they want? The computers, Max! The fixtures and fittings. The coffee, the beef, the vegetables, the bread, the toilet paper, the engine parts, the light bulbs that *do* work. Everything. Millions of roubles' worth.'

'And then? How will they hide what they have done?' demanded Max.

'That's the beauty of this place. Mys Zhelaniya. It's one of the remotest spots in the entire world. And it's the biggest arms dump on the face of the globe. They'll simply sink her. Here in the middle of it all. Slowly, I'd say. So they can get well clear before she bottoms. No one'll ever find her. Even if they suspect, they'll never dare to look. There's even a fair-to-middling chance she'll land on explosives and get blown to pieces.'

'Rusanova!' spat Yagula.

'Yes. She covered her tracks well and was – what shall I say? – calculatedly distracting. I suspected her least and last. Especially as you kept fitting yourselves in the frame. Max, what is it about Norilsk? Norilsk Nickel? I suspected you were in bed with them even though they're your biggest rival in all sorts of areas. And they're working on the one thing that can sink this whole deal, aren't they? And sink it legitimately – especially if the oil-transport system proves so dangerously unreliable.'

'The new fuel. Yes. Since Christmas 2002

341

they've been working with the Academy of Science in Moscow to develop a hydrogen-based fuel. Infinitely renewable and almost free. But it's like cold-fusion nuclear power – they're years away from production.'

'But you still need a foot in both camps, just in case. That's why the coincidence of Peter Korsakov's hospital treatment was so unsettling. Still, I'm glad to know just whose side you're really on. And whose side Rusanova is really on. You have to bear some responsibility for that yourself, Regional Prosecutor. A fiercely intelligent, ruthlessly ambitious woman living only for her job. People like that are like the tall trees you keep talking about. They grow or they die. All she lives for is recognition; promotion. And you'd slammed a glass ceiling on her like I've never come across before. She was better than anyone else of yours but she was going nowhere, was she? She'd tried everything, but she was going nowhere. So. A little bribery, a little graft, and what has she got? The chance of a nice retirement fund at least. A project worthy of her talents – even if it is in the black economy and aboard a black ship. But there's already been lots of undercover work, and no reason why someone quick-thinking couldn't get credit for a little more. So, if she's lucky and she plays her cards right, she may even have the chance of breaking a case that'll get headlines from here to Vladivostok – just at the very moment there's a vacancy in the post of Regional Prosecutor. She's tried to murder you once already. She was a little impatient there and got her fingers burned. But she can take her time now. At least until they've finished stripping *Titan 10*. And that's all the time we've got too.'

'Well, how are we going to get out of this?' demanded Murphy. 'From the look of things there are only four guys on our side – the two bodyguards and the two forensics men – and they're nowhere to be seen. And there's a full fucking crew against us who have already slaughtered God knows how many poor bastards and shoved them back on *Titan 10*.'

'A crew and a half,' said Max. 'The men who didn't die on *Titan 10*, if I follow Richard correctly. The men who followed Ivan Smirnov.'

'I'd say Bronowski's our best bet,' answered Richard.

'Why should he bother?' demanded Yagula. 'He's stayed safe all this time. All he has to do is to keep his head down—'

'Fear, quite apart from anything else. He's trapped in the middle of a murderously dangerous situation. We're the only people who know it, and we represent the only way out he's got. It's what motivated Rusanova, I think. It was a clever plan. She was in charge of the kitchen and she had seen the cyanide. There was real coffee there – black and bitter enough to mask what taste there was. She thought she could control who drank it – she was certain she could get it to you, Yagula, and then she'd take over the investigation herself. But Pugin got it instead. She found that out first because she found him dead when she was clearing the cups away. So she sipped a bit and made herself sick too. But in the confusion of it all she lost sight of the spoon. She was very sick – spectacularly so. But she was never really unconscious. She heard what we said about finding the spoon and realized what else we might find. So she waited until she could wrap herself in that long black coat and flit from shadow to shadow. There was one perfect print to be put over hers on the spoon. Pugin's. And that's what she was doing – putting Pugin's print on the spoon – when Uncle Vanya walked in on her. She was in the shadows, dressed in black. He didn't see her at first. He turned away and started to look for something. She caught up the scalpel from beside Pugin and stabbed Uncle Vanya from behind. Right to left.' He gestured, as Yagula had done, showing the location of the blade through Uncle Vanya's throat. 'At first I thought it must have been you, Max, with your left hand. Another little thread of suspicion in there with Norilsk Nickel. But no. She did it from behind. No blood, you see. It would all have shot sideways and forward – down his throat and out of his mouth. And she did it for the same reason Bronowski is going to try and help us. Because she was trapped and it was the only way out she could think of.'

'Well, let's hope you're right – on both counts,' said Murphy. 'Because if you're wrong, then Mr Asov here *did* do it. And if he murdered Uncle Vanya, then that means he's on the other side. And you've just told him everything we know.'

'How about that, Max?' asked Richard. 'I wondered about that left hand of yours another time too. When Peter Korsakov got killed. The third thread of suspicion. What do they say? *Once is happenstance, twice is coincidence – three times is enemy action.*'

'Not guilty! Peter turned and saw some guy on the far end of the gangplank. That really staggered him – literally. I don't know why, but there it is. And there *he* is. That tall guy by the servery there. You see him? With the long blond hair and the reddish stubble. That's the guy Peter saw just before he went over.'

'Then that'll be the last of our enemies in all likelihood,' said Richard quietly. 'Remember his face, if you get the chance. It's the one Peter Korsakov least wanted to see here, I should guess. It must therefore belong to his good friend and ex-lieutenant Ivan Smirnov.'

As if to confirm Richard's words, the second treacherous lieutenant, Alexei Skylerov, joined Ivan and they stood shoulder to shoulder, everyone around them falling back uneasily, while they swept the room with their cold stares. Until they settled like midwinter on the little group round Richard.

Abruptly, Rusanova joined them and there was a brief, passionate discussion. The ex-Special Investigator put a point of view forcefully – passionately, even. The lieutenants laughed at her. Sneered at her. When she turned away, apparently defeated, Alexei reached down and lingeringly patted her bottom. It was a possessive, proprietary gesture. As she stormed out, a group of five grim-faced men replaced her.

'Maria Ivanova's found another glass ceiling,' observed Richard.

'And she's found someone else in need of her particular talents,' gloated Yagula. 'First him, then the rest of them.' He gave a grim chuckle.

'Hang on to that thought,' said Richard. 'It'll help you to die laughing.'

Alexei and Ivan turned, together, addressing the five grim men nearby, jerking their chins back and forward as they spoke. The gestures were so clear – and the response to them so unmistakable – that Richard and his companions were standing waiting when their well-armed escort arrived. With no discussion or hesitation, they fell in between the lines of armed guards and walked out in a little phalanx, Max and Murphy behind Richard and Yagula, like convicted soldiers heading towards a firing squad. For the first time since they arrived aboard, nobody seemed to be watching them. Even the guards only glanced at them from time to time.

Out of the door by the servery they went and into the corridor along which Richard had followed Bronowski. Step by step, with numbing inevitability towards the big, cold steel-walled compartment where the first crew had been gunned down before being taken back to *Titan 10*'s water-filled tanks. By a kind of common consensus, the corridor was empty. The crew of *Karakov* were thugs, not psychopaths. They all had nightmares enough no doubt, thought Richard, without adding yet another one now. Just as no one in the canteen wanted to look at them, so no one wanted to watch them as they marched towards their death.

Which made it all the easier for Bronowski, 'Tom' and 'Audrey' when they came out of one side corridor using their feet and fists with ruthless precision – while the Darwin Twins erupted from the doorway to a store-room opposite, swinging lengths of metal pipe with equally powerful effect.

Richard immediately waded in with the massive fists that had settled many a bloody argument all those years ago when he had been First Mate on any tramp that would have him. And Yagula was almost as quick to react – and almost as effective. Max and Murphy caught guns and bodies before they fell too noisily to the floor. So it was that within a very few bloody, violent, but almost soundless seconds the execution squad was out for the count and hidden in the massive storeroom more dead than alive themselves, while four helpless victims had been transformed into a small, well-armed unit of nine desperate men.

'What now?' demanded Bronowski.

'We go on to the execution chamber, quickly!' snapped Richard. 'They're expecting to hear gunshots. They have to hear gunshots. Then up on deck with all of us. Hurry! I'll explain as we go.'

Two minutes later there came the lethal rattle of automatic fire contained in echoing steel. The sound of it was overpowering but brief, and was accompanied by several choking screams that carried almost magically into every corner of the ship. Max and the Darwin Twins had found out the hard way how painful on the eardrums the concussion of contained fire can be. But the sound of their distress added priceless authenticity.

Soon after that, five men came staggering up on to the deck, carrying four dead bodies between them. Again, no one nearby was paying too much attention – certainly not enough to see that the four bodies were giving their five bearers some very necessary help. So they made it up and out into the arctic afternoon. Here the strength of the porters understandably gave out and they dumped their grisly burdens out of sight under the keel of a well-snugged lifeboat and put their guns beside them while they caught their breath and looked around.

The day had closed in from the brightness of the morning. The wind had strengthened, driving the mist away and causing the sea to heave more threateningly under the heavy covering of growling ice. It was getting rapidly colder. The scudding, slate-grey clouds were closing down on the world like the steel jaws of a vice – and Captain Smirnov's storm looked as though it would be arriving almost any minute now.

The starboard side of the factory ship was all brightly illuminated. All the more so because the original gangplank had been joined by a second down to the submarine's deck – her lading hatches were open now – and these two had been joined by a third, from *Karakov*'s weather deck to the top of *Titan 10*'s sail. The laden crew toiled wearily between them.

'They're still busy with *Titan 10*,' said Richard. 'Max, how long will it take them to strip all the equipment out of her?'

'There's a hell of a lot of them and they look as though they know what they're doing. How long have they had?'

Richard glanced at his watch. 'Nearly four hours.'

'That should just about do it for my equipment. Depends what else they want to go for.'

'Logic suggests they must be more or less finished. They just want to tie up loose ends, dump the bodies aboard and cut loose. We'll be out of time any moment now.'

'We'll be out of time when they go to get the men I released and find them all gone,' whispered Bronowski.

'With luck, there'll be just one execution squad aboard and that'll be us,' said Richard. 'Certainly it looked like there was no one else after a piece of the action. They'll be expecting us to put the first four bodies aboard *Titan 10* before we go back for the rest. So let's start doing it two at a time. Murphy, we'll leave you here. And you Bronowski. Use your afterlife to check out this lifeboat, will you? We may want to use it and we certainly want to use the radio inside it. Remember *Prometheus 4*'s wavelength, Murphy? Good man. Now ... Wait a second. Bronowski, what's that equipment right at the back there?' Richard gestured past the end of the after bridge house to a solid-looking complex of winches, cables and netting perched apparently precariously across *Karakov*'s broad, square stern.

'That's the extra trawl.'

'How interesting. Max, you're standing guard on a couple of corpses. Why not just drift down aft for a well-earned cigarette and take a look-see at the mechanism while you're there, OK? Right, Regional Prosecutor, if we take this apparently deceased forensic scientist and your bodyguards take the other, we can do a little more exploring with any luck.'

But their luck ran out almost at once, for as they finished crossing the deck and prepared to heave the slack bodies over on to the gangplank between the deck and the submarine's sail, so Ivan and Alexei came bustling out of the forward bridge house, calling and gesturing. Richard and Yagula stopped, putting their burden down. Both pairs of eyes darted back to the useless pile of weapons

350

under the now deserted keel of the lifeboat; then down to the aft where Max was just going past the after bridge to look at the trawl.

'That's it,' said Richard. 'We're rumbled.' He tensed himself for action, ready to fight until the bitter end.

But another voice carried over the deck, with just enough authority to stop the lieutenants in their tracks. Rusanova bustled past them, so swiftly that Alexei's pat missed her bottom this time. She flung some Russian over her shoulder, her words enough to turn the others back. 'She says the Captain sent her down to hurry us along,' growled Yagula. 'Good. When she comes near I shall kill her at once.'

But she stopped well clear. Stopped and stood and looked at them for an instant. 'They told me you were dead,' she said to Richard.

'The reports may have been exaggerated,' he said easily.

'What will you give me if I help you?' she asked.

'First place in line for the firing squad,' spat Yagula.

'Ha!' she spat in return. 'First you need to stay alive. And then you need to catch me! Neither looks likely to happen. Richard?'

'Free passage. A head start. But why the change of heart?'

'You saw, did you not? How they treated me? That will be the rest of my life if I am not

351

careful. The rest of my short but active life.'
She turned to Yagula suddenly. 'You told me
something once. The only good advice you
ever gave me and I am here because I didn't
listen. But I'm willing to listen now. You said,
It is better to sleep with the devil you know...'

'*...than screw with the devil you don't,*' completed Yagula.

'How true,' said Richard thoughtfully. 'How
true.'

CHAPTER THIRTY-THREE

Prometheus

The three of them went down to *Titan 10*'s
sail. Richard and Yagula stood in the outer
command cockpit while Rusanova checked
below. As they waited, so they planned their
escape – or rather Richard did, as he kept
pulling Yagula back from increasingly brutal
plans for legal and illegal revenge. 'We can
settle things later,' he said, at last, frustrated.
'What we have to do now is get back aboard
Karakov and set my immediate plan in action
before they find out what's going on. It'll only
take someone to check on the storeroom or
the execution room. Or to check up on the

other four still awaiting execution, as Bronowski said.'

'You have a plan?'

'Of course. With any luck, Murphy will be
able to get through to *Prometheus 4* on the
lifeboat's radio. At the very least he'll be
broadcasting a distress locator she can pick
up – on her company frequency so it won't
interfere with *Karakov*'s radio traffic unless
we're very unlucky indeed. So *Prometheus 4*
will be here before dark and looking for a
lifeboat at the very least. Then we want to set
things up so we can drop the lifeboat overboard – so that it'll be waiting for us if we
need it. We'll have to arrange a distraction to
do that.'

'That'll have to be a hell of a distraction.'

'All clear below here!' called Rusanova.
'There seems to be no one left aboard at all.
The next part of their plan, as I understand
it, is to get all the stuff from here securely
stowed away on *Karakov*. Then I guess they'll
come back aboard for the final time.'

'She guesses!' snarled Yagula. 'As though
she's not been in this up to her treacherous,
murderous, slutty little neck!'

'They'll send Alexei and Ivan, I'm sure,'
said Richard, firmly.

On Rusanova's call, the apparent execution-
ers seemed to dump their burden down the
gaping shaft. They gestured to the next pair as
the forensic scientist actually climbed below,
then followed their body down.

Titan 10 was gutted. Dark, but not pitch-black. The emergency lights were mostly gone – only one or two remained, dully aglow, testifying to screws and catches painted into inviolability. But their brightness also demonstrated that there was life in the batteries. And where there was life, thought Richard, there was hope. But then he remembered his own description of the plan that logic was dictating here. The long, slow scuttle to the bottom of the explosives dumping ground must necessitate power – to open the seacocks. To turn the motors over and let the sinking vessel make a little way while the *Karakov* escaped. And that of course meant that the motors and the basic motor-control systems must also be left functional.

And that fact completed his plan, for it gave him his vital distraction.

The next three came down, and he took a narrow-eyed look at the resources he now had down here. Two forensic experts and two Spesnaz men. Or ex-Forces if not ex-Special Forces, at the very least. 'Yagula,' he said, recalling the Regional Prosecutor from a terrifyingly violent glower at Rusanova's back. 'Can either of these two bodyguards of yours work a simple motor control if I show them how?'

Yagula spat out a string of Russian. 'Audrey' and 'Tom' exchanged glances, then both of them nodded, 'Da.'

'OK,' said Richard. 'Explain to the others that we're leaving these two aboard, so they now have to pretend to be the execution

354

squad. Yagula, you stay and help me explain the motor controls. The forensics men go with Maria Ivanova and make a big show of fetching the other two bodies. Go as slowly as you can. Let us catch up with you after we've finished here. If Rusanova's right, everybody else will be pretty busy. Then *Titan 10* is going to get up to her old tricks again and sail away all on her own. And if that doesn't distract them, nothing will.'

In actual fact, the motor control was set to 'Slow Ahead All', as Yagula read the Cyrillic labelling. All the two men had to do was pull the switch to 'On'. Beside the motor control panel was a new one Yagula read as being the 'Flood Control' panel – obviously designed to open the seacocks and send *Titan 10* to her final resting place. But it took only an instant to distinguish the two and make sure that 'Audrey' knew which switch to throw and 'Tom' knew what the signal would be.

So it was easy enough for Richard and Yagula to untie the topmost gangplank without anyone noticing, then get back aboard *Karakov* and catch up with Rusanova and the others, safe in the knowledge that one set of sharp ears waited at the open hatch and one set of steady hands hovered over the motor control switch.

They were lucky with the lifeboat in several ways. First, as Murphy gleefully informed them, there was a good radio aboard through which he had contacted *Prometheus 4* on the secure company wavelength. Richard was welcome to talk to Captain Hand if he so wished, but he would merely confirm that the tanker was just below the horizon and making all speed towards them. Secondly, the lifeboat was not suspended by davits. It was sitting at the top of a double slide. Two strong guide strips like the centrepieces of any children's playground sat cocked upright fore and aft. At the touch of a button they were designed to slam down to water-level and the boat would career along them until it hit the waves and floated free. Thirdly, this particular boat was well supplied with diesel, which in Bronowski's view was first-grade – and a motor that, in Murphy's opinion, would fire at first turn.

Richard nodded. Good. That only left Max and the interesting equipment aft. 'What do you say, Maria Ivanova, shall we check it out?'

They left Yagula and the Darwin Twins hesitating beside the lifeboat and went aft together. 'Jesus!' said Max. 'I thought you'd never get here. I was thinking of going back to the lifeboat. What's with this stuff anyhow? It's just a set of trawl nets, from what I can see. Simple lever launch. Take the safety off there and pull this. The chute slides down there and vomits the whole lot over the stern. Quick and efficient.'

'Quick release in actual fact,' added Richard, taking them from the open-sea side, to the side above *Titan 10* herself. 'Those hawsers are coiled by the capstan there, you see? Just the same on both sides. Coiled

356

beside the capstans not round them. The system is designed to winch in, not out! And judging by those weights on the bottom it'll all sink like lead.'

'Is that good?' asked Rusanova.

'Couldn't be better,' answered Richard, almost aglow with excitement. 'Let's do it!' He put his fingers into his mouth. The index and second finger of each hand. And, leaning over to look down at *Titan 10*, he whistled. It was as simple as that. As though he was the leader of a gang of boys in the woods of his youth, he whistled. The sound was strident, piercing. It cut through the grumble of the ship's generators and the bustle of movement aboard. It reached *Titan 10* with ease. He saw a flash of movement on top of the fin in answer to the signal. And yet it was only a whistle. A childish, non-threatening thing. Nobody aboard would pay much attention to it. At least, that's what Richard was banking upon. 'The rest of you, back up to the lifeboat,' he ordered. 'I've got to wait here just for a few more—'

There came the most unnerving *CRASH!*

'That was the fin gangplank,' he shouted. '*Titan 10*'s moving. Now move, the rest of you, too. All hell's about to be let loose.'

As they ran to obey, Richard looked over the side once more, just in time to see the parting of the two massive hulls tear the lower gangplanks loose, snapping the great hawsers like so much thread. With an almost majestic inexorability, *Titan 10* was turning away.

357

Tearing herself free and sailing north into the ice. The roundness of her low, half-submerged hull seemed to lift the floes and set them sliding aside as she gathered way.

For an instant there was silence aboard *Karakov*. Silence – then pandemonium. For the second time, the stubborn submarine was refusing to lie dormant beneath the weight of the terrible plans the Smirnov brothers and their cohorts had for her. Still representing a terrible threat to them, full of bodies, fingerprints and who knew what other evidence, she was sailing away beyond their control.

Even before he heard it, Richard felt the throbbing of *Karakov*'s engines as she too came under way. Dragging the three gangplanks as though using them for leverage in her turn, the ship began to wheel about, her bow settling on to the northward track left by the fleeing submarine. Mouth dry, heart racing, he crouched by the lever waiting for the penny to drop. Waiting for the black ship's crew to realize that they were under attack and increasingly at risk.

But long moment dragged into long moment and still the Babel of confusion continued without the ordered sounds that would come when they realized, and started looking for the missing men. And Rusanova. He felt little enough responsibility for her – she was a murderess twice over – but the things that either side would do to her if they caught her meant that according to his own old-fashioned lights she deserved some help

358

from him. Deep in the grip of his almost Victorian Sir Galahad complex, he strained round the winch housing and looked across the deck to where she should be crouching by the lifeboat waiting. But the aft bridge house was in the way.

At the moment of his movement, *Karakov*'s bow slammed into the first thick floes above the ammunition dumping ground of Mys Zhelaniya. Richard hit the lever that dumped the deep-water trawl and sprinted towards the lifeboat. The sound of his movement was lost beneath the thunder of the net's departure. The whole of *Karakov* lurched as the simple mass of weighted nylon tore outwards and downwards behind her. Her whole frame shuddered, for the nets' deployment had been done just as she was coming to full-speed. The hawsers screamed and strained as they plunged inexorably downwards. The bows reared upward over ice – and upward again as the weight tugged at the stern. Richard slipped and scrambled while the deck heaved under him, torn this way and that by the conflicting forces of engine-thrust and net-drag. He slithered out from behind the aft bridge house, regained his footing and began to power up the length of the port-side rail towards the lifeboat. 'Launch!' he bellowed as he came. And Rusanova rose to do his bidding, just as planned.

But the instant that she did so, Yagula reared to tower above her. His great fist drove down on to the back of her head, hurling her forward across the deck towards Richard. The Regional Prosecutor looked down for an instant upon his judgement and his brutal execution, 'Let them have her and welcome!' he yelled. 'They deserve each other!' And he added something in Russian that sounded like a curse. Then he hit the 'Launch' button and leaped aboard the lifeboat. The slides slammed down and the little vessel began to race sideways down them. Richard had timed it perfectly. Had everything worked to his dictates he would have been leaping aboard her at that very moment, just as she slid away from the port-side rail. But instead, he was kneeling beside Maria Ivanova, pulling her inert body up off the bucking deck. Her eyes flickered. 'Leave me,' she whispered. 'I'm scuppered anyway...'

Alexei and Ivan came bursting out of the aft bridge house. By the grace of God neither of them had seen the situation clearly – or thought the whole thing through. So they had neither guns nor any real idea of what was just about to happen. But they had not come alone and, although only Richard really appreciated precisely what was going on, one of the men behind them had brought a gun. And he opened fire at once.

The first bullets exploded off the metal deck and howled away, trailing sparks like tracers. Their brightness under the gathering gloom allowed Richard to see the approaching arc of fire. He wrenched Maria Ivanova aloft and slung her over his shoulder, staggering towards the nearest of the vacant slides left by the lifeboat. He remained focused – fixated – on that. Only a man of his insuperable strength and concentration could have made it. With the mob of them howling at his heels and the bullets snarling past his ears like rabid dogs – and the deck bucking increasingly madly beneath his feet, he attained the left-hand slide. The instant that he did so, he pushed Rusanova on to it and reared upright, turning back to face them; to hold them at bay if he could as she slid safely away.

Under the first flash of lightning on the wings of the approaching storm they froze in his mind – the line of angry sailors with the gunman at their centre, Ivan and the familiar Alexei a pace or two in front, blessedly in the line of fire; almost close enough to grab him. Almost but not quite.

'You're dead, you stupid bastards,' he yelled at them with a voice that seemed to echo from the clouds and mix in with the immediate thunder. 'Where are your nets? Your *nets*?' He gestured on the first word, and they slowed, confused, turning to look back.

On the repetition, he flipped back on to the slide, blasted over the side not only by his own twisting power but by the impact of a bullet high in his right shoulder. He felt the pain as though a door had slammed shut on his upper torso. He felt the slipping and the sliding fall all the way down the slick, strong plastic to the almost solid coldness of the icy water. But he saw in his mind like a photograph the faces of the two bad lieutenants, riven with realization and with horror, turning. And the stupid stares of the raging crowd behind, who did not understand.

Then he felt the firm grasp of a pair of hands tearing him up over the stern of the lifeboat as the engine caught and she powered away southwards. He blinked the icy water out of his eyes and saw Max Asov looking anxiously down at him.

'Rusanova?' he asked. And by way of answer, Max gave a grin and the ghost of a wink.

And the instant that he did so, *Karakov*'s trailing trawl hit a pile of submerged explosive. In a strange kind of slow motion, light spread through the water, great submarine beams of brightness, as though they had discovered the city of Atlantis down there – and then had turned on all the lights. Then power began to spread. Not sound, but a kind of subliminal throbbing which wove itself into the very fabric of the universe, as the tapping of the feet in *Titan 10*'s tanks had echoed through her frame. Then the gathering physics of the massive detonation blew a great foaming hill of water upward. A weird luminous, throbbing, volcano of water mounted, its sides laced with foam and shattered ice. Its crest containing *Karakov* like Noah's Ark aground on Mount Ararat. And then the volcano erupted; exploded – sending up a column of boiling foam that threatened to top the cliffs of Mys Zhelaniya themselves.

The force of it was devastating enough to break the black ship's back, tear off her stern and send her down like the *Titanic*. The mountain of water closed around her, fell in upon her, crushing her, sucking her down as the lights went out and the rumbling faded.

The explosion sent great foaming waves northwards under the ice, where they made *Titan 10* pitch dangerously. A blizzard of foam and crushed ice fell rattling with the first of the rain against her safe-closed command hatches. It sent waves eastwards and westwards, where they were lost beneath the weight of the south-flowing Polar pack. And it sent them southwards, where the stout little lifeboat kicked up her heels and went surfing safely closer to the lights of the approaching *Prometheus 4* as she powered up over the horizon in answer to Murphy's call, running wildly north to rescue them and coming up at full, flank speed.